*A hunch—and maybe a furtive
hope—led Burn to Antelope Basin.*

He saw her horse first, tethered near the crystal-clear pond. Next he saw Allie's clothes—jeans, a T-shirt, some tantalizing scraps of silk—draped over a branch.

His belly grew hot and his heart started pounding even before he edged his mount closer.

Her hair floated on the water like corn silk. Her bare skin was tawny. In spite of her high-class, big-city roots, Allie Halston seemed as at home as the cypress and the creatures rustling in the brush.

Burnett Monroe had always been attracted to anything a little wild, a little untamed....

He watched silently until Allie became aware of him and turned. Her eyes widened.

"You need someone to stand guard, Boston," Burn said softly.

Dear Reader,

Welcome to Silhouette **Special Edition**...welcome to romance.

Some of your favorite authors are prepared to create a veritable feast of romance for you as we enter the sometimes-hectic holiday season.

Our THAT SPECIAL WOMAN! title for November is *Mail Order Cowboy* by Patricia Coughlin. Feisty and determined Allie Halston finds she has a weakness for a certain cowboy as she strives to tame her own parcel of the open West.

We stay in the West for A RANCHING FAMILY, a new series from Victoria Pade. The Heller siblings—Linc, Beth and Jackson—have a reputation for lassoing the unlikeliest of hearts. This month, meet Linc Heller in *Cowboy's Kin*. Continuing in November is Lisa Jackson's LOVE LETTERS. In *B Is For Baby*, we discover sometimes all it takes is a letter of love to rebuild the past.

Also in store this month are *When Morning Comes* by Christine Flynn, *Let's Make It Legal* by Trisha Alexander, and *The Greatest Gift of All* by Penny Richards. Penny has long been part of the Silhouette family as Bay Matthews, and now writes under her own name.

I hope you enjoy this book, and all of the stories to come. Happy Thanksgiving Day—all of us at Silhouette would like to wish you a happy holiday season!

Sincerely,

Tara Gavin
Senior Editor

Please address questions and book requests to:
Silhouette Reader Service
U.S.: 3010 Walden Ave., P.O. Box 1325, Buffalo, NY 14269
Canadian: P.O. Box 609, Fort Erie, Ont. L2A 5X3

PATRICIA COUGHLIN

MAIL ORDER COWBOY

SPECIAL ✦ EDITION®

Published by Silhouette Books
America's Publisher of Contemporary Romance

For Claire DiFranco, of the Oaklawn Library, with special thanks for her friendship and encouragement.

 SILHOUETTE BOOKS

ISBN 0-373-09919-3

MAIL ORDER COWBOY

Books by Patricia Coughlin

Silhouette Special Edition

Shady Lady #438
The Bargain #485
Some Like It Hot #523
The Spirit Is Willing #602
Her Brother's Keeper #726
Gypsy Summer #786
The Awakening #804
My Sweet Baby #837
When Stars Collide #867
Mail Order Cowboy #919

Silhouette Books

Love Child

Silhouette Summer Sizzlers 1990
"Easy Come...."

PATRICIA COUGHLIN

is also known to romance fans as Liz Grady and lives in Rhode Island with her husband and two sons. A former schoolteacher, she says she started writing to fill her hours at home after her second son was born. Having always read romances, she decided to try penning her own. Though she was duly astounded by the difficulty of her new hobby, her hard work paid off, and she accomplished the rare feat of having her very first manuscript published. For now, writing has replaced quilting, embroidery and other pastimes, and with more than a dozen published novels under her belt, the author hopes to be happily writing romances for a long time to come.

Chapter One

Cowboys were her weakness.

They always had been, and, having reached the advanced age of twenty-eight with no lessening of her fancy for mavericks of the two-legged variety, Allie Halston was resigned to the fact that they probably always would be.

She wasn't complaining. There was something intrinsically fascinating about cowboys. Maybe it was their cosmic link to the Old West, their tenacious dedication to a dying way of life or their legendary code of honor and rugged individuality. Then again, she thought with her usual frankness, maybe it was simply that she was a sucker for the rear view of a pair of saddle-worn blue jeans.

Allie's fantasies had been shaped by countless wagon-train romance novels and old Clint Eastwood westerns. She had long ago committed to memory all the classic scenes. One of her all-time favorites had the tall, steely eyed stranger—riding a black stallion named Diablo or something similarly menacing—happening upon the beautiful virgin as she swam naked in a pristine stream. It was such a favorite, in fact, that when Allie first lifted her head and blinked the water from her eyes, she thought for an instant she might be having an especially vivid daydream.

The only problem was that the scene before her differed from her fantasy in several notable ways. For one thing, there was no horse in sight. This particular stranger was driving an open Jeep and wearing designer sunglasses. Then there was the unsavory fact that the water she'd resorted to bathing in was more mudhole than stream. And lastly, she was no virgin.

"Nice day for a swim," the stranger called to her.

A cautious woman would ignore him and pray he'd go away, or else order him off her property. Or, at the very least, sidle closer to the clothes she'd draped over a branch of a nearby tree. But Allie wasn't a cautious woman. Quite the opposite. She was a risk taker who didn't mind working without a net. She was impulsive and easily bored and no darn good at resisting temptation.

The man eyeing her from no more than twenty feet away was definitely a temptation. Like some starry-eyed green-horn, she'd foolishly expected the streets of the nearby Texas town to be paved with Clint Eastwood clones. But although she'd glimpsed plenty of ten-gallon hats and scuff-toed boots on the long drive from the airport, this was the first man she'd seen who actually delivered that old cowboy rush. And he delivered it with a vengeance.

Her knees slightly bent to keep her shoulders below the water, she did a quick assessment of what she and her friend Liz had long ago dubbed the SQ—Stud Quotient. Broad shoulders, thick dark hair long enough to stick out from beneath his hat, a mouth that hovered between cruel and tender and a face with enough chiseled angles and hard lines to meet the definition of ruggedly handsome... All in all, her intruder presented a brand of raw, masculine allure of which Allie was an enthusiastic connoisseur.

Unless she was mistaken—which she very rarely was in such matters—he was doing an equally detailed counterassessment of his own. The opaque lenses of his sunglasses hid his eyes from her view, but even if they hadn't, the dusty brim of his black cowboy hat would have shaded them. Only the slant of his mouth gave away his smug amusement. To Allie, accustomed to a different, more enthralled reaction from members of the opposite sex, it was tantamount to waving a red flag.

"I am not swimming," she informed him in the regal, how-dare-you-intrude tone that she considered her most useful memento of her years at Miss Baxter's Academy For Young Women. "I'm bathing."

"Boston?"

"I beg your pardon?"

"No need to beg. I can come closer if you can't hear."

"No," she retorted as he made a move to climb from the Jeep. It was not that she feared he would see anything through the murky water. Even if he did, modesty was not one of her greater virtues. But he was still a stranger and a lot bigger than she was, and being manhandled was not part of her game plan.

"I can hear you just fine from where you are," she explained. "I simply didn't understand your question."

"I asked if you're from Boston."

"As a matter of fact I am."

"Thought so."

"Let me guess—my accent gave me away, right?" she asked, her slightly bored tone suggesting that she'd heard the line a hundred times before. She had.

"Nope."

Allie stared at him in silence.

It stretched until she felt a chill, something that an hour ago, driven by the midday heat into this dubious pond to cool off, she hadn't expected to feel for the duration of her stay. Her only previous experience with the Lone Star State had been a two-hour layover at the Dallas airport. Bandera was closer to Mexico than Dallas, and the summer temperature here could be blistering.

"All right," she conceded at last, her impatience edging toward irritability. For Allie, who didn't particularly like to be kept waiting even when she wasn't standing ankle deep in mud, it was a quick leap. "So it wasn't my accent. Are you going to tell me how you did know I was from Boston?"

"Want me to?"

"Would I have asked if I didn't?"

"I don't know, would you have?"

Her sigh was exquisitely exasperated. "This is ridiculous . . . and I'm getting cold standing here."

"Then come on out. It's plenty warm over here," he said in a slow, rough-around-the-edges tone that gave new meaning to the word *drawl.*

"I will. Just as soon as you move along."

"I'm not in any hurry," he countered, slouching behind the wheel in a way that underscored that fact.

"Well, I am. So unless you have some business here, I'm going to ask you to leave."

"Funny."

"What is?"

"I was just wondering the same thing about you. That is, whether you have business here on the Circle Rose or just stopped by to take a bath."

"I would hardly have sought out such rustic facilities," she muttered, then lifted her chin with as much dignity as she could muster naked and wet. "I happen to own the Circle Rose."

Sunglasses and all, Allie swore she saw his eyes narrow to slits. In surprise? Disbelief?

"Since when?" he asked before she could fully dissect his reaction.

"Since the beginning of the month. On July 1," she added, with a sweep of her arm that seemed to command his full attention, probably because of the way her breasts lifted dangerously close to the water's surface in the process, "I became the proud owner of this three-hundred-acre paradise known as the Circle Rose. Of course, after seeing what I bought, I confess to being considerably less proud and a great deal more understanding of the term 'buyer beware.'"

"Why's that?"

"Let's just say I've learned that beauty isn't the only thing that's in the eye of the beholder. So is the definition of 'working ranch.'"

"The Circle Rose is a fine working ranch," he said quickly, "provided you have the right man working her."

"You could have fooled me," Allie countered dryly. "In fact, from the second the key jammed in the front-door lock until I tried turning on the water in the bathroom and got a shower of rust, I haven't found one thing on the entire place that works properly."

He shrugged. "So she needs a little TLC. A ranch is like a woman. You can't neglect her year after year and expect she'll give you her best. But the right man—"

"Will you stop saying that?" Allie snapped. "As if only men own ranches or know how to run them."

He touched the brim of his hat. "Sorry," he said without sounding it. "I guess you're proof that's not true."

"Exactly. I own the Circle Rose now and I intend to do whatever it takes to get it up and running again."

"All by yourself?"

"Of course not. I've arranged for my attorney to hire a foreman. He should be arriving—" She stopped short and took a closer look at him...the hat, the boots, the way he appeared right at home against a backdrop of sagebrush and dust devils. "Are you the man Mr. Rosen hired?"

"Rosen?"

"My attorney in San Antonio. He handled everything, placing the ad in trade papers, screening applicants. I just thought perhaps you were the man he selected."

Thought, tweaked her conscience, *or hoped?* If this man should indeed turn out to be what her friends back East had rather snidely dubbed her "mail order cowboy," life on this disaster of a ranch could prove to be decidedly more interesting than it had appeared an hour ago.

Allie wasn't sure if she had imagined a split second's hesitation before he bared straight, white teeth in a smile and said, "You thought just right."

"You mean you are my new foreman?"

"Signed, sealed and delivered." He reached up and pulled off his sunglasses. "Name's Monroe. Burnett Monroe, but most everyone just calls me Burn."

Burn. *How appropriate,* thought Allie, heat sizzling through her as, for the first time, her gaze met his directly.

His eyes were blue, dark and hooded in a sensual way that would make any woman's mind wander. Before hers wandered too far, Allie acknowledged his introduction with a ridiculously formal nod.

"I'm Allie Halston."

He nudged the brim of his hat. "Miss Halston."

"Please. Call me Allie. It seems ridiculous to stand on ceremony when we'll be working together so closely."

Burnett Monroe nodded. "You're the boss."

He said it with the soft affability of a man indulging a woman. Allie's spine stiffened.

"That's right, I am. Why don't you head on back to the house while I finish up here? When I get back we can talk over the arrangements in more detail."

"Arrangements?"

She frowned impatiently. "As in how and where we're going to begin fixing up this place, how many men you think we need to hire to start, even bunking arrangements. I should warn you that the roof of the bunkhouse is one more thing that needs repair. In fact, that might be the best place to start. I know Mr. Rosen has already talked to you about salary and all that—"

"Actually," Burn interrupted, "he said I should work out those details with you."

Allie rolled her eyes. "Figures. Word of advice, Burn— never hire a lawyer because he's the friend of a friend."

"I don't have much call to hire lawyers, friends of friends or otherwise."

"I see." For some reason, Allie felt subtly chastened. "All right then, when I get back we'll sit down and work out all the details."

"I think I'll just wait here and give you a lift back."

"That's really not necessary. I can walk."

"You said you were cold."

"I also said I can walk."

"See that dust?" He indicated the cloud of it blowing across the road at his back. "You'll be as dirty as when you started before you walk twenty feet. I'll wait."

It was, Allie realized, a battle of wills draped in chivalry. He wanted to wait and she wanted to walk. All right, she really would prefer not to have to walk all the way back to the house. What she wanted was to find a graceful way to get out of the water and into her clothes...without losing the battle.

She supposed she could always ask—no, *order*—him to turn his head while she dressed. After all, she was the boss. He'd said so himself. It was simply that the way he'd said it was still echoing tauntingly in her head.

Something warned her that buried somewhere beneath the lethal blue gaze and cordial manners, Burnett Monroe had a Neanderthal streak wide enough to herd cattle over. She was familiar with the breed. For all his millions and sophistication, her father, Richard Maxwell Halston III, was simply a more urbane, polished member of the same male tribe. He didn't think she could run a ranch by herself and Allie had a hunch Burn Monroe had already drawn the same conclusion.

It made her wonder why on earth he'd taken a job working for a woman in the first place. Or had he? His surprised expression when she'd announced that she was the new owner of the ranch suggested that Cal Rosen had neglected to discuss more than salary. Maybe it had been intentional. Maybe Rosen had known that telling a cowboy up front that the boss was a woman was a sure way to sour the deal.

If that was so, thought Allie, it was even more crucial that she get off to a strong start. Being coy or begging him to turn his head and grant her some privacy didn't strike her as the way to do that. Having never before been a boss—or for that matter, never having answered to one for longer than a few weeks at a time—she wasn't sure exactly how one should act when cornered. She was quite sure, however, that using the tried-and-true methods of cajoling and manipulation were out. Instead, words like *fearlessness* and *forthrightness* came to mind.

Squeezing water from her hair as a stalling technique, she asked herself what would be the most fearless and forthright way to handle the situation. Nothing sprang to mind. She tried asking herself instead what her father or Burn Monroe would do if they were in her position. Much better. Without a second thought, she began moving through the water toward where her clothes were hanging.

"I think I'll take you up on that ride after all," she announced.

The gentle slope of the small pond brought her out of the water at a right angle to where his Jeep was parked. As her shoulders, then her chest, then her hips emerged from the water, she stood tall and felt the heat from either the sun or his stare warming her skin.

While she was by no means an exhibitionist, all the time she'd spent traveling in Europe had broadened her mind considerably. Besides, when it came to her body, she had nothing to hide. In every way possible, Aphrodite had been generous with her, and Allie knew it. She was tall and lean and golden from two recent weeks on a private beach in Greece. Her cheekbones bore the exquisite mark of her mother's distant Gypsy heritage, and her hair, which dusted her shoulders and appeared dark when it was wet, would dry to a silky curtain of sun-streaked gold. Her eyes were a rare pale green, the exact shade of the delicate chain of citrine and gold that encircled one slender ankle.

Allie walked naked from the water because she was comfortable with her body and exceedingly uncomfortable with the idea of giving her new foreman any reason to think she was too prissy or vulnerable or easily intimidated to run the Circle Rose.

She dried off, pulling on her jeans and white T-shirt with businesslike speed, and turned to find his hat tipped low, dark glasses back in place and his mouth a straight, unreadable line... all of which told Allie exactly what she'd hoped. That she had taken him by surprise and made him think twice about the woman who would be giving him orders. If not, she reasoned, he wouldn't be taking such care to hide his reaction from her.

"All set?" she asked, pushing her feet into a pair of brown leather boots before slipping on her own sunglasses.

He nodded, reaching across to push open the passenger door for her. Allie slid in beside him and slammed it shut.

Instead of starting the engine, however, he got out and walked toward the spot where she'd gotten dressed.

"Where are you going?" she called after him.

"To start earning my pay."

As he spoke, he bent to pick up something and headed back. Glancing sideways from behind her sunglasses, Allie did her best to see what he was holding without appearing too interested. He approached her side of the Jeep, held his hand in front of her and opened it palm down so that her bra swung by one narrow strap from his finger. It was demi-cupped and flowered and embarrassingly flimsy.

"You forgot something," he said, his voice a smoky drawl that was all the more eloquent for its flatness.

The almost imperceptible twitch at the corners of his mouth might as well have been an out-and-out grin for the dampening effect it had on the smug self-satisfaction Allie had been basking in only seconds ago.

He let the lacy scrap dangle until she snatched it from him, scrunching it into a ball on the seat beside her.

"Thanks," she snapped.

"Anytime... boss. Anytime."

Chapter Two

"So tell me, what made you decide to buy the Circle Rose?"

Burn had two reasons for asking. First, because he was itching to know exactly what would make a city woman, one whom he'd bet had never gotten closer to a steer than reading some fancy restaurant menu, think she could tame a piece of land that had beaten men a lot tougher and stronger than she was.

And second, because he figured that as long as he kept talking, he wouldn't start drooling. Even if he did, if he was lucky, she might be too distracted by his questions to notice.

The truth was his mouth was watering so bad he might well be drooling any second. He'd been this way since she'd moved out of that pond, gliding more than walking, as smooth and graceful as a ballerina.

Not that Burn had ever actually seen a ballerina. Only a picture of one once, and that was a long time ago. He couldn't have been more than ten or eleven when his mother had hung the dime-store painting over her dressing table. Another lifetime. Still, like lots of things from that other life, the image of the ballerina dressed all in white lived on in that stubborn corner of his memory where things he'd rather not remember resided. And everything that ballerina had represented to him—beauty and grace and femininity—was embodied in the way the woman seated beside him moved.

That was part of the reason that looking at her made his mouth water.

The other part had nothing to do with ballerinas in white dresses and everything to do with the red-hot fantasies a man resorts to when he spends too much time alone. Burn had spent a lot of time alone lately, and every sweaty fantasy he'd ever conjured up had sizzled to Technicolor life inside him when Allie Halston stepped out of that water naked.

She was hands down the most beautiful woman he'd ever seen. All soft apricot curves and tempting hollows, with the kind of endless legs that could tie a man's imagination in knots. A natural blonde, too. He'd noticed that fascinating little detail about a split second before he'd shoved his sunglasses back on so she wouldn't catch him gaping like some saucer-eyed teenager at his first peep show.

Yep, she was about as close to perfect as a human being could get. Which was why Burn was so irritated with himself for becoming addle brained over a little flash of T & A...even temporarily, and even if her butt was a work of art and her breasts were coral tipped and beaded with drops of water he could still almost taste. He'd been around enough to know that all that outward perfection invariably covered up a real pain-in-the-rear interior. And if he hadn't already learned that lesson, the arrogance that dripped from Allie Halston as she rose from that pond should have warned him. Getting involved with her kind of woman was sort of like riding in a Caddy with horsehair upholstery.

Knowing all that, he was surprised at the power of his response to her. He didn't need to check the labels in the lady's clothing to know she belonged to an elite group of rich, beautiful, spoiled women with too much time on their hands. Everything from her pronunciation to the way she tossed her head broadcast money and plenty of it. Over the past year or so he'd become something of an expert on the subject of wealthy, demanding women, and he had foolishly believed he'd built up an immunity to the spells they cast so effortlessly.

Of course, he'd also thought that being able to sit dead still without anesthesia while a doctor stitched up whatever piece of his skin had gotten torn open meant that he had absolute control over all his body's responses. The past few minutes had proven him wrong on both counts.

He wanted Allie Halston, fast and hard and right this minute. Watching her step into her panties back there, he'd gotten so aroused he thought was going to explode with wanting her. He still felt plenty combustible and he figured it was going to take a while to defuse the feeling. At the moment, talking was the best way he could think of to cool off.

They had nearly covered the distance from the pond to the house, and she was either still mulling over his question about her reason for buying the ranch or else flat-out ignoring him.

"I'd really like to know," he prodded. "Did you just get a sudden hankering to rough it or have you been saving your pennies for this ever since you were a kid?"

Her sudden smile signaled that if she had been trying to ignore him, she'd failed.

"Neither," she replied. "A very dear aunt—just about my favorite person in the whole world, actually—died recently and left everything she had to me."

"I'm sorry to hear that—about your aunt, I mean."

"Thanks," she acknowledged, her smile softening. "I really do miss her."

Burn nodded without saying anything. He understood about missing someone and how it was a hurt that nothing anyone else said could make easier. Burn wasn't one to waste his breath.

"I still don't get it, though," he went on as they circled around the back of the main house. It was a one-floor dwelling with a wide porch on the front, a big kitchen facing east so it would stay cool on hot afternoons and three bedrooms with a view of the endless plain stretching south. Nothing fancy. A family home, Burn thought with a twinge. "Why didn't you use your inheritance to buy something closer—one of those Boston brownstones or a nice big chunk of oceanfront property? Why a ranch? Why Bandera, for Pete's sake?"

Allie tossed her head. "I'm really not surprised you don't 'get it.' I wouldn't expect you to, any more than my father or anyone else in my family did. But I get it and Verdy would have gotten it perfectly, and as far as I'm concerned that's all that matters."

"Verdy?"

"My aunt Verdy. She was great, a free spirit, one of a kind. When I was a kid," she said as he pulled up in front of the house and stopped, "my parents were always warning me that if I wasn't careful and didn't stop doing whatever it was I wanted to do and instead did what they deemed proper, I would end up like Verdy. It was meant as a threat, of course, but instead it only urged me on. For the life of me I could never figure out why everyone didn't want to be like Verdy."

"Still working on it, are you?"

Her withering glance bounced right off him. "Not at all. I figured out a long time ago that most people don't have the guts to live like Verdy did . . . to reach out and grab for what they want most in life."

"Or the money," he said dryly.

"Money has nothing to do with it."

"Right," he retorted with something close to a snort. "As if you bought the Circle Rose with guts and a handful of magic beans."

Allie shrugged, tossing her long, straight blond hair, which was already nearly dry from the midday heat. "All right, money is one factor, but only one. I know lots of people who have plenty of money and still don't have the guts."

"If you're looking for someone to speak on behalf of the backbone of the idle rich, you picked the wrong guy."

"I'm not. I have no doubt that my entire family is back in Boston right now, clucking their tongues and telling each other how right they were, how just what they always warned me would happen has—that I've ended up like Verdy. And maybe I have." She gazed around at the empty stable and the ramshackle building that served as the bunkhouse. "All I know is I'm here and I couldn't be happier."

Burn pushed his hat back to scratch his forehead. "So Verdy owned a ranch, too. Is that it?"

Rolling her eyes in disgust, Allie climbed from the Jeep and slammed the door behind her.

"Hold on," Burn called out.

Not bothering with his door, he swung over it and hurried after her. His imprudence cost him, and he clutched his lower back as all those misaligned disks the doctor was always warning him to treat with TLC seemed to clatter together like so many stacked plates. They didn't crash, though—not this time, at least—and Burn said a quick prayer of thanks that the combination of steel pins and stubbornness that held him together was evidently going to last awhile longer.

"I'm just trying to understand," he said, reaching to pull open the screen door for her. "Run it past me again, slow this time. Your aunt Verdy was the black sheep of the family and—"

"She was not a black sheep," Allie interjected, her eyes flashing a shade of green Burn had never seen before, paler than a brand-new leaf and iridescent, like ice and fire at once. "I told you—she was a free spirit."

"Got it. A free spirit. And in her will she left you..."

"Everything," she supplied. "Everything she had. Which admittedly wasn't much by my family's standards."

"Your family has pretty high standards, I take it?"

"When it comes to money, they're high enough. Verdy gave up her share of the family fortune to do what she pleased with her life. And by leaving me her nest egg, she was giving me a chance to do the same. Follow your dream," she said softly, her eyes filling as she stared off across the scorched earth, crisscrossed with broken fences. "That's the message she left for me in her will...follow your dream."

Burn's mouth twisted. "So you followed it all the way here to Bandera?"

"Very funny." She stepped inside and let the screen door close on his arm.

"I'm not trying to be funny," he told her as he followed her inside and along the corridor he knew led to the kitchen. "Honest."

"I see. You're just naturally obtuse?"

He grinned amiably, stopping just inside the kitchen and removing his hat. The ceilings in the house were high, at least ten feet, Allie gauged, putting him at six-two or six-three.

"I guess maybe I am," he agreed. "Stubborn, too. You're going to find that comes in handy on a ranch. Let me try this again. Your aunt Verdy left you some money to follow your dream and you dreamed of owning a ranch?"

"Where's my box of little gold stars when I need one?"

"I'll take a rain check on the star. For now, tell me why a girl from back East would dream of owning a ranch."

Allie pulled open the refrigerator door. "That's a long story. Do you want a soda or a beer?"

"A beer. And I've got time to listen."

"No, you don't." Turning with two bottles of beer, she nudged the refrigerator door shut with her hip. A very distracting move. "You're on my time, remember?"

Her time? Burn was puzzled until he realized she was referring to the fact that he worked for her now. Actually, he hadn't remembered, and the idea was going to take some getting used to. He'd become so engrossed in her story that he'd forgotten all about the little bit of impulsive fabrication he'd engaged in back by the pond...not to mention all the complications it was going to create in his life if he went ahead with it.

He couldn't even explain why he'd pretended to be the foreman she was expecting in the first place, other than the fact that the opportunity had presented itself and the quick reflexes he'd developed in order to survive on the professional rodeo circuit had kicked in automatically. For twelve years he'd lived by those reflexes, and he'd done more than survive—he'd dominated.

"Of course, I remember that I'm on your time," he said, diving in even deeper. "It's just that you yourself said we're going to be working together closely. I thought it might be a good idea if we got to know each other a little better."

"All right." She lowered herself into one of the chairs at the kitchen table and kicked out another one in an unspoken invitation for him to join her.

Burn tossed his hat on the table and sat. He didn't recognize the maple kitchen set and was thankful for that. As it was, so much here was familiar that he was having trouble concentrating on the moment at hand.

"Let's get acquainted," she said, holding the open beer bottle close to her lips, her gaze steady on his. "I bought this place on a whim...a crazy, half-baked whim, as my father put it. Sometimes that's where dreams start—on a crazy, half-baked whim. Why Bandera? Because I read that it was the cowboy capital of the world and I liked the sound of that." She arched her brow at his cynical expression. "You don't agree with that description?"

"I guess it depends on your definition of cowboy."

"What's yours?"

"Not someone who spends his days making nice to the guests on a dude ranch. And that's what Bandera is filling up with these days."

"Maybe. But from what I've seen, there's more to Bandera than dude ranches. Like the Circle Rose, for instance."

"You were the one who said the Circle Rose hardly qualifies as a working ranch anymore."

"But it will," she retorted, an intriguing glint in her eyes. "You can count on that. Now it's my turn to ask a few questions."

"Go right ahead."

"Where's your horse?"

Burn laughed out loud. "My horse?"

"Right. I've never seen a cowboy without one."

"You have now. Welcome to the nineties, Miss Halston. You don't necessarily need a horse to run a ranch." He took a swig of his beer and tipped his chair onto its back legs. "Next question."

"What makes you so sure it's 'Miss'?"

His chair slammed back onto all fours.

"You called me Miss Halston," Allie explained in response to his perplexed frown. "Twice now. And I was just wondering what made you assume I was Miss and not Mrs. Halston."

Wishful thinking, said a small voice inside Burn. That's what made him think it. Now he considered the alternative, the fact that there might be a Mr. Halston somewhere in the picture. He thought about what he'd said and what he'd been thinking about a woman running a ranch all by herself, not to mention some of the other things he'd been thinking about this particular woman, and he felt like a damn fool.

"Is it?" he asked in as offhand a tone as he could manage. "Is it Mrs. Halston?"

For reasons he didn't want to think about right then, Burn knew that her answer would definitely influence whether he decided to continue with this little charade or move on.

She let him wait, hitching the heel of one boot onto the seat of her chair and circling her bent knee with her arms.

"No," she said at last, her eyes gleaming with satisfaction. "It's Miss. I just wondered what made you so sure."

Witch. Burn placed his bottle on the table and leaned forward.

"Same reason I was sure you were from back East," he said softly.

She stared at him, her golden brows arched with curiosity. She could arch all she wanted. Based on the way she'd held her chin up as she walked naked from that pond, Burn was gambling that no matter how badly she itched to know, she wouldn't give him the satisfaction of asking.

He watched curiosity war with pride in her steady gaze and saw his gamble pay off. Reaching some private decision, she leaned back in her chair and sipped her beer. Anyone not paying attention to the slightly feral gleam in her eyes would think she couldn't care less what mysterious factors had led Burn to his conclusions about her. She cared. She was simply biding her time. Burn thought he would do well to remember that as impulsive and headstrong as she clearly was, the lady could override her impatience when she chose to.

"So where was the last place you worked, Burn?" she asked.

"The Double D," he replied. Damn. His legendary reflexes had failed him that time. He should have thought quickly and lied.

"Is that here in Bandera?"

"About fifty miles northeast of here."

"What made you decide to leave?"

He shrugged. "A better offer came along."

"Meaning the job here?"

Burn nodded.

"Better in what way?"

Good question. He could hardly tell her the truth—that he had his own reasons for driving to the Circle Rose today, and that looking for a new job wasn't even close to being one of them. Or that his grounds for staying were a murky mix of hormones and nostalgia.

"The Double D is a going operation," he said finally. "It runs like clockwork no matter who's at the controls. I prefer a challenge."

She flashed him a wry smile. "Looks like you've found one."

Or two, Burn mused silently. Time would tell.

"I just want to say up front that it's not too late to back out now that you've seen for yourself what's in store for you here," she pointed out. "Frankly, I'd rather you do it now than in the middle of the job."

"I'm not going anywhere." So that was that, he thought with only a momentary sensation of having stepped off the top of a mountain.

"You're willing to take the job even knowing that it will be a long time and a lot of hard work before things around here run like clockwork?"

"I can handle hard work."

"How about answering to a woman boss? Think you handle that, Burn?"

"A boss is a boss," he replied with a laconic shrug. "The person who gives the orders and hands you your check at the end of the week. Fact is, I hardly noticed you were a woman."

"Well, that's good," she said, looking more amused than injured by the remark. Self-confident as well as arrogant, thought Burn.

"All right then," she continued, "let's get down to the nitty-gritty. I don't plan to haggle over salary. Rosen told me the going rate for a foreman of a ranch this size. Considering the condition of the Circle Rose, I've increased it twenty-five percent and that's as much as I'm prepared to pay."

She named the figure and quickly ran through what would be his general responsibilities.

"Sounds fair enough," Burn said when she was through.

"Good."

"As far as it goes."

"What else is there?"

"Trust me, there's about a hundred things you haven't thought of and won't until they rear up in your face. At the moment, however, I'm mostly concerned with two small oversights and one request."

"What oversights?"

"Where do I sleep and where do I eat?"

"Of course." A frown shadowed her fine features. "Sleeping is a problem. You saw the bunkhouse."

"Looks sort of inhospitable."

She shuddered. "Worse. I wouldn't ask a dog to sleep there under those conditions, so I guess until we get it fixed up you'll have to stay here in the house. I took the largest room at the far end of the hall. You can have the next biggest one here off the kitchen. I'll show it to you if you like."

Burn shook his head. He didn't need to see the small room with its view of the corral and the wall of built-in shelves just the right size for displaying model cars. "I'm sure it'll be fine."

"You know now why I suggested that the bunkhouse might be the obvious place to begin work. I can hardly hire a crew until I have a place to put them up. In the meantime maybe we can arrange for some temporary help, perhaps a few carpenters."

"I'll take care of it," he said. "First let me check out exactly what needs to be done and how much I can handle on my own."

"All right. It will be a relief to have you oversee that end of things," she admitted. "For the time being I'm going to have my hands full redecorating in here."

"Redecorating?"

"You know—furniture, curtains, floors. I like the rough wood planks in the living room, but I was thinking a tile floor, something with Aztec overtones, perhaps, would be better in the hallway and here in the kitchen. More light would help, too." She glanced past him toward the living room. "I see skylights, perhaps a double set of French doors leading to a patio and—"

"Sounds great," he said with undisguised disgust. "Want to know what I see?"

She gave him a pained, expectant look.

"Money being poured down the drain...money that, unless you have unlimited resources, you're going to need if you're serious about getting this place up and running again."

That struck a chord that his earlier crack about not noticing she was a woman had missed by a mile. "I've already told you I'm serious. This is my chance to prove I can do whatever I set out to do. To prove that I'm more than—"

"More than what?" Burn prodded when she broke off abruptly.

Allie shrugged. "More than a body with a pretty face and an empty head. More than my father's daughter."

"Well, lady, you won't prove it by squandering money on curtains and knickknacks that you're going to need for fence posts and grain and cattle."

Her brow furrowed. "Cattle?"

"Right, cattle. You know—those big awkward things that wind up on a barbecue in some backyard in Topeka." His sneer deepened. "Or were you planning to herd skylights?"

Tossing her hair back, her eyes narrowed to slits, she said, "Sheep."

"Sheep?"

"Right, sheep. You know, those cuddly, furry things that make such great sweaters."

Burn couldn't have been more stunned if she'd announced she planned to turn the Circle Rose into a farm and grow artichokes. In fact, he'd prefer artichokes to sheep.

"The Circle Rose is a cattle ranch," he blurted out.

"How would you know?"

"I did some research."

"Fine. The Circle Rose *was* a cattle ranch."

"That's what I just said. You can't raise sheep here."

"Oh, really? Why not? Is this some sort of sacred cattle ground?" she demanded, waving her arm in the direction of the window and the land beyond.

"Something like that," he agreed, exasperation in his tone.

"Well, for your information, this type of terrain is suited for raising either cattle or sheep."

"Says who?"

She reached and snatched something from the counter behind her. "This."

"A book?" Burn demanded, openly incredulous. "A damn book?"

"A guide," she corrected, her cool show of control doing little to aid his.

Burn glanced at the title. "*The Beginner's Guide to Ranching*? Who the hell would use a book to learn about ranching?"

Even as he asked the question, the answer came crashing in on him. His new boss, that's who.

He stared at her in silence for a moment, trying to judge whether she was really serious. She was. And then he was trying to figure out what the most diplomatic response would be. He'd never been accused of being overly tactful, but even his instincts warned that his natural reaction— laughing out loud—would not bode well for employee-employer relations.

"What made you settle on sheep?" he asked at last, opting for safety by tossing the ball back into her court.

"They're smaller than cattle, for one thing, and it just seemed to me they'd be easier to manage."

"You don't manage cows, you herd 'em."

"To slaughter," she retorted. "I'd prefer shearing."

He smiled faintly. "Less messy?"

"You might say that."

"Well, Allie, you don't have to worry about the mess, or the herding, and you sure as hell don't need a book to tell you what to do," he added, taking it from her and tossing it back onto the counter. "That's what you've got me for."

"I see. Meaning that you'll be telling me what to do instead?" she asked in that snotty back-East way that had the same effect on his senses as if he was climbing on a wild pony and waiting for the chute to open: an urge to conquer and dominate.

"When it comes to running this ranch, you bet I will," he replied. "Isn't that what you hired me to do?"

Their gazes locked across the table and, for no reason he could put a name to, the air between them became heavy and charged, as if a storm was coming.

"Of course, that's why I hired you," she said finally. "But I still make the final decisions."

"Fine. Just remember there's a lot to be done before a final decision has to be made. Why don't we talk about that?"

Allie nodded, then listened quietly as he outlined what sounded like a very logical approach to the myriad repairs and general maintenance that needed to be done. From his mention of specific problems in areas of the ranch she had yet to explore, she realized he had checked the place out thoroughly before he stopped by the pond. Probably wanted to know what he was getting into, she mused.

All in all, she was impressed, both by his obvious knowledge of ranching and his keen eye for controlling the cost of their undertaking. Like modesty for modesty's sake, frugality was not high on her list of virtues. His earlier comments about her redecorating plans had prompted her to realize for the first time since she'd plunged into this project that Verdy's nest egg might not be enough.

Grimly, she acknowledged that to play it safe she would have to scale back a bit on her plans for the house. At least until the ranch was closer to becoming self-supporting. With Burn running things, it sounded as if that wouldn't take too long. The French doors she had envisioned could wait for now, she decided, only half listening as Burn talked about grain sheds and irrigation ditches. But the skylights were a must. She made a mental note to check the phone book for a local contractor to handle the job.

"One question," she asked when he'd finished running through the jobs he considered most essential. "You haven't said anything about hiring a crew."

"Because I don't plan to. Not yet, anyway."

"Then who's going to do all this work?"

"I am."

"Alone?"

"You tell me. Can you afford the alternative? Take what you're paying me and shave off a quarter to a third, then multiply it by six men, which is an average-size crew for a spread this size. That's a pretty big outlay of cash with no profit coming in for at least a year."

"A year?" Allie exclaimed, shocked.

"That's right. Maybe a little less if everything breaks our way, and believe me, on a ranch it never does."

She quickly did the suggested math in her head and felt her heart sink. "There's no way I can afford that, not along with repairs and loan payments."

"I had a hunch you couldn't. Most folks have no idea what it takes to run a ranch. Not the money or the sweat or the..."

"Or the what?" she prompted when he trailed off, his gaze on the landscape outside.

"Or the frustration," he said, turning back to her. "The frustration of nursing a sick calf through a long winter just to have the coyotes get her come spring. The frustration of having a rainstorm take the roof off the grain shed, soaking the feed you just spent your last dime to buy. The frustration of . . . lots of things.''

His voice had become taut as he spoke, giving rise to questions Allie didn't know him nearly well enough to ask.

''Sounds like you've had a lot of experience on ranches,'' she said. *Brilliant, Halston,* she thought the instant the words were out. Of course he had ranching experience. Why else would Rosen have chosen him from all the other applicants?

''All my life,'' he replied.

''No kidding? You grew up on a ranch?''

He nodded.

''Did your family own it or—''

He nodded again before she could finish. ''Yeah, we owned it all right. Along with the bank.''

''And you liked ranching enough to want to make a career of it?''

He gave an amused snort. ''I'm not so sure you'd call what I've had a career, but I've spent my life working around horses and cattle. I can get the job done for you here, Allie, you can count on that.''

''I am counting on it.''

He pushed his chair back far enough to slide his long legs from under the table.

''I'll need a couple of days to tie up some loose ends where I'm staying now,'' he said.

''I'd really prefer that you start right away,'' Allie protested, disappointed at the prospect of having to put everything they'd discussed on hold even for a couple of days.

Burn eyed her consideringly before replying. ''I just might prefer that myself. It's simply not possible.''

''Fine,'' Allie retorted. ''When can you start?''

''Why don't we plan on Wednesday?''

She nodded, resisting the urge to point out that since this was only Saturday, that was more than a couple of days.

"Also, while I meant what I said about getting by without a crew for the time being, I will want to hire one man."

"Of course. Shall I ask Cal Rosen to handle it or would you prefer to interview applicants yourself?"

He grinned. "There's no interviewing needed. I know just the man for the job. Frizzy Stockton. He's old and he's ornery, but he'll give you more than a day's work for a day's pay. Plus he can cook, and I've got my doubts that you can."

Allie crossed her arms across her chest, her gaze cool. "What would you say if I told you that I happen to be a Cordon Bleu chef?"

"I'd say you were lying through your teeth," he said, dismissing the subject by heading for the door. He paused with his hand on the knob and turned to Allie, who was standing a few feet behind him. "One last thing... about that request I mentioned."

"Oh, right, what is it?"

"I'll need Saturdays off."

"Every Saturday?" she asked, instantly curious.

He nodded. "Unless something changes."

"I guess that would be all right. Sounds as if you have something very important to do on Saturdays."

"Very important," he agreed, swinging open the door.

Allie followed him onto the porch, her curiosity billowing around her, but he didn't elaborate. She hated the strong, silent type....

"You know, Burn," she said, "it just occurred to me that we discussed the fact that I'm not married. How about you?"

"You mean how about me being married?"

She nodded.

"Nope."

"Never?"

"Never."

"I guess that old Willie Nelson song is right. You know, the part about cowboys being hard to love and even harder to hold."

He regarded her speculatively over the open door of his Jeep. "Seems to me like you know a lot about cowboys for a woman from back East." He touched the brim of his hat. "See you Wednesday."

Allie hoisted herself onto the porch rail and contemplated the cloud of dust his tires left behind. Burn was wrong. She'd been here only a day and that was long enough to convince her that she didn't know nearly as much about cowboys—or ranching—as she'd thought. But she did know what she liked, she thought, grinning, and that's what counted.

Chapter Three

Even more than it needed redecorating, the ranch house needed cleaning from top to bottom. Allie handled the matter the only way she knew how—by phoning a local cleaning company and requesting a crew be sent out first thing Monday morning. By charming the service manager and agreeing to pay extra, she even arranged for them to haul away those furnishings left by the previous owners that she positively could not live with.

From Cal Rosen she'd learned that the ranch had been put on the market by an older couple who had retired to Florida a year earlier, leaving behind all the ranch equipment and nearly all the furniture. Allie could understand why they'd abandoned most of it. She spent Sunday afternoon marking those items that had to go. A wooden floor lamp with built-in magazine rack, a lopsided Danish-modern coffee table, two ugly brown plaid wing chairs and more than a dozen other items were all tagged for removal.

There were a few pieces she was happy to claim, however. Her favorites were the rolltop desk in the office off the living room and a pair of pine bookcases that fit perfectly with the airy but rustic look she had planned for the house. She also hung onto an old rocking chair covered in fabric reminiscent of a gray chenille bedspread, which was just homely enough to be a conversation piece.

After inspecting the house, which had accumulated more than its share of dust and grime during the months it had sat vacant, the cleaning-crew foreman announced that it would be a two-day job. While they cleaned, Allie shopped. San Antonio was an easy drive away and she arranged to spend Monday night in a downtown hotel.

Her first purchase was a new red pickup truck. Burn Monroe wasn't the only one who knew how to ranch in the nineties. That was followed by enough designer towels and sheets to stock the linen closet, and a down sofa covered in nubby cream linen to replace the old lumpy one she'd had carted away. She also bought a set of earthenware dishes to match the amber border of the new designer dish towels. She wandered around the kitchen department for nearly an hour, but having no idea what else might be needed, she finally decided to wait and deal with it later.

She finished shopping for essentials around two on Tuesday and spent the rest of the afternoon having her nails done, complete with Ombre Rose polish, which struck her as appropriately western and also coordinated perfectly with the color scheme of her new place. She made a quick stop at a grocery store near home and arrived back at the ranch to find the cleaning crew gone and the entire house sparkling like a jewel in the setting sun. For the first time since she'd arrived at the Circle Rose and found it was not quite what she'd expected, the haunting feeling that she might have made a huge mistake began to recede. This was going to work, she thought excitedly. She was going to make it work.

Lugging her purchases into the house took nearly an hour. Armed with a tall glass of iced tea, she made up her bed with the new sheets and comforter and struggled to hang the matching balloon shades. She'd settled on a gold-and-cream color scheme for her room, planning to accent with some pieces of antique lace, which she had also inherited from Verdy. Finally satisfied that the shades were hung as well as she could manage, she decided to leave Burn's room and the linen closet for the next day and tumbled exhausted into bed. Odd, she thought, yawning against the silky softness of the new cotton pillowcase, shopping didn't usually leave her so tired.

She woke in the morning entirely too early and to the sound of someone knocking on her door. Actually, it sounded more as if someone was trying to kick it in. The loud, insistent banging suggested that whoever it was had been going at it for some time and was clearly losing patience.

Maybe they would give up soon and go away, Allie thought sleepily, pulling the pillow over her head.

Then a second thought hit her.

Burn. This was Wednesday, the day he was supposed to return, and a rush of anticipation brought her fully awake in a hurry. She leapt from the bed, finger combing her hair and grabbing her robe as she hurried to the door. Smiling as she swung it open, she came face-to-face with a total stranger waiting on the other side.

Her excited expression immediately gave way to a frown, prompting an apologetic smile from the chunky, dark-haired man standing on the front porch. He was dressed in dark blue work clothes and looked to be in his late forties.

"Sorry to wake you, ma'am," he said, "but I'm supposed to be doing some work here this morning."

He held out a printed work order from the Acme Construction Company. Just the sight of it was enough to jar Allie's memory.

"Of course, my skylights," she exclaimed. "I've been so busy I completely forgot you were coming first thing this morning. Sorry you had to knock for so long. I overslept."

It was a slight twisting of the truth, since she usually slept until whatever time she felt like getting up.

"No problem," the man assured her as he motioned to his co-worker waiting in the truck to begin unloading their tools.

Allie opened the door wider and stepped aside. "Come on in and I'll show you where I want the windows."

He followed her inside and let her point out three places in the living room and hallway where she wanted the skylights installed. One spot he deemed fine, the second he suggested moving several feet and the third he advised forgetting about entirely because of the angle of the roof at that point. Allie bowed to his expertise and agreed to go with a larger skylight in the spot he suggested as an alternative.

She showered and dressed to the whir of electric saws as the two carpenters sliced holes in the roof. By midmorning the sunlight streaming through the raw openings assured Allie her instincts were right. Already the entire house seemed brighter and more spacious.

Dressed in old jeans and a red T-shirt, she stocked the linen closet with her new purchases. She was acutely conscious as she stacked towels and sheets that Burn had not yet arrived. Frankly, she was irked. She tried telling herself that her irritation stemmed from the simple fact that she was paying him a full day's wages and expected a full day's work in return, but she wasn't gullible enough to believe it. Deep down she knew her reaction wasn't so much that of an irate employer as an impatient woman, one who'd been waiting four days to see Burn Monroe again. Allie didn't like to be kept waiting.

As she pulled out the sheets she'd chosen for his room, she consoled herself with the thought that at least work on the inside of the house was progressing nicely. En route to the room Burn would be using, still undecided as to whether she ought to make his bed or simply toss the sheets there and let him fend for himself whenever he bothered to show up, she heard Vernon, one of the carpenters, call to her.

"I'm afraid we've got a problem over here," he told her, beckoning Allie to where a ladder stretched through one of the newly cut openings in the ceiling. "Ants."

"Ants?"

"Yes, ma'am. Carpenter ants, from the looks of them."

"That doesn't sound good."

"Not good at all, ma'am. Those suckers can just about bring a house down if you let 'em go at it long enough. They've already done a lot of damage to one of your support beams. It's a lucky thing you found 'em when you did."

"Mmm," Allie agreed, not feeling all that lucky. "So what do you do now that you've found them?"

"We don't do anything, ma'am. We're carpenters, not exterminators."

"I understand that you're not exterminators, but can't you just spray them with something?"

"I don't think you understand. There's a whole mess of them up there, ma'am. You want to climb up and have a look for yourself?"

"Not particularly."

"Well, someone ought to," he told her. "You got a husband or something?"

She shook her head, feeling an instinctive urge to do what she usually did when she encountered a problem in her life—dump the entire inconvenient matter on someone else's shoulders. Then she remembered that this time there was no one else, that she was in charge here and that this was what she wanted—a chance to prove she was capable of handling things all by herself, a chance to prove that when the going got tough, the tough got going, and that she was as tough as they came.

"Hold the ladder for me," she told Vernon.

"We've got it clamped up top so it's not going anywhere," he assured her, "but I'll hold it just the same."

He waited until she had climbed high enough that her head was level with the opening.

"Okay, now duck and look to the right," he instructed. "Farther right. See that support beam that runs the length of the house? Hunch down a little ... turn ... right there!"

"How the heck am I supposed to know which one is the support ... oh, yuck."

She spied the ants, a frantically moving mass of them, just as someone slammed the front door.

"What the hell do you think you're doing?"

This time there was no mistaking Burn's arrival. Allie would know that gritty, angry drawl anywhere, and she lifted her head so quickly she banged it on a rafter. Rubbing where it hurt, she glanced down to find Burn glaring up at her from the bottom of the ladder. At times over the weekend she'd wondered if any man could truly be as utterly sexy and all-out tempting as she recalled him being or if it was merely her imagination running away with her. Now she knew.

It wasn't her imagination.

"I asked what the hell you think you're doing up there?" he repeated, just about growling.

Allie's breath caught to think he would get so worked up over her. "Relax," she said, "I won't fall and break my neck, if that's what you're worried about."

"Hardly. If you did, it would save me the trouble of breaking it myself."

Allie eyed him coolly. "Thanks for your concern."

"Save your sarcasm. It so happens I'm plenty concerned. About the roof."

"Well, don't be," she snapped. "The roof isn't your problem, while just about everything else on this ranch is. Which brings me around to asking why you're so late for work?"

His eyes narrowed. "Sorry. I was under the impression you hired me to punch cattle, not a clock."

"So far I don't see you doing either. Exactly what time do you plan to start your workday in the future, Mr. Monroe?"

"Same time I started today, Miss Boston."

"It's Halston, not Boston."

"I know. Boston just seems to fit better."

"So you plan to start work at noon?" she asked, ignoring his jibe.

"No, at daybreak. Same as today, like I said."

"Daybreak?" she countered with a disbelieving shake of her head. "You Texans sure have a strange sense of time."

"Lady, I've been working my butt off since sunrise. If you don't think so, why don't you just come right out and say so?"

"Fine. I don't think you've been working your butt off since sunrise. I know you haven't been working it off here."

"Take a look outside."

All Allie had to do was step up one rung and turn her head to see in the direction he indicated. Outside, parked behind his Jeep, was a horse trailer and a flatbed truck loaded with . . .

"Cows," Allie stated from between clenched teeth. "Those are cows."

His mouth twisted. "In a manner of speaking."

"I told you I was going to raise sheep."

"And I told you the Circle Rose was a cattle ranch. And we left it undecided."

"You might have been undecided. I've decided on sheep."

He shrugged. "You'll come around after you've been here awhile and gotten a feeling for the land."

Allie was furious. "And in the meantime you just took it upon yourself to buy cows on my behalf?"

"Nope. I bought them on my behalf. Came across a deal I couldn't refuse."

"So if those are your cows, what are they doing on my land?"

He scowled, then gave another shrug. "I figured we could work something out, seeing as you're going to have to re-seed that acreage up by Pebble Creek if you want to graze anything on it come next spring. I figured I'd move the cattle and their feed up there after the seed goes down. They'll tramp it in better than any roller you can buy and their hoofprints will hold the rain from running the seed right off."

"Oh," Allie replied, not having any better response to offer. "You still should have checked with me first."

"Sorry," he said without sounding it. "I didn't think you'd be awake at dawn."

"Well, I was."

Allie prayed that Vernon knew enough to keep his mouth shut about having to bang on the door to get her out of bed. He seemed to. As a matter of fact, both he and his partner were hanging back, staying well out of the line of fire.

"Fine," Burn told her. "Now that I know you're up at sunrise, I won't hesitate to call on you early. Just so you'll know, I also brought along two horses of my own and picked up the supplies to get started on the corral, the stable roof and the seeding. You can just deduct from my salary whatever part of the morning's work you figure wasn't ranch related."

"Don't be ridiculous. I suppose I may have jumped to the wrong conclusion."

"Apology accepted."

Allie was about to point out that she hadn't exactly apologized, when he returned to his original question.

"Now that we've got that settled, would you mind telling me what's going on here?"

"Not at all. What would you like to hear about first, the skylights or the ants?"

He frowned, squinting in the direction of the open ceiling. "Ants?" He looked at Vernon. "What color are they?"

"Brown," she replied.

"Black," said Vernon.

"Black." Burn grimaced. "Carpenters, you think?"

"I'd say," said Vernon.

"A nest?" Burn asked.

Vernon nodded. "From the looks of it."

Allie cleared her throat. "Would you like to hear what I think? Since I am the one who's up here viewing the situation firsthand?"

"Depends," said Burn. "Do you know as much about ants as you do cowboys?"

"Probably not," she countered. "After all, ants are much more complex creatures. For instance ants—ouch."

She drew back sharply as an ant flew at her from the dark space inside the open ceiling, then she began hurriedly groping her way down the ladder. She had made it about halfway when a second ant dive-bombed her directly, getting caught in her hair. As she shook her head frantically, trying to get it out, her foot slipped and she slid ungracefully down the remaining rungs.

Burn stepped forward to break her fall, but instead of ending up cradled in his arms—which wouldn't have been half-bad, actually—she was trapped between him and the ladder, his hard chest pressed against her back. As she landed, she bumped her chin on one of the metal rungs and split her lip with her teeth.

"Oh, now see what you made me do!" she cried.

"Sorry. I don't know how I could have been such a clod."

Allie shot him a withering look over her shoulder. "Don't be smug."

"Just trying to please my new boss."

"If you really want to please me, help me get this bug out of my hair."

"Calm down."

"I am calm, damn it."

"If you say so. It's just that I've never seen anyone so scared of a few little ants."

"It's not a few, they're not little and I am not scared of them."

"Then how come you jumped?"

"I didn't jump, I slipped."

"Because you were scared."

"Because I was startled. Call me crazy, but I don't like having bugs crawling around in my hair. Now will you get it out?" she demanded, brushing her fingers across the top of her head as she twisted around to face him.

"Say please," he prompted, laughter in his voice.

"I don't have to say please. I'm the boss," she reminded him.

Burn shrugged and took a step backward. "I'm afraid that picking bugs out of your hair isn't in my job description."

"Please," she uttered, her teeth gritted.

He raised his hands to her hair, weaving his fingers through the full length of it, lifting it off her neck in the back in a way that brought his palms against the sides of her throat. His skin was warm and rough, and Allie felt a slow fluttering of her senses that escalated madly when her gaze met his.

"It's out," he said, his voice deep and close.

"Thanks."

Neither of them moved or, it seemed to Allie, even breathed, for the endless stretch of time until Vernon cleared his throat.

"You folks want us to maybe come back tomorrow?" he asked. "After you take care of the ants?"

"No," Burn replied, dropping his hands at last.

"Yes," Allie said at the same time. They exchanged another look, this one less searching and more inflammatory. "They have to come back to finish installing the skylights."

"The house doesn't need skylights."

"Since the holes have already been cut in the roof, I'd say it needs something."

"I can patch the roof."

"I want skylights."

"Do you know what three skylights that size will cost you?"

"To the penny." A small lie, since she'd simply told Acme Construction to install the skylights and bill her.

"I thought we agreed that ranch expenses would take precedence over redecorating," he reminded her.

"And I thought I'd made it clear that I was calling the shots around here."

Burn's jaw came up as if she'd landed a blow on it.

"You're right. Sorry I overstepped my bounds." He reached for the hat he'd tossed aside when he came in. "I'll go see to the cattle."

"Burn, wait," Allie called after him, regretting that she'd pulled rank in such a pointed and public way. But damn it, she was the boss around here. The whole point of buying this place was to do something on her own, in her own way, not to simply go from taking orders from her father to taking them from some cowboy with a seductive drawl and great shoulders.

He stopped by the door and turned just enough to shoot her a silent, narrow gaze.

"What do you think I should do about the ants?" she asked.

She knew she was giving him a perfect opportunity to tell her exactly what she could do with them, but she chanced it. After all, he was the foreman, and he was also the one who'd convinced her to hold off hiring more help for the time being because he could handle whatever problems arose. Here was his chance to prove it.

He glanced up at the opening in the ceiling. Allie suspected his look of disgust had more to do with the hole than the ants.

"I'll take care of it," he told her. "Better put some ice on that lip," he added as he strode away.

With Burn out of the way, Vernon and his partner quickly went about covering the ceiling openings with plastic, then left, promising to be back first thing in the morning. Alone, Allie sighed and kicked the leg of a table, not at all happy with the way things had gone. Which was ridiculous, since she had won. Burn was going to take care of the ant problem, and the skylights would be installed tomorrow just as she wanted. So why wasn't she happy?

It had something to do with Burn, that was obvious. But what? She was certain she was right and he was wrong about the skylights. Besides, she wasn't much interested in his opinion of how she chose to decorate her house. There was no denying that she was very interested in him, however.

Over the weekend she'd had more than one daydream about her next meeting with Burn Monroe, and not one of those daydreams had included a bloody lip, ants or an audience of two clearly bemused carpenters. Not that any of that should have mattered. She may not have been at the top of her class in school or a fast riser in the business world, but where men were concerned, Allie was usually in full control.

Usually, but not with Burn.

It wasn't because he wasn't attracted to her. Her infallible sixth sense about such things assured Allie that he was. And she was attracted to him as well. Very attracted. But that didn't explain why was she thrown so off-balance when he was around. Or why she was uncertain what her next move should be.

The answer was obvious: roles. Or rather, what Burn no doubt considered a role reversal. She had a hunch that his notion of man-woman relationships ran more along the lines of Me-Tarzan-You-Jane than having to take orders from a woman boss.

It didn't help the situation any that being in charge was a totally new experience for Allie. Not that she didn't like holding the reins. It was just going to take some getting used to. For both her and Burn. It was going to require some attitude adjustment on both their parts.

It occurred to Allie that her past success with the opposite sex was a result of the fact that she always had a definite idea of what she wanted from a man and how to get it. So what did she want most from Burn Monroe?

The answer came immediately. She wanted Burn's help getting the Circle Rose up and running. Romantic daydreams and tummy flutters aside, that's what she wanted most from him. For her sake and for Verdy's. Privately, she was now willing to concede that her father might have been right: that buying a ranch with her inheritance was just one more impulsive act in a lifetime of shortsighted impulsive acts on her part. But it didn't have to end there.

If she had arrived to find the Circle Rose as she expected, more like a scene from an old "Bonanza" episode than a ghost town, she might have dabbled at playing rancher for a while, indulged a cowboy fantasy or two and grown bored. Instead she was presented with more of a challenge than she'd bargained for...and more of a chance to prove herself. In the process she would also be proving that her aunt Verdy's faith in her was well placed. After all these years, Verdy deserved to have everyone in the Halston clan recognize that while her methods might be unorthodox, her judgment had always been sound. Rusty pipes and carpenter ants be damned. There was no way Allie was going to quit and let Verdy down.

There was also no question that to make a go of this she was going to need Burn's help a lot more than she needed a fling with a cowboy. It might be possible for some men to take orders from a woman with whom they were romantically involved, but that same canny sixth sense told Allie that Burn wasn't one of those men. She was going to have to earn his respect, and that meant she couldn't give any mixed signals or allow any more fevered looks like the one they'd shared a few minutes ago. The West was full of cowboys, she reminded herself, and as soon as the ranch was squared away, she would have time to meet some of them.

For now she had to concentrate all her attention and energy on ranching. For starters that meant proving to Burn that she meant business, and that when she gave an order, she knew what she was talking about. It would probably help, she mused, if she had a better idea of what he was talking about most of the time. Cal Rosen had given her a crash course in grazing rights, and while she had an idea of what permits and allocations had come with the deed to the ranch, Burn's talk of reseeding the area around Pebble Creek proved she had no notion of the specifics of how that land could best be utilized. But she soon would, Allie decided, going off in search of her *Beginner's Guide to Ranching.*

Until now she had only scanned the guide, mostly interested in the pictures of roping and general ranch life. Now she paid careful attention to each word. She also consulted some other books she'd brought along, as well as the ranching magazines she'd picked up at the airport. She learned about reseeding and grazing rotation, and that a lot of what Burn had been telling her yesterday incorporated new methods of mixing ranching with conservationism.

By the end of the afternoon she'd been thoroughly disabused of any notion she might have had that ranching was a romantic or easy way of life. It was hard work, with the frustrations Burn had tried to explain being both built into the job and added on to by a confusing system of government rules and regulations concerning grazing permits. Strangely, however, instead of being discouraged, Allie was more enthused than ever about the challenge ahead.

She was even willing to consider the possibility of keeping the Circle Rose a cattle ranch. Her reading had impressed upon her what a time-honored and essential role the cattle industry had always played in this country, and she felt an unexpected stirring of pride at the thought of being a small part of that tradition...of being part of something unique and important.

Her mood was buoyant as she put the books aside and went in search of Burn to tell him about her change of heart on the cattle question. She spotted him through the kitchen window. He had his shirt off, and his bare shoulders and back glistened with sweat as he bent over the engine of what appeared to be a tractor. Allie grabbed two beers from the refrigerator and headed outside.

"Hi," she said, stopping by the side of the tractor across from him.

Burn looked up and reached for the bandanna stuck into his waistband, using it to wipe the sweat from his face. Allie did her best not to notice his gorgeous chest, the way sweat had dampened the dark hair covering it into curly tendrils or the intriguing scars he bore. He was an employee, period, and thoughts of how his powerful arms would feel wrapped around her were totally inappropriate.

He nodded in response to her greeting and Allie held out the bottle of beer.

"No, thanks," he said. "Not while I'm working."

"You must be close to quitting for the day."

He glanced skyward. "Not while there's still sunlight."

"But you've been working for hours...since sunrise. You said so yourself."

"That's what you're paying me for, remember?"

"I'm certainly not paying you to work yourself to death."

"I'll keep that in mind."

"Seriously, Burn, I want the ranch up and running as much as you do, but this is still a job like any other job. I don't expect you to work around the clock."

"That's where you're wrong. Ranching is not like any other job. There's no whistle that blows at the same time each day to tell you that you can just drop everything until another whistle blows the next morning. Not when you're dealing with nature, and with animals in particular. With ranching there are times when you have to all out bust your butt to get everything done in time, and times when you can take it a little easier for a spell.''

"When do you think that taking-it-easy-for-a-spell time will come today?''

"After I get this carburetor back on and drive the cattle up to the creek. I managed to haul their feed up there and get the eastern slope turned over before the engine acted up. I also got the stable roof fixed in case it rains tonight.''

"Is it supposed to rain?''

He shrugged and wiped the metal rod in his hand on a rag he had handy before glancing up at the sky. "Doesn't feel like it. But my horses don't like to play the odds when it comes to getting wet.''

"I can't believe all you've gotten accomplished in one day.''

"Not nearly what I set out to accomplish,'' he countered, a grim set to his mouth. "And I haven't forgotten about the ants. I drove into town a while ago and picked up a couple of bombs that ought to do the trick.''

"Bombs?'' Allie echoed, startled.

"Insecticide bombs. You put them in the infested area and set them off, and they release a gas that will kill anything within range.''

"But what's to stop the gas from spreading to the rest of the house?''

"Nothing.'' He looked up from the engine, his smile mocking. "That's sort of the point. Did you think the ants restricted themselves to the one little area where you wanted to put a skylight?''

"I didn't really think about it.'' She watched in silence as he replaced the bolts he had painstakingly cleaned. "How long will the fumes last?''

"Twelve hours.''

"Twelve hours?'' she exclaimed. "But it's nearly five now. How will we be able to sleep in there tonight?''

"We won't,'' he said matter-of-factly.

"We won't?" Allie echoed, growing a little weary of his taciturn routine. "Then exactly where do you suggest we spend the night?"

This time he didn't bother to lift his head, just shot her a look that seemed to question her intelligence. "Out here. Where else?"

Chapter Four

"Me? Sleep out here?" Allie gave a short laugh. "In the dirt?"

"No. In a sleeping bag."

"I don't have a sleeping bag... at least not with me."

"Then it's lucky for you I have two."

"Why is it that lately whenever someone tells me how lucky I am, I end up doing something I don't want to do? Having to look at ants or sleep in the dirt or—"

"You want to hand me that rag?" he interrupted, both his hands gripping what she assumed was the carburetor.

"Yuck... here."

"Thanks."

"What if it rains?"

"It won't."

"But what if it does? It could, you know. Isn't that why you fixed the stable roof for the horses? I'd say that I deserve at least as much consideration as you give your damn horses."

His expression suggested otherwise, but all he said was "If it rains, we'll sleep with the horses. But I'd think of that as a last resort, if I were you. The air's fresher out here."

Allie made a disgusted noise and turned toward the house, both unopened beers in hand.

"Where are you going?" Burn called after her.

"Back inside. Before I get any luckier."

"What's for supper?"

"Supper?"

"Right, supper. You probably call it dinner. I didn't say anything about missing lunch, but one meal a day is all I care to skip."

"I haven't even thought about it," she confessed, feeling guilty that she also hadn't thought to at least offer him an apple for lunch when she had one. She wasn't accustomed to looking after anyone's needs but her own. "You said you were going to hire a man to do the cooking."

"I tried, but he's going to need some time to clear things up before signing on here."

"How much time?"

"Hard to say. In the meantime I'll take my chances with your cooking, Miss Boston."

"Very funny." Much as she had no idea of what to cook or how to go about it, it seemed to be the least she could do after the day he'd put in. "I have some canned soup. How does that sound?"

"Can't think of anything better on a hot night."

"It's either that or an apple," she told him.

"Then soup it is."

It could have been worse, Allie reasoned after serving dinner and adding the dishwasher to the growing list of things on the Circle Rose that did not work. But it couldn't have been much worse. If anyone had ever asked, she would have said that even she couldn't mess up canned soup. That's the main reason she had stocked up on cans of soup in the first place. But she was wrong. First she neglected to add water and then added too much, and somehow she managed to drop the lid of the can into the pan so that it ended up in Burn's bowl.

The only bright spot in the whole meal was that he fished it out before he cut his mouth on it. To his credit, he didn't complain once, and he even finished his entire bowl of soup. Of course, since he'd gone without lunch and done physical labor in the sun all day, she'd bet there wasn't much she could have put in front of him that the man wouldn't have eaten.

After dinner he excused himself to go feed the horses without so much as offering to help with the dishes. He did clear his place, however, and to her surprise Allie wasn't able to work up even a trace of feminist outrage. Things were different out here, she reflected, more clear-cut and less open to the sort of philosophical debate her friends back East so often engaged in. Here the nature of a man's work wasn't simply fodder for intellectual conjecturing, it was hard reality. Liberated woman of her time though she was, Allie found it impossible to chafe too much over washing a few dishes for a man who'd been breaking his back in the sun all day.

Washing dishes still wasn't her idea of fun...or what she'd bought the Circle Rose to do, she reminded herself. She might not be able to haul grain up a hillside or drive a tractor, but she could ride a horse, and she was a fast learner. There had to be something she could do to help even at this stage. On second thought, she decided, tossing the dish towel over a hook, maybe she *could* drive a tractor. Tomorrow she would find out.

It was beginning to get dark fast when Burn came back inside to tell her she had twenty minutes to use the bathroom and get together whatever she would need for the night before he set off the insecticide bombs. He checked the kitchen himself, stowing the fruit bowl and a bag of bagels inside the refrigerator for safekeeping and tightly closing all the windows. When he joined her outside, he was carrying the two beers he'd refused earlier. He offered her one.

"Does this mean you're officially through for the day?" she inquired as she took it from him.

"Pretty much. I'm just going to grab the sleeping bags from the Jeep."

He carried them to a patch of scruffy-looking grass near the corral.

"I thought we could sleep on the porch," Allie called to him.

"Be my guest," he said as he unrolled the first of two navy blue sleeping bags. "Personally, I'd rather look up at the stars than a bunch of chipped paint."

"How very Western of you," Allie muttered, not quite so enamored of the cowboy mystique at the moment.

Burn chuckled as he stood and opened his beer, taking a long swallow before turning to her with the second sleeping bag in his hand. "So where's it going to be, Miss Boston?"

"Stop calling me that. It makes me feel like a beauty queen."

"Bet that's a real stretch," Burn murmured.

"What was that?" she demanded, eyes narrowing in irritation.

"I said—"

"Never mind. I heard you the first time. Think what you please."

"I always do. Now, do you want to tell me where you plan to bunk or shall I just toss this to you and you can spend the rest of the night making up your mind?"

Allie shrugged. "I guess I'll join you over there after all," she said. Although she'd never admit it to Burn, she wasn't quite comfortable enough with the prospect of sleeping outside in unfamiliar surroundings to brave it alone on the porch.

"There you go," Burn said when he'd finished unrolling her sleeping bag for her.

"Thanks," replied Allie.

She slowly walked over and dropped her pillow on the makeshift bed. Burn finished his beer, tossed the empty bottle in a trash can he'd been using earlier to collect brush and debris from the corral and stretched in a way that reminded her of a grizzly bear about to settle in for the winter. Then he climbed into his sleeping bag and rolled to his side away from her.

"Good night," he said.

"Good night?" she countered in surprise. "Do you mean you're planning to go to sleep? Now?"

"Just as soon as you stop yakking."

"But it's barely nine o'clock."

"Since I woke up at four and plan to do the same tomorrow, nine sounds just about right to me."

"But going to bed at this time is... uncivilized."

"Oh yeah? Well, tell me, Ms. Boston," he said, levering up just enough to glance over his shoulder at her, "what sort of civilized plans did you have for this evening? The ballet? Opera? Or maybe crouching by the front window and watching a little television...that is, if you can see the screen through the fumes in there."

"I thought we could talk."

"I don't have anything to say."

That didn't come as a big surprise. Burn was clearly a man of as few words as possible. Unfortunately for him, Allie enjoyed the art of conversation and she wasn't the least bit sleepy. She lowered herself to her sleeping bag and sat with her legs folded under her.

"Well, I do have a few things I'd like to discuss with you."

"I'm listening," he said, lowering his head to the ground, still turned away from her.

It wasn't exactly the sort of rapt male attention she was accustomed to, but then Burn was hardly the sort of male she was accustomed to. Which was probably for the best, under the circumstances. *Think attitude adjustment,* Allie reminded herself.

"For starters, I'd like to know what I can do to help."

"Help with what?"

"The ranch," she retorted impatiently. "With all the work you're doing."

"Stay out of the way and feed me on time," he countered.

"I mean seriously, Burn."

"I am serious."

"I want to really help. And..." She hesitated, not wanting to make the same mistake she had that morning.

"And?" Burn prompted after a minute.

Allie shrugged in the darkness. "And it's my ranch."

She wasn't sure if the sound she heard was a chuckle or an oath.

"In that case I guess you can do whatever you damn well please. That must make you happy."

"Look, maybe you think this is all just some sort of game, but—"

"Isn't it?" he cut in, rolling over to face her this time.

"Of course not. I—" Allie broke off in the middle of the automatic denial. "All right, it may have started out that way," she admitted, "but it's more now. I know I've been here only a few days and some of my ideas may seem silly to you—maybe some *are* a little silly—but I'm changing. This place is the first thing I've ever had to call my own and that changes things."

"The first thing you've ever had to call your own?" he echoed with undisguised skepticism.. "I make it a practice never to call a lady a liar, but honey, the way you throw money around, I find that real hard to believe."

"Oh, I'm not saying I haven't owned things before. You're right, money has never been a problem for me. All my life, whatever I've wanted I could have—provided my father approved. Buying this place is the first thing I've ever done all on my own, without having to get his approval."

"Do I smell a rebellious streak?"

"Maybe. Maybe I'm sick of being thought of only as my father's daughter. Not that I've ever given people much reason to think anything else," she added in a voice heavy with self-recrimination.

"Now what's that supposed to mean?"

"Oh, I don't know.... I fooled around in school and never did manage to get a degree in anything. The only jobs I've ever had have been positions my father arranged for me. I have no profession, no real talent or field of expertise. Which is probably why buying a ranch didn't strike me as being as outrageous as everyone else seems to think it is. I've certainly tried my share of other things that I didn't know anything about. Why not this?"

"Excuse me if that sounds just a little like you're out here playing a game of some sort."

"Like I said, think what you please. I know the truth and that's what counts."

"And what is the truth, Allie?"

She thought for a moment, hardly understanding herself the subtle changes she felt taking place inside. "The truth is that for some reason it's become very important to me to make a go of the Circle Rose. I have two sisters—one's a pediatrician and the other's an architect. Even my mother has her volunteer work. I'm sick of being the only one with nothing she can point at and say, 'Look, that's mine, I did that,' and feel proud."

She wrapped her arms around her legs, hugging them to her chest, her sigh pensive. "For years I told myself it was because I was younger than my sisters, that sooner or later I'd find something I wanted to do with my life. But hell, I'm twenty-eight. Lauren was setting broken bones at my age and Nola was building skyscrapers."

"I take it Lauren and Nola are your sisters?"

Allie nodded. "I guess when you come right down to it, the reason I want so badly for this to work is to prove to myself and everyone else that I can...and maybe also to prove that Verdy was right for trusting me in the first place. Is that so wrong?"

She heard him sigh as he rolled onto his back, settling his hands beneath his neck as he stared up at the star-studded sky. "No, it's not wrong, Allie."

"I'm willing to do whatever it takes, Burn. I want to help. I'm willing to work . . . to do anything you tell me to do."

He slanted her a dubious look. "Anything?"

"Anything except stay out of the way."

"And you're serious?"

"Absolutely," she assured him, encouraged. "So what do you say?"

"I'll sleep on it," he replied, then groaned as she whacked him on the shoulder. "All right. I'll think of something. Can you ride?"

"Yes."

"I don't mean can you sit on a horse and let it take you along some picturesque trail in the park. Can you ride well enough to move cattle?"

"I think so."

"Well, we'll find out for sure first thing in the morning."

"Burn?"

"Mmm?"

"About the cattle."

"Mmm?"

"I decided you were right. The Circle Rose is a cattle ranch."

"Maybe there's hope for you after all, Miss Boston."

"And Burn?"

"What, Allie?" A sleepy note of irritation deepened his already deep voice.

"What did you plan to do with those cattle? I mean eventually."

"Sell them to you," he murmured.

"But—"

"I knew you'd come around sooner or later," he said before she could voice her protest. "And I also knew that when you did, I'd be out shopping for the right steers to get a herd started. Figured I'd just save myself some time and trouble down the road.''

"Oh. I thought maybe you bought them because you were planning to save for a ranch of your own."

"Nope."

"Not ever?"

"Not ever. If that's what I wanted, I have enough to buy a small place of my own right now."

"But I thought you liked ranching."

"Ranching's fine. It's owning I have a problem with."

"What sort of problem?"

He sighed resignedly, once more turning onto his back. "When you own something, you always stand the chance of losing it. I don't like losing."

Allie, unable to suppress a small smile of amusement, was glad for the darkness. Unless she was mistaken, she was hearing a Wild West version of the fear of commitment that afflicted so many men she knew. "Nice theory, Burn, but you can't go through life without owning anything."

"I have."

"What about your Jeep? And your horses?"

"I'm talking about things that matter. Things that can't be replaced. I admit I'm attached to my Jeep and my horses, but when you come right down to it, they can be replaced."

"And a ranch can't?"

There was a long silence, during which Allie felt sure that she had him, that he would be forced to concede she had a point. But when he spoke, his tone was as rough and uncompromising as hardened concrete. "No, a ranch can't."

After another silence, he amazed her by elaborating.

"A ranch isn't just a bunch of buildings and some land," he told her. "It's a home and a business—it's a way of life."

He lay flat on his back, one knee slightly bent. Allie watched his chest rise and fall and waited. This was clearly something about which he felt deeply and about which she knew next to nothing. She wouldn't trivialize it by pretending otherwise.

"When I was fourteen," he said at last, "my mother died."

"That must have been awful for you, Burn. That's such a tough age anyway."

"It wasn't nearly as tough on me and my brothers as it was on my father. He fell apart. He lost the woman he loved and then he lost the ranch he loved, bit by bit, until there was nothing left but a stack of bills he couldn't hope to pay even if he was given another lifetime to do it. And all I could do was stand by and watch it happen."

"You were just a kid," she said in an attempt to comfort him.

"Yeah, I was a kid. And my father was the strongest man I knew. When I saw how a loss like that could break him, I knew I never wanted to lose that way."

"It sounds to me like it's more than owning property you avoid."

"I avoid a lot of things."

"Yet you followed in your father's footsteps and worked on a ranch."

"Not hardly," he replied, his laughter rough. "The work always came easy to me—at least the showier parts of the business, roping and riding—and I never was one to fight what came easy. I went to college on a rodeo scholarship—"

"A rodeo scholarship?" Allie exclaimed. "I didn't know there was such a thing."

"I'll bet there's lots of things you don't know about, Boston."

"What happened to the Miss?"

He shrugged. "I figure since we're sleeping together I can drop the Miss."

"That's progress," Allie said with a laugh. "Now, if I can get you to remember my real name . . ."

"I remember it just fine. Allie."

The way he said her name, soft and rough at once, turning his head to look at her in the darkness, made Allie tremble unexpectedly and for all the wrong reasons.

"So, tell me what someone on a rodeo scholarship studies in school," she said quickly.

"I don't know about everyone else. I studied conservation agriculture and I competed in rodeos for the school. It's pretty much like any other sport."

"Somehow I don't think so. It's hard to equate riding a steer with lacrosse."

"Careful, your roots are showing."

"So are yours. I can't imagine being so blasé about something as exciting as competing in a rodeo."

"Yeah, well, after the first couple hundred or so the excitement dwindles."

"Couple hundred? How long were you in school?"

"Four years, same as everyone."

"Not everyone," she interrupted in a wry tone. "I went for six."

Burn looked amazed. "And you still didn't get a degree?"

"No, but I think I hold the record for the number of majors I almost have a degree in."

He chuckled at that. "Sounds like what you have is a short attention span."

"My one flaw," she joked. "Tell me more about the rodeos you competed in."

"There's not much to tell. After getting out of school, I competed on the professional circuit for another ten or so years."

"Ten years? You must have been very good to last that long."

"I did all right."

Allie had a hunch he'd done a lot more than all right, but that Burn wasn't the type to talk about his own past glory. Frowning slightly with confusion, she asked, "How old are you?"

"Thirty-four."

"If you competed in rodeos for ten years, when did you manage to fit in time to learn ranching?"

"I learned it growing up, learned it from the best. It's not something you forget. Then a few years ago, a doctor buddy of mine fixed me up when I dislocated a shoulder and told me that I ought to think about walking away from competition while I could still walk. I've been working on one ranch or another ever since. End of story."

"Sounds like that doctor must have had reason to be concerned. Just how badly were you hurt?"

"Never too badly all at once. Just bad enough consistently."

"Is that how you got the scar on your chest?"

He nodded, and flashed her a grin. "Among others. That particular one happened when a steer I was getting ready to ride taught me a lesson in paying attention. Like losing, that's another lesson a smart man doesn't have to learn twice."

"Do you miss competing, Burn?"

"I miss winning."

"Did you win often?"

"Wouldn't have hung around if I didn't. It's like I told you before, I don't like losing. And that's enough discussion for one night," he said, pointedly turning away from her. "'Night."

Allie grudgingly slipped into her sleeping bag, which was positioned about a foot from his. She didn't have to speak loudly to get his attention.

"Burn?"

Silence. No one fell asleep that quickly, but for a few seconds she thought he might be pretending he had.

"What now, Allie?" he said at last.

"I was just thinking. You never did get around to telling me how you knew I was from Boston."

"You never did get around to asking."

"Well, I'm asking now."

"Simple. Only a woman from back East would go swimming naked in a pond around here without a gun within reach. And I just figured Boston's about as back East as a woman can get."

"A gun?"

"Right. For shooting snakes," he said before she could ask.

"Oh, gosh. Burn, I never even thought about snakes."

"I know you didn't, Boston."

"I'm definitely thinking about them now, though. You don't think there are snakes around here, do you?"

"No, I don't think it."

Allie frowned at the sharp emphasis he placed on the word *think*. "What does that mean?"

"It means I don't think there are any around here," he retorted, sounding very exasperated as he rolled to face her. "I damn well know there are. This is Texas, Allie. There are snakes in Texas. Didn't any of this occur to you before you decided to play Annie Oakley?"

"No."

"Well, it should have."

Silence.

"Burn?"

"What?"

"I'm worried."

"I wish to hell you'd done your worrying before leaving Boston, not now, while I'm trying to sleep."

"Aren't you even a little worried?"

"No."

"Then you're crazier than I thought."

"Maybe, but at least with me around, you don't have to worry about snakes."

Allie jumped as he pulled his arm from inside his sleeping bag and stretched it across her so that the gun in his hand lay flat on her chest.

"That's a gun," she whispered.

"Now who's the one who should be handing out little gold stars?"

"Burn, if a snake did come, could you really—"

"In a heartbeat," he whispered before she even got the question out. "Now go to sleep, Allie."

Burn was half-afraid she wouldn't be able to sleep after he'd gone and opened his mouth about the snakes. Most women like her would get hysterical at the mere thought and end up spending the night in the car. But Allie stayed, and she slept.

When Burn heard her muffled breathing adapt a regular pattern that signaled she was asleep, he was surprised and a little impressed. Allie Halston was a puzzle, all right. Which, considering the way his life was going lately, was entirely appropriate. Why should she be any easier to understand than anything else? Ironically, the biggest puzzle of all was turning out to be himself. These days he was one big bundle of questions with no answers.

Only a few months ago he'd been just another cowboy, albeit a washed-up one, collecting a shameless paycheck for smiling at rich women and leading trail rides at the Double D dude ranch. Correction: guest ranch. The Double D management kept telling him that referring to the clientele as guests rather than dudes sounded less condescending. Now he was a washed-up cowboy breaking his back on a piece of land he'd once sworn he never wanted to set foot on again, working for a woman who made him horny and angry in about equal measure. And then there was the little matter of a fourteen-year-old son he didn't even know and who made it clear he didn't have any interest in getting to know him.

At the moment, however, it wasn't those things keeping Burn awake long after Allie had fallen asleep. What was bothering him now was why the hell he had gone and told this woman, whom he'd known was treacherous from the moment he laid eyes on her, more about himself than he'd ever before told anyone.

The night passed without Burn having to shoot any snakes. He woke as the sun was dusting the horizon, the gun by his side where he'd placed it before falling asleep, his arm stretched across Allie's chest. His hand was numb and he wanted badly to flex his fingers. Not quite as badly, however, as he wanted to leave it where it was, nestled against Allie's very warm, very soft breasts, for just a minute longer.

Watching her sleep, her perfect face so serene, made him think of poetry. At that moment it was easy for Burn to forget about the skylights, how she was bound to mess up the Circle Rose, the hundred or so other ways she made him angry. That left him feeling only horny. There was nothing he liked better than rowdy morning sex, and the urge to wake his new boss and find out if she was really as uninhibited as she had appeared that first day down by the pond was so strong that Burn had to stand up and walk around to bring it under control.

He headed for the house, opening all the windows to air the place out and putting on a pot of coffee before taking a cold shower that left him feeling it was safe to wake Allie. From her own description of her life before coming to Bandera, he had a hunch that if she'd ever seen a sunrise before, it had been on her way to bed, not because she was just getting up.

She frowned and mumbled when he called to her, and tried to scrunch deeper into her sleeping bag. Burn finally put the coffee mugs he was carrying aside, knelt down and shook her hard.

"Go away," she muttered, giving him a sleepy push.

"Can't. It's morning."

"I hate mornings."

"Yeah, I sort of figured that," he chuckled, deciding his first impression of her had been right, after all. "You still have to get up. You're going to help me move those cattle this morning, remember?"

"I'll move them later."

"Uh-uh." Burn dragged the sleeping-bag zipper open and rolled her out onto the ground. "Hungry cattle wait for no man...or woman."

"Damn you, Burn," she cried, shooting to her feet, her green eyes flashing in a way that told him she was wide awake now, all right. "Don't ever, ever—"

She broke off as he held out one of the mugs of coffee to her and smiled. "Hope you take it black."

She wavered, then accepted it with a shrug. "I do. Thanks."

She took a sip and the soul-satisfied look that came over her made Burn chuckle again. Silently, of course—it was still too early to risk inciting a skirmish. But the fact that she could drink coffee as strong as he made it, black, first thing in the morning, was one point in favor of her adapting to life on a ranch. Whether there would be others, enough to counter the hundreds of strikes against her, was something he figured he'd soon find out.

"I already ate. Soup," he explained in response to her questioning look.

Allie shuddered.

"Yeah," Burn concurred. "We're going to have to do something about the food situation until Frizzy gets here. But we'll worry about that later. For now, you go get cleaned up and grab something to eat while I get the horses saddled. I'll meet you by the stable in twenty minutes."

"Twenty minutes?" she echoed, her tone incredulous. "It takes me twenty minutes to wash my face."

"Then I guess you've got a choice to make—wash it or feed it. Just be out here in twenty minutes or I leave without you."

As he turned away she said, "Aren't you forgetting that I'm—"

"The boss?" he snapped, whipping back around. "Not likely, with you throwing the fact in my face every time things aren't going your way. I remember that you're the boss, all right, but you better remember that I'm the foreman around here. You hired me to do a job. If you've changed your mind and think you can do that job better yourself, just say the word and I'm out of here. But if you want me to stay, there are going to be a few new conditions.''

"Such as?'' Her expression was both haughty and cautious.

"Such as no more pulling rank. If you don't like the way I'm handling things, tell me. We'll talk it out. If you still don't like it, fire me. But don't keep—''

"All right, all right. What else?''

"If you want to sit up there on the porch with your decorating books, that's fine. I'll handle the work load. But if you expect to be out here working by my side, then you have to take orders same as any other hand would have to.''

"But that's—''

"That's the only way it will work. At least, that's the only way I'll work. Give me my head or give me my walking papers. It's your call, Boston.''

She folded her arms across her chest and pursed her lips in a way that in Burn's estimation she really shouldn't chance around men she didn't know well. More an invitation than a pout, it made her lips look soft and moist, and filled his head with very distracting possibilities.

"All right,'' she said at last. "Since I need help here and Rosen obviously thought you were the best man for the job, it's a deal.''

"Good,'' Burn told her. "I'll meet you by the stable in fifteen minutes.''

"But you said...oh, never mind,'' she muttered, starting for the house. "Fifteen minutes.''

To Burn's surprise, she made it back outside in time, looking good enough that no one would ever guess she'd dressed in such a hurry.

Her faded jeans fit her backside a little too closely for his concentration, but other than that he couldn't find fault with her appearance. She was wearing boots made for business, not for looking pretty, a hat with a brim broad enough to shade her face from the sun and a long-sleeved white shirt with a bandanna looped under the collar. Like him, she was wearing sunglasses.

"Did you eat?"

"I had an apple and some cheese. That's more than I usually eat for breakfast," she added when he raised an eyebrow.

"Maybe. But I'll bet you don't usually spend the day herding cattle."

"Is that what we're going to do this morning?" she asked, such a note of anticipation in her voice that Burn wondered whether he would be able to leave her behind even if it turned out she didn't know which end of the horse to sit facing. It would sure make for a long day if he had to baby-sit her along with the cattle.

"That's what I'm going to do," he replied, trying to sound tougher than he felt at that moment. "Whether or not you come along remains to be seen." He led over to her the smaller of the two already-saddled horses, a cinnamon-colored beauty with a white mane. "Think you can mount up by yourself?"

"I'll do my best," Allie retorted, rolling her eyes. She swung into the saddle with an encouraging degree of ease. Many of the women he'd dealt with during the past few years couldn't even do that.

"Hold her tight," Burn cautioned. "She's frisky in the morning."

"What's her name?"

"Fortune, because that's what she cost me. She comes from a strong line of rodeo champions and someday I'd like to breed her. This here's Vagabond," he added as he mounted the espresso-colored stallion who stood patiently waiting. "Because that's what he is."

While he spoke, he took note that Allie appeared comfortable and that she held the reins lightly and correctly. This just might work out after all.

"Okay," she said, controlling Fortune's tendency to dance in place, "where do we start?"

"With a little test ride."

"For heaven's sake, Burn, can we skip the preliminaries? I know how to ride a horse."

"Then you shouldn't mind indulging me with a little demonstration. Just let me warn you that riding out here is a lot different than on a trail back home."

"Gee, I'll try and hold on real tight."

Lady, you'd better, Burn thought as he spurred Vagabond into a quick trot. He'd intended to choose an easy path—along the drive back out to the road and then into the woods across from the ranch. But her cocky attitude changed his mind. Instead he broke into a full gallop across the fields behind the house, heading for the rocky hills that cut the Circle Rose's grazing lands in half and made for riding rough enough to demand even his full attention, and he'd ridden it hundreds of times before.

It was not only a tougher stretch than he'd planned to test her on, but a much longer one as well. A waste of time, he realized when she stayed with him a hell of a lot better than he expected. But by then his pride was involved in some crazy way and he'd be damned if he'd give in—even if he was wasting time he couldn't afford to waste. Not any way to run a ranch, he chided himself even as he drove Vagabond forward. Not any way at all.

He gave Allie credit for having the sense to let Fortune pick her way up the steep and narrow brush-covered trail that brought them to where a tributary of Pebble Creek flowed into a clear pool in an area known as Antelope Basin. In spite of a lot of painful memories associated with the Circle Rose, this just might be Burn's favorite place in the whole world, and he wasn't sure why he had brought Allie there.

"Did I pass the test?" she demanded, not any more winded than he was.

"You aced it," he admitted. "Where did you learn to ride that way?"

"Boston," she countered triumphantly.

Burn chuckled. "Point taken. We'll just let the horses drink a minute and then head back down." He walked Vagabond to the edge of the pond and loosened the reins for him to lower his head and drink. Allie followed suit.

"I wish I'd known about this place when I wanted to take a bath the other day."

"Wouldn't have done you much good even if you knew about it. That's a long climb without a horse."

"True," Allie agreed, gazing over her shoulder to where the path disappeared among the steep cliffs.

"You should be able to stick to indoor bathing now, anyway. I didn't notice any problem with rust when I took a shower this morning," he remarked.

"I know. It disappeared once I left the water running for a while. I guess I was just too hot and impatient that first day. And now that I know about the snakes..." She grimaced and looked around.

"Just keep a pistol handy."

"I don't happen to own a pistol, or any other kind of gun, for that matter. I guess I should tell you up front that I'm opposed to guns of any kind."

"Me, too," Burn agreed readily. "Just not quite as opposed to them as I am to snakebites."

Allie's laughter had an edge of self-mockery. "I can't argue with that."

She reclaimed the reins as Fortune raised her head, finished drinking. Together she and Burn turned their horses back toward the path, but Allie drew up to gaze out over the panorama spread before them. The view seemed to go on forever, mile after mile of unspoiled terrain dotted with an occasional ranch, green pasture running into yellow grain field and wide patches of raw brown earth—a cowboy's rainbow.

Allie was silent. Speechless, thought Burn, understanding completely. Sitting there, taking it all in, was enough to make a man or woman feel very insignificant indeed. Ironically, the same view had a way of making a boy feel like he was king of the world. Burn had felt exactly that way once, a long time ago. That feeling had been ended by the wailing siren of the ambulance that had come to take his mother to the hospital. That afternoon was when they'd discovered her headaches weren't caused by bad allergies, but by a brain tumor that took her life before a doctor could operate.

At least, Burn thought, there'd been a time when he had got to sit up here and feel like a king. He thought suddenly of Rory, his son. *His son*... Burn didn't think those words would ever stop making him feel as if he was wearing someone else's hat. But no matter how ill-suited he felt for the role, the biological fact remained that he was Rory's father. Rhonda might have been about fourteen years late in getting around to telling him that fact, but she wasn't lying about it, of that he was certain. Just as certain as he was that the quiet, sullen Rory had never gotten his chance to feel like the king of anything. Was it too late for him now? Was it too late for both of them? Burn wished to hell he knew.

An ocean of yearning, for what he wasn't quite sure, opened up inside him as he sat there beside Allie. He felt Vagabond shift beneath him, eager to get moving, and the small rockslide caused by the horse's movement broke Allie's concentration. She turned to Burn, the sense of wonder she was feeling evident in spite of the dark glasses hiding her eyes. She looked the way he used to feel, he thought, wanting that feeling back again.

"Burn, this is the most beautiful thing I've ever seen," she said.

Without speaking, without even thinking, Burn reached out and grasped the back of her neck, heedless of the horses' reflexive jockeying for position as he pulled Allie close enough to kiss her. If he'd planned the kiss, it might have been executed with more finesse. Instead it was hard and searching and a little desperate, like his mood. It was as if by kissing her long enough and hard enough, he could draw from her those feelings he'd lost somewhere along the way.

Allie neither protested nor participated, although Burn was certain he felt the pulse in her throat racing as hard as his own just before he finally pulled back.

"Want to tell me what that was all about?" she asked placidly.

Good question, one more for which he had no answer.

He tipped his hat up a notch, safe behind his own dark lenses. "Blame it on the moment...and the fact that you're just about the most beautiful thing *I've* ever seen."

"That's very flattering," she told him, "and totally inappropriate."

Burn did his best to pay attention as she delivered a predictable little speech on the pitfalls of mixing business with pleasure, all of which made perfect sense to him and none of which made him at all sorry he'd kissed her. After just one taste, Burn didn't think there was anything that could make him sorry, or make him stop wanting more of her.

"I just want to make it clear from the start that I came out here to learn about ranching," she concluded. "Period."

"Really?" Burn couldn't resist countering in a drawl. "Then you really are unique. I've known a lot of ladies who come out west to learn what it's like to sleep with a cowboy."

"I already did that. Last night," she reminded him when his eyebrows shot up.

Last night. Burn felt the sudden crazy tightness in his chest brought on by the mere thought of her sleeping with another man ease a bit. "Last night doesn't count."

"Then I guess I'll just have to pass on the entire experience, as mesmerizing as I'm sure it would be," she added in a tone dry as dirt. "Now, shall we get to work?"

Chapter Five

It took them most of the day to move the cattle across dry hilly terrain to the spot where Burn planned to graze them over the summer. To Allie's surprise there were already cattle nearby, along with a man on horseback.

Burn explained to her that the Circle Rose shared this particular grazing allotment with the Longo family, who owned the neighboring ranch, and that the cattle she saw were theirs. They were being tended by a range rider who kept them from overgrazing any one spot and destroying all growth in that area. She was impressed to learn that Burn had already spoken with Ben Longo about splitting the cost of the rider's salary and having him move their cattle as well.

For now, Burn told her, the Longo brand would be sufficient to differentiate the herds, but branding would have to be one of the first tasks attended to as soon as they hired more hands. It was one more fact of ranch life that was new to Allie and one more reminder that she was lucky to have

Burn running the Circle Rose. She made a mental note to write Cal Rosen a note of thanks.

Lunch was eaten late and consisted of bagels and apples. They ate sitting on the front-porch steps after she had badgered from Burn a rather brusque acknowledgment that the newly installed skylights did brighten the house considerably. He made sure the workmen had repaired the damage done by the ants before she wrote the check to pay them.

Allie was tired and sore from the unaccustomed hours in the saddle and, once her stomach was full, would have liked nothing better than to indulge herself with a cool shower, crank up the air conditioner in her bedroom and take a long nap. Unfortunately, she had a hunch that afternoon naps weren't part of a rancher's life. There was no doubt her riding ability and her work that morning had come as a surprise to Burn, earning her a modicum of grudging respect that she knew could be wiped away by a single whine. She didn't intend for that to happen. When he stood and announced that he was going to see what could be done about the bunkhouse, she was right by his side, delighting in the unspoken astonishment clearly registered in his expression.

They worked side by side, hauling debris from the bunkhouse and dragging bedding outside to air until the heat of the day had passed and Allie's stomach was issuing frantic growling reminders that it was once again time to eat. The empty feeling grew steadily stronger. She couldn't recall ever before being this hungry. Of course, she noted wryly, she also had never before put in so many consecutive hours of hard labor.

When she couldn't take it any longer, she tossed her broom aside and tracked down Burn, who was working under the sink in the bunkhouse's oversize bathroom.

"Burn?"

"Yeah?"

"I'm hungry."

"Me, too."

"What shall we do about dinner?"

"Keep working and don't think about it."

"I've been trying not to think about it for over an hour. Now I can't think of anything else. Even canned soup sounds exciting. Let's call it a day."

"Not until I'm finished here."

"How long will that take?" she asked, determined not to quit until he did.

"Hard to say."

"Well, try, damn it. I'm starving."

That got his attention away from the pipes. He glanced up at her, and Allie was suddenly conscious that she hadn't combed her hair since that morning and that her clothes and her face sported more dirt than she usually came in contact with in a month. She expected him to laugh. Instead his expression softened and his eyes seemed to warm with admiration. Either cowboys had strange tastes or he couldn't see very well in the shadows.

"I thought maybe we'd skip the soup tonight and go into town for a real meal," he said. "How does that sound?"

Allie's heart pumped as if he'd suggesting flying to Paris for dinner. "It sounds like heaven." She glanced down, grimacing. "But I can't go like this. I'm a mess."

"Not quite," he countered in a deep, dry tone. "But if it makes you feel better, go get cleaned up. I'll just clamp this last pipe back in place and join you."

He didn't have to urge her twice. Allie showered quickly, washing her hair and letting it air dry, and dressed in a pair of cream-colored jeans, boots and a tawny silk shirt. With the addition of a simple gold chain and earrings, she was ready for anything from fast food to a more formal restaurant, and she found herself wondering which Burn would suggest. It would be a signal of sorts, she mused. Would they get on line for a burger and each pay for their own like any two people stopping off for a bite after work? Or would he suggest someplace where they could sit and talk and linger over their meal, the sort of place a man might bring a date?

A date with Burn Monroe. Over and over during the day she had been reminded of how much the Circle Rose needed his dedication and expertise, and of how much she needed him if she was to succeed with her plans for the ranch. Still, just the thought of sharing a romantic dinner with him made her senses flutter with excitement. For at least the hundredth time since it had happened she closed her eyes and relived the moment when he had kissed her.

Perhaps if they hadn't been mounted at the time it would have seemed to her like any other kiss she'd ever experienced. Maybe it was the awe-inspiring beauty of their surroundings or her awareness of the restless energy of the horse under her that made it seem more powerful, more devastating, larger than life and twice as dangerous. Burn's kiss had left her hot and hungry and babbling mindlessly about how it absolutely could not happen again. Fortunately, he hadn't seemed to be paying much attention to her desperate little speech, his blasé expression throughout telling her he was taking her words about as seriously as he might his daily horoscope.

This change-in-attitude stuff wasn't going to be as easy as she hoped, Allie realized as she went to meet him. He was waiting by his Jeep, dressed in fresh jeans and a soft cotton shirt so white it made his lean face look even tanner. And more irresistible, she thought cautiously. His dark hair was wet and he was holding his hat.

"Did you shower in the bunkhouse?" she asked.

He nodded. "It's not really in as bad a shape as it looked at first. In fact, once the roof is repaired and a few floorboards are replaced, it will only need some cosmetic work. That can be done while it's in use."

That meant he would soon be moving in there, Allie thought, not sure if that was more of a relief or a disappointment.

He opened the passenger door for her as if they were on a real date, and on the drive into town asked if a local steak house would meet with her approval.

"I thought I should ask in case you turned out to be a vegetarian," he joked, taking his attention off the road long enough to shoot her a grin. He seemed more relaxed than usual. "I figured that your idea of a good meal might be a few goat-cheese ravioli and a sprig of watercress arranged with panache on a bed of *radicchio.*"

Allie, who had to laugh at his mocking version of a restaurant review, decided not to confess that she had indeed flirted with vegetarianism awhile back. But watercress certainly wasn't on her mind tonight.

"Not quite," she said. "At the moment I can thoroughly understand the concept of the meat-and-potatoes man. In fact, the thought of a nice juicy steak makes me feel a little savage."

"Welcome to Texas," Burn drawled. "Riding herd does have a way of changing your perspective . . . not to mention your appetite."

"Let's talk about something besides food and my appetite. I'm starving."

He chuckled softly and glanced her way again, but this time he wasn't grinning. "You have a right to be hungry. You did good today, Boston. Real good."

For the rest of the ride they talked about what they had accomplished and all that remained to do, while Allie privately basked in the afterglow of his praise. *You did good,* he'd said, and somehow those few words thrilled her more than hundreds of more eloquent and flowery compliments she'd received through the years.

Ruby's Steak House turned out to be a combination of fast food informality and fine dining. It was, Allie decided, exactly the sort of place Burn would take a woman on a date, and that pleased her beyond reason. They both ordered steak and baked potatoes, and for the first half of the meal they both devoted more attention to their food than to each other.

Over coffee they continued their discussion of the future of the Circle Rose. Allie noted that Burn spoke of the ranch with such concern and foresight that a listener might assume he was the owner or that he and Allie were equal partners. From listening to the frequent diatribes of her father, the quintessential businessman, she understood that such dedication was a rare quality in an employee. In fact, she thought a bit sheepishly, Burn seemed more devoted to the Circle Rose than she had ever been to any of the assorted family businesses where she'd put in time.

They finished their meal with strawberry shortcake, Allie for once not even thinking about the calorie avalanche involved. She estimated that her recent activity would have burnt off the daily calorie intake of a small country. As they walked back to the Jeep afterward, Allie understood why Burn had wanted to turn in so early the night before. The thought of putting her head on her pillow was so pleasurably tempting that the sensation was almost physical. As Burn climbed into the driver's seat beside her, she yawned and stretched contentedly.

"Tired?"

"Mmm."

"Too bad," he countered dryly. "We've still got shopping to do before we head back."

She straightened in her seat. "Shopping?"

"Grocery shopping," he reminded her. "I don't know about you, but I can't survive on a diet of apples and bagels for too long."

"I'm stuffed," she grumbled. "I can't even think about food now."

"Fine," he said, driving a short distance down the road and swinging the Jeep into a parking space outside a brightly lighted supermarket. "You push and I'll think."

It was a workable compromise. Allie pushed the shopping cart, glad to have something to lean on, since she was really beginning to feel the aftereffects of the day's activities. All that riding, hauling and sweeping had evidently used very different muscles than her twice-weekly dance-aerobics class back home.

As they moved up and down the aisles, she vetoed Burn's choice of white bread and tossed in an occasional bag of cookies or bottle of mineral water that caught her fancy. Burn frowned each time she did so, pronouncing her impulsive selections a waste of money. While they were skirmishing over a four-dollar jar of gourmet mustard, an elderly woman stopped her cart to tell them that she and her husband had argued the very same way when they were newlyweds.

"Let him win, honey," she advised Allie with a knowing nod and a smile. "I always did and I've been married over fifty years."

Allie and Burn smiled and nodded in return, waiting until the woman was out of sight to look at each other.

"Is that what we're acting like?" Burn muttered with disgust as he replaced the jar of mustard on the shelf. "Damn newlyweds?"

"Perish the thought," Allie countered, reaching for the jar and putting it back into the cart.

The thought persisted, however, that that was precisely how they were acting. Like it or not, there was something oddly intimate about shopping together for food they would also eat together, and the way Burn retreated into his typical taciturn mode for the remainder of the time they were in the store told Allie that he was equally unsettled by the notion.

They had checked out and bagged their groceries and were wheeling the cart out the door when a woman called out Burn's name. They both stopped and turned.

The woman, who had just entered the store and now circled around the bank of shopping carts to reach them, was wearing tight jeans, a tight yellow sweater and a tight smile. Her long red hair was about the only loose thing about her, Allie observed as the newcomer addressed Burn in a rather tense tone.

"Burn, you have no idea how glad I am to run into you."

"Hi, Rhonda. I didn't know you did your shopping way over here."

"Well, I don't usually," she said impatiently, "but I had to drive over here to pick up some seed that was on back order and to stop at the K-Mart for... Oh, never mind all that. The fact is it's a blessing I ran into you. I tried calling you at the Double D, but they said you don't even work there anymore—can you imagine that? And—"

"I don't work there anymore," Burn interrupted to confirm. "I did leave a new number where you could reach me if you needed to, though."

"Well, they sure didn't give me any new number when I called. I swear, Burn," she said with a sweep of her arm that sent a drift of very strong, very sweet perfume Allie's way, "those people at that place are just so damn rude. Dude ranch my butt, it's more like an asylum. For the life of me I can't figure out why anyone would want to spend his vacation at that place. And pay through the nose for it while he's at it. I mean—"

"Rhonda," Burn broke in, slanting an uneasy glance Allie's way.

She stood by silently, two words of the woman's rambling lodged front and center in her mind. Dude ranch?

"I haven't got all night," Burn told the woman. "Why don't I call you tomorrow and you can tell me what's bothering you?"

His tone was gentle and patient, Allie noted, and he was calling the woman by her name, not some stupid condescending nickname like Boston. The soothing tone worked on her, too. Rhonda's expression relaxed a bit as she nodded.

"All right, that probably would be best. It's a long story and maybe sort of... you know," she added a little awkwardly as she darted a glance at Allie. "Private."

"I could wait in the car," Allie felt obliged to offer.

Burn shook his head. "Rhonda, this is Allie Halston. Allie, Rhonda Sue Gibbons."

That was it, just Rhonda meet Allie, Allie meet Rhonda. No subtitles, such as "This is Allie, my boss," or "This is Rhonda, my..."

My what? The big question mark about who this woman was to Burn was like a fever spreading through Allie as she and the other woman exchanged polite greetings. Friend? Lover? Sister? She looked to be about his age, so any of them was possible. Allie observed both the woman's and Burn's body language as they made plans to talk the following day, but she couldn't draw any substantial conclusion. Her curiosity was so strong that it almost—*almost*—distracted her from the thought still uppermost in her mind.

Dude ranch?

"I really do appreciate it," Rhonda told Burn with what struck Allie as unnecessary fawning after he had assured her for the third time that he wouldn't forget to call her first thing in the morning. "I don't know how to thank you."

"I told you there's no need to thank me, Rhonda," Burn countered quietly, sounding and looking more ill at ease with each passing second. "I want to be involved in this."

"And you'll come on Saturday? That's definite?"

"Yeah, I'll come on Saturday."

The mention of Saturday was like a shot of adrenalin to Allie's already exploding curiosity. So, she thought, whatever the very important things were that Burn did each Saturday, they involved this woman.

Allie and Burn loaded the bags of groceries into the back of the Jeep in silence and drove home the same way. Burn turned on the radio, but the sounds of a country station did little to alleviate the heaviness in the air. Allie wanted to ask him about Rhonda Sue Gibbons and how he spent his Saturdays, and about the Double D ranch. As his employer she certainly had a right to ask if his previous experience had been on a dude ranch, but for some reason she held back.

If she'd been confident that she would be able to talk like an employer questioning an employee, she might go ahead and do it. But she wasn't at all sure that most of what she was feeling and thinking right then had anything to do with Burn's ability to perform his job. An ability which, to be fair, he'd already proved no matter where he'd worked before now. It was the suspicion that what she was feeling was more personal than professional and that it might be obvious in whatever she ended up saying that held her back.

Burn helped her put the groceries away in the kitchen cupboards and then said a hasty good-night.

"Burn, wait," Allie called as he left the kitchen.

He stopped and took a step back toward her, his mouth grim. "What is it?" he asked, a wary edge to his expression and his tone.

"About dinner tonight," she said. "Thanks for suggesting it."

"Sure."

His relief was almost palpable, and maybe, Allie mused later, alone in her bed, it had been that sense of relief, of not being cornered, that prompted him to open up to her even a tiny bit. She vowed to remember that, where Burn was concerned, it was better not to push too hard. That knowledge was bound to come in handy for her as his boss, and maybe as a woman as well.

He had started to leave again when he once more turned to her, his broad shoulders as rigid as his jaw. "And Allie, about Rhonda..."

"Yes?"

"She's just an old friend."

He didn't give her a chance to respond or probe the matter further, which she would have dearly loved to do. He disappeared into his room, and all Allie could do was turn off the lights and do likewise.

She half expected to lie awake for hours, tossing and turning the way she often did when she was troubled by something. Instead she fell asleep instantly and didn't wake until the sun was an orange blaze outside her window and Burn was rapping on her bedroom door. In spite of the emotional turmoil she'd felt going to bed, there hadn't even been a bad dream to disturb her sleep. First dessert without guilt and now a peaceful night's sleep. There was, she decided, a lot to be said for hard work.

"Rise and shine, Boston," Burn called to her through the door.

Allie reached for a slipper by the bedside and hurled it, wishing it could have hit his head instead of the wall.

She heard his retreating boot steps stop and return.

"Care to repeat that?" he drawled.

Grinning, Allie tossed the other slipper.

He chuckled on the other side of the door. "Yeah, that's what I thought you said."

By the time she'd showered and dressed, Burn had breakfast on the table. Scrambled eggs, bacon and toast.

"It looks great," Allie told him, sitting down across from him. "This was really nice of you."

"Not nice, fair. If you're going to be working with me, I figure I ought to do half the cooking. You've got dinner tonight . . . and since the cupboard's well stocked, there's no excuse to resort to soup."

"Sure there is. I can't cook. How's that for an excuse?"

"Yesterday at this time you couldn't herd cattle, either." He took a bite of toast. "You'll do just fine."

Allie wished she had as much confidence in her ability as he seemed to have. She did go so far as to take a package of chicken from the freezer, with no idea what she would do with it once it was thawed. She turned to find Burn loading the dishwasher.

"That doesn't work," she told him.

"It does now. I fixed it."

"Is there anything you can't do?" she demanded irritably.

He glanced over his shoulder at her. "Plenty."

"Such as?"

"I'd be a fool to point out my shortcomings to the boss now, wouldn't I?" He swung the dishwasher door shut. "Ready to get to work?"

"I am," she said pointedly, "but don't you have a phone call to make first?"

"I already made it."

"My, my, Rhonda Sue must be a very early riser."

"Yeah," he agreed, his mouth slanting into an amused smile as he brushed past her on the way out. He dipped his head to add, "But she can't herd cows worth a damn."

Burn spent most of the day repairing the roof on the bunkhouse, while Allie continued to work on making the inside livable. For the first time in her life she used a paint-brush, putting a fresh coat of paint on the interior walls and on most of herself in the process. The exterior walls were constructed of log planks, and while Burn assured her that whoever she hired wouldn't much care what color wall they bunked next to, she thought the pale sand shade she'd selected coordinated perfectly with the rough wood.

She left Burn hammering shingles into place while she fixed sandwiches for lunch, and again later when she knocked off early to face the more daunting task of turning the thawed chicken into a meal. After consulting a cookbook left behind by the former owners, she decided for Burn's sake to curb her impulse to attempt Chicken Mexicana and settled on oven-fried chicken and baked potatoes. To her own amazement, and, she surmised, to Burn's as well, the meal was a success.

Allie felt ridiculously triumphant. Get a grip, she chided herself. Millions of women around the world produced edible meals every night of the week. She was still proud of herself. It wasn't exactly brain surgery, but it was about as close as she'd ever come to doing something worthwhile completely on her own. And, she acknowledged, aware that Burn's enthusiastic response had more than a little to do with her feeling of satisfaction, it was the first time she could recall a man truly appreciating her for something besides her looks or her bank account.

Again she went to bed exhausted and sore, a combination she was growing accustomed to. But she was also happy. She even woke early on her own, still happy and actually looking forward to another day of washing walls and feeding horses. Maybe she could even persuade Burn to take a break and go riding with her later on. She wouldn't mind visiting the pool at Antelope Basin again. With Burn along she would even feel safe enough to go for a swim.

The house was quiet when she got out of bed, full of her grand plans for the day. Too quiet, thought Allie as she entered the kitchen and found none of yesterday's activity or good smells. That's when she remembered that this was Saturday, and Burn was gone.

Chapter Six

Allie spent the morning working, but somehow, without Burn around, it wasn't nearly as enjoyable or as satisfying. Not really the martyr type, she knocked off around noon and changed her clothes, deciding to drive into San Antonio and do some shopping.

She now had a much better idea of what was needed in the way of kitchen supplies, and she was amazed at how long she could spend happily puttering around that department. She had dinner in the city and decided against going to a movie by herself. She wandered past shop windows, wondering what on earth she was doing in Texas, alone, when back home she'd had a perfectly comfortable life and friends to see and parties to go to. She hadn't come up with a really good answer by the time she arrived back at the ranch around nine-thirty. Burn was already there, and suddenly the answer didn't seem to matter so much. Any regrets she'd been on the verge of feeling vanished at the sight of his Jeep parked in its usual spot.

She'd had no idea what time he would be returning to the ranch or even if he would return that night at all, and relief was a big part of her reaction in finding him there. Opting to ignore the exact nature of the excitement that immediately bubbled inside her, she bounded into the house all smiles.

"Burn? I'm ho—back." She caught herself at the last second, deciding that calling out "I'm home" was just a little too cozy, considering the limits she herself had placed on their relationship.

She hurried through the living room, lighted only by a lamp in the window, and practically bumped into Burn as he came striding out of the kitchen.

Gripping a steaming mug of coffee in one hand, he squared off against her in the cramped confines of the house's central hallway.

"Where the hell have you been?"

The question, delivered in a gruff and unmistakably angry tone, took Allie so much by surprise that she laughed out loud.

Burn's scowl deepened. "What's so funny?"

"You are. You look all uptight and enraged, sort of the way my father used to look when I came in late from a date."

"Maybe he had good reason to be uptight and enraged . . . if he'd spent hours worrying about you the way I just have."

Her smile melted away, replaced by a tentative, perplexed expression. "You've been worried about me? But why?"

"Why? Hell, woman, I come home to find you gone—no note, no message, the sink full of dishes and clothes thrown all over the place, as if you'd either been called away in a big hurry or dragged out of here against your will. I don't know about you, but that strikes me as plenty of reason to worry."

"I'm sorry," she said, her small smile sheepish. "I just drove into the city to pick up a few things. I didn't even think about the dishes or the clothes and how it might look to you if you got back first. I guess I'm not the neatest person in the world.''

Even in the dark hallway she could see his eyes narrow in disbelief. ''You mean all that was just a normal mess for you?''

''I'm afraid so. My mother used to say that when I left in the morning it looked like a cyclone had hit my room.''

''And would your mother pick it all up?''

''Oh, no. Louisa would take care of it when she did my room.''

''Louisa?''

Allie nodded. ''Our housekeeper.''

Burn said nothing, but the look that flickered in his deep blue eyes was close enough to contempt to make Allie realize how callous her reply sounded. Never mind how it sounded. Now that she'd had a chance to spend hours on the business end of a broom and a dustrag, she had a much better understanding of how Louisa earned her living. For the first time ever she paused to think how callous it truly was to blithely leave a big mess behind for someone else to clean up, and she felt her face grow warm.

''Let's just forget about it, okay?'' she said, sliding past him and into the kitchen, which she noticed was now very tidy. ''I'll try and do better with the dishes and confine the rest of my mess to my own room...at least for as long as you're staying here.''

''And you'll leave word about where you're going when you go out.''

''Why?'' she countered, feeling prickly. ''You didn't.''

''That's different.''

''Why is it different?''

''Because...''

''Because?'' she prompted, eyebrows delicately arched. ''Because you're a man? Because you were the one doing the wondering and worrying this time? Because you don't want to talk about where you go and what you do with your free time, but I'm supposed to let you keep tabs on my every move?''

His jaw was rigid as he crossed to the sink and tossed the rest of his coffee down the drain. "You're right. I had no call to ask you that."

"No, you didn't. But," she added, her mood softening as suddenly as it had turned irate, "it was still sort of sweet of you to worry about me."

He shrugged. "It wasn't something I planned on, believe me. I guess I've gotten used to you being here, and I couldn't imagine where you'd have gone for so long all on your own."

He moved so that he was standing directly in front of her, his booted feet braced apart. His faded chambray shirt was open at the neck, the tails tucked into a pair of snug, low-slung jeans. He was the embodiment of every cowboy fantasy Allie had ever had and her breath had gone shallow and shaky on her even before he lifted his hand and lightly brushed the hair from her face.

"You know," he said, "living here together like this sort of confuses things for me. It's hard to know what's work and what's not, where being friendly ends and overstepping my bounds begins."

"Don't worry. I'll let you know," Allie said, her voice suddenly a whisper.

"You do that, Boston," Burn murmured as he bent his head.

His mouth was almost touching hers, so tantalizingly close she could smell the coffee on his breath as it warmed her cheek. Allie's instinct was to simply close her eyes and surrender to what she wanted, to what they both wanted, and it took more self-control than she usually bothered to muster to place her palms flat against his chest and stop him.

"No," she said.

Burn didn't move any closer, but he didn't pull away, either.

"How come?" he asked, his tone a deep, husky drawl that played havoc with Allie's will to resist.

"Because," she said. "I explained the other day about how business and pleasure don't mix. Right now I need you to fix the roof, hire a crew and get this place up and running."

"Fixing roofs and making love are not mutually exclusive activities," he pointed out dryly.

"They are as far as we're concerned."

"Besides," he said, cajoling with his words and with the slight pressure of his body looming over hers, "you might decide you need me for a lot of other things, too, if you'd give me a chance."

"That's exactly what I'm afraid of," Allie acknowledged ruefully as she tried and failed to slip from the narrow space between him and the counter.

His wide, tempting mouth twisted into a frown, but it lacked the fierce anger she'd glimpsed earlier.

"Does this mean you're not going to let me kiss you tonight?" he asked plaintively.

"You got it." A lifelong penchant for taking chances prompted Allie to add, "Besides, what would good old Rhonda Sue say if she knew you wanted to kiss your new boss?"

"She wouldn't have anything to say about it at all," he countered, a hint of heaviness returning to his tone. "Like I told you, Rhonda's just an old friend."

"Then you must have a lot in common," Allie said, pointedly sniffing the air. "You're wearing her perfume, Cowboy."

Burn pulled away. "There's an exit line if I ever heard one."

"Burn, wait," she said. "Now I'm the one who's out of line. I was just teasing."

"Then we'll call it even."

"But..."

"But?" he echoed, his tone wary.

"As long as I've gone and brought up the subject—"

"You can bring it up all you want," he broke in. "I've told you the truth about Rhonda and me. I don't much feel like discussing it any further."

"Fine," she said, her curiosity burning white-hot. "But I would like to discuss the Double D."

"What about it?" he asked more calmly than she expected.

"The other night Rhonda referred to it as a dude ranch. Is it?"

He shrugged and nodded. "You didn't have to wait all this time to ask. In fact, you could have checked it out for yourself just by looking in the phone book."

Darn. She hadn't thought of that.

"I don't expect to have to go checking up on you. Why didn't you tell me yourself that your last job was working on a dude ranch?"

"I didn't see how it mattered where I worked last. I knew I could do the job here. Period."

"But why a dude ranch?"

Another shrug. "Why not?"

"I don't know. It's just that the very idea of a dude ranch seems affected and pretentious and not at all like you."

"It's not at all like me. But it pays better than straight ranching."

"Then why give it up to work here?"

He shrugged again, uneasily this time. "Things changed, that's all. And I guess I'd had my fill of spending my days pleasing a pack of spoiled women by the time this opportunity came along." There was a teasing edge to his drawl as he added, "I figured that for a while I'd try my hand at pleasing just one spoiled woman."

Ignoring the jibe, Allie asked, "Did you tell Cal Rosen the truth about the Double D or did you simply lie about your previous experience?"

"I never lied to the man about anything," he said, folding his arms across his chest. His eyes flashed dangerously. "Look, if this is such an issue, then maybe—"

"It's not," Allie cut in. "I just wondered, that's all."

"Now you know." He turned toward his room. "See you in the morning, Allie."

The discussion with Burn left Allie without any deeper insight into his life away from the Circle Rose or what he did on his days off. The fact that it was none of her business didn't lessen her curiosity one iota. Time after time throughout the following week Allie considered phoning Cal Rosen and asking what he knew about the man he'd seen fit to hire. Two things held her back.

First, Burn was right when he said that he could do the job he'd been hired to do. With each day she was more convinced of that. He was talented and tireless, and uncanny in his knack for anticipating problems on the ranch even before they arose. It was as if he had a sixth sense for the land he was working. After inspecting their southwest grazing allotment, he predicted that it would be dry and useless by next year unless they repaired an existing ditch and ran pipe to pump water to it from Pebble Creek. He even approached the forest service about sharing costs for the project.

Next year seemed so far away to Allie, who in spite of all her determination to stick it out on the Circle Rose had no precedent for seeing herself sticking with any one venture for that long—especially not one this tough. But Burn insisted that it would take nearly a year to get the proposal he'd submitted approved, reminding Allie all over again how invaluable he was as foreman.

Her second reason for not picking up the phone and calling Cal Rosen was less sensible and more personal. It was quite simply because Burn had been concerned enough to worry about her when he'd returned and she wasn't there last Saturday night. After she'd finished bristling and being indignant, it had occurred to her just what such concern could mean to a woman living out here alone. It made her feel safe to know that Burn was looking out for her. It was a good feeling, and she didn't call Cal because she really didn't want to find out anything that might spoil it.

By the end of the week the bunkhouse was ready for business, the roof sound and the inside so fresh and clean Allie wouldn't have minded bunking there herself. Along with the routine chores associated with a ranch, Burn got the tractor running to his satisfaction and began preliminary repair work on the ditch that ran out to the southwest allotment. Allie helped out when and where she could, spending any free time on her overhaul of the house, always with the prospect of a solitary Saturday hovering just beneath the surface.

She knew it was crazy to be upset about Burn having a life of his own, a life that obviously included Rhonda Sue in some fashion and did not include her. It was especially crazy when she herself had rebuffed him both times he'd shown an interest in her as something besides his boss. But knowing it was crazy to feel as she did didn't stop her any more than all her logical explanations as to why they couldn't get involved had stopped Burn from being interested.

True, he hadn't tried to kiss her again. He hadn't even touched her, unless you counted a friendly whack on the back at the completion of a tough job or a hand offered to help her down from her horse. Allie was still astute enough to know when a man was interested, and Burn was definitely interested. He was interested in her in spite of her rejection and, she had a hunch, in spite of himself. She suspected that, deep down, Burn Monroe didn't find her any more suitable for romance than she found him. It made for some interesting chemistry, the mutual wanting and not wanting all at the same time. As Burn had said, living there alone together had a way of confusing things.

One thing Allie wasn't confused about was that the ranch wasn't the same when Burn was away. She had taken the trouble to meet some of her neighbors, but with the ranches spread so far apart it was hardly the same as popping in for an impromptu visit with a neighbor back home. Besides, on most ranches Saturday was as busy as every other day.

Allie purposely planned ahead and saved up errands for Saturday, only to find herself as restless being alone in the city as she was alone at home. Bored, she headed back early and ended up beating Burn back to the ranch by several hours. Several *long* hours, during which she phoned her mother to assure her that she was fine and hadn't bitten off more than she could chew.

She also telephoned a few old friends to catch up on all she was missing and ended up impulsively inviting them to come for a visit. They accepted, and arrangements were made for a weekend two weeks away. Allie reasoned that by then Burn would probably have moved into the bunkhouse and she would have three available guest rooms. She looked forward to seeing her friends and showing off the Circle Rose.

After making the calls, she thumbed through several wallpaper books she'd brought home, ate a pint of chocolate ice cream and came to the conclusion that the loneliness she felt wasn't going to be alleviated by phone calls or calories, only by Burn's return. There was no denying it, she realized glumly. She missed him like hell.

Braving the late-afternoon heat, she took the mystery she was reading outside and settled into the old rocker she'd moved to the back porch. In the mood she was in, she did more rocking and staring off into space than reading, and that's how she spotted the unexpected splash of color in the dirt about fifteen feet away. Curious, she ambled over to it and was astonished to find that growing amidst the brush was a rosebush. Spindly and frail, to be sure, but a rosebush just the same.

Poking around in the dirt, she found the trampled remains of what looked like a second bush and possibly the stump of a third. Even the earth seemed different in that patch, she observed, poking it with her toe. It was looser, as if at one time it had been a garden, the usually dry soil enriched and carefully tended. She had wondered where the name Circle Rose had come from, and something told her she'd just found the answer.

Allie instantly decided to restore the rose garden to what it must once have been. She had no idea what that might entail, but she reasoned that if she could learn about ranching from a book, then she ought to be able to learn a little about growing roses from one. And Burn would help, she was sure. She'd yet to find anything about which he didn't know at least a smattering. Why should roses be any different?

She drove into town in a blaze of fresh determination, found a book on gardening at the bookstore and sat in the truck outside a local nursery as she scanned the section on roses. The man who ran the nursery was even more help than the book, and Allie returned home with special fertilizer, several bulky bricks of something called peat moss and an irresistibly pretty set of gardening tools with blue-and-white delft handles. She also bought two new rosebushes, which the nursery man assured her were guaranteed to grow locally.

It turned out to be a bigger project than Allie had anticipated, and several times she was tempted to give up, at least for the day. She wasn't sure what spurred her on, digging and hoeing and getting dirty right down to her broken fingernails in the process. When she was just about finished, she heard the sound of Burn's Jeep approaching, and she knew in a flash what had driven her. Pride.

The rose garden was now weed free and well tended, a site of potential beauty, and Allie knew that a big part of her pleasure in it would be in seeing her accomplishment reflected in Burn's eyes.

He parked in front and came through the house to the back porch, arriving just as she was gathering her tools. His sunglasses concealed what she assumed to be the look of surprised wonder that she'd been envisioning all afternoon, but he stood silently staring at her reclaimed patch of dirt for so long that Allie knew he was surprised.

"What is this?" he asked finally, turning to her.

"A rose garden," she replied, trying to keep the lilt of pride and excitement to a minimum.

"I can see that. But why? And why here, of all places?"

Allie explained how she'd found the first feeble bush, which now stood pruned and fertilized and supported with a dowel, and had decided to tend it and plant more.

"I'll bet this was once a gorgeous garden," she concluded. "That must be why the ranch was named the Circle Rose in the first place." She beamed expectantly as he once again surveyed the results of her labor. "What do you think?"

"I think you're wasting your time," he said.

His harsh, brittle tone pierced something fragile that had been swelling inside Allie all afternoon as she dug and lugged bricks of peat moss and waited to share her discovery with him.

"Why?"

"Because this is a ranch, not a damn hothouse." Burn kicked the dirt with the toe of one boot, sending a dusty cloud of it raining down on the darker mulch covering most of Allie's garden. "Look at this dirt. You can't expect anything as finicky as roses to grow in it."

"That's why I used fertilizer and peat moss and mulch," she shot back with mounting irritation. "And I bought bushes especially bred for this climate. They're guaranteed to grow here."

His laugh was short and rough. "Nothing in life is guaranteed, Boston. If you don't know that by now, you damn well ought to."

"Well, I do know that the man at the nursery in town knows more about growing roses than you and me together, and he says they'll grow here. Flourish. That's the word he used, in fact—*flourish.*"

"Yeah? Well, I might not know much about roses, but I know the Circle Rose. I don't care what bill of goods he sold you along with the fertilizer. Those roses don't belong out here . . . any more than you do."

His words cut deep. They were like the final blow in a sudden, brutal boxing match that Allie didn't fully understand. Roses had seemed a harmless enough diversion. Sure, Burn had objected to remodeling the house with skylights and installing the new tile, which she had temporarily put on hold in favor of buying pipe for the irrigation ditch. But she hadn't expected him to react so strenuously or bitterly to a rose garden.

Dropping the pail holding her tools, she turned and stalked away. She had no idea where she was going until she reached the stable. Before coming to the Circle Rose, she'd never saddled her own horse, but during the past couple of weeks, doing so had become second nature to her. She saddled Fortune quickly and efficiently, without giving a damn what Burn might think of her taking his horse without permission.

The high-spirited Fortune seemed to sense Allie's mood. Her movements were jerky and anxious until Allie gave her her head, and she broke into a gallop before they had even crossed the corral. She took the fence at the far side in a smooth graceful leap that Allie's Bostonian riding instructor would have deemed magnificent. Allie didn't even turn her head to see if Burn was watching. Anger and resentment were quickly edging out her initial wounded reaction to his words, and at that moment she couldn't care less what Burn Monroe was doing or thinking.

What Burn was thinking as he watched her tear off on horseback was that he was an even bigger bastard than he'd thought when he arrived back here today. He crossed the yard at a run, calling Allie's name even though he knew it was too late. The way she was riding, she probably couldn't hear him, and even if she could, he had a feeling she wouldn't bother to turn around to hear anything else he might have to say.

This sure didn't seem to be his day for winning friends and influencing people. It had started earlier with Rhonda, kicked into high gear with an argument with Rory over a pierced ear, of all things, and now this. He'd ended his visit with Rory—if you could call three hours of hostile silence a visit—in a bitch of a mood and had headed back to the ranch with some stupid, half-baked notion that seeing Allie would make him feel better. That just being around her would bring back the sensation that he was doing all right, and that just maybe he was good for something besides providing a crowd with cheap thrills by risking his neck on the back of a bull.

What a jerk.

Turning back to the house, he noticed Allie's gardening tools scattered in the dirt where they'd spilled from the bucket when she dropped it. He bent to pick them up, pausing as he lifted a small spade to examine the handle.

His lips curved. The tools suited Allie, pretty and feminine and yet also bright and bold. She'd proven to be quite a surprise, all right. She was willing to dig in the dirt or swing a mop or help tear down moldy paneling in a bunkhouse, and she did it all with her own brand of style and grace. He finished collecting the tools and stood, reluctantly turning his attention to the rose garden.

It was a sad, brave sight. She must have worked on it most of the day, he thought, wincing as he recalled the callousness of his reaction. She'd clearly been proud of her work and had expected some sort of acknowledgment that she'd done well. And she deserved it. Instead, he had belittled her efforts. Worse, he'd used them against her, striking in the place he knew she was most vulnerable—her decision to move to a ranch in the first place.

Those roses don't belong here any more than you do.

That's what he'd told her, and he supposed he meant it, although he damn well hadn't meant to hurt her feelings. It was just the shock of seeing a garden here, in this particular spot, and Allie standing beside it, so full of life and pride. It had stirred up some of the worst memories—and fears—he'd ever known.

And so he'd lashed out and hurt her, the one person who didn't deserve any of his aggravation. With Allie's care, he wouldn't be surprised if the roses did flourish, just as the salesman had predicted. After all, roses had flourished here once before under the tender care of a woman very much like Allie, feminine and lively, a woman who knew what she wanted out of life and wasn't afraid to reach out and grab for it. Burn swallowed the sudden lump in his throat and stared off in the direction in which Allie had disappeared.

The difference between Allie and her roses was that they were specially bred for the harshness of southwest Texas and she wasn't. Oh, there was no denying that she'd surprised him so far with her willingness to work hard and follow orders, but it wouldn't last. It couldn't, he assured himself, thinking how that would throw a major hitch into his plans. Plans that were becoming more and more real to him with each passing day. Plans for the Circle Rose and for himself and for Rory.

Those plans didn't include a woman, especially not a woman like Allie, a woman too flighty and delicate for the long haul. A woman who'd made no secret of the fact that she had a short attention span and was more accustomed to housekeepers than to keeping house. And, he thought disgustedly, a woman he couldn't get off his mind, night or day, a woman who held the power to possess him in a way he knew wasn't safe for any man to be possessed.

After just one kiss she haunted him. He couldn't imagine what it would be like if he ever actually made love to the woman, or how he would ever manage to let her go afterward. He went to sleep at night thinking about her, wanting her, and woke every morning the same way. What's more, in spite of all her talk about a purely professional relationship, he knew that Allie thought about him in the same steamy way. All the haughty and aloof expressions she tossed in his direction couldn't hide the fact that she wanted him almost as much as he wanted her.

Of course, he also knew that she would stop wanting him in a hurry if she knew the truth. When he'd first come to work for her he had spent a great deal of time looking over his shoulder, waiting for her real foreman to arrive, prepared to either get rid of the man if he could or confess what he'd done and hope his performance—and Allie's sense of humor—would work in his favor. No one had ever shown up to claim his place, however, and for long stretches of time he actually forgot that he wasn't supposed to be here, that coming and staying might prove to be the biggest mistake he'd ever made.

At the moment, however, the only mistake on his mind was the one he'd just made by hurting Allie. All he could think about was the mixture of shock and injury that had flashed in her eyes when he'd lashed out at her. Burn didn't think he would ever forget it.

If there was a way to screw up something, he thought bitterly, even something as simple as a flower garden, he'd find it.

Placing the bucket of tools safely on the porch step, he headed for the stable, moving almost as quickly as Allie had. His words had hurt Allie's feelings and stolen some of the pleasure she'd found in creating the garden. Never a master at personal relationships, Burn wasn't entirely sure how he could make that up to her or even *if* he could, but he had to try.

A hunch led him to Antelope Basin. A hunch and maybe a furtive hope that Allie might share his feelings for the place. He saw Fortune first, tethered to a tree near the crystal-clear pool. Next he saw Allie's clothes, jeans and a T-shirt and tantalizing scraps of silk, draped over a branch the way they had been that first day he'd come upon her bathing.

His belly grew hot and tight and his heart started pounding even before he edged Vagabond close enough to see her, her hair floating on the water like corn silk, her bare arms tawny. In spite of her high-class, big-city roots, at that moment she seemed to him to be as at home there as the cypress trees surrounding them and the creatures rustling in the bushes nearby. He'd always been attracted to anything a little wild and untamed. Maybe that explained his feelings for Allie. Then again, thought Burn, maybe there was no explanation.

The waning sunlight cast a soft glow over the scene, making it feel almost like a dream. He watched her in silence until she became aware of him and turned, and their eyes met. At that instant, with every clamoring fiber of his body, Burn knew that this was no dream.

"You need someone to stand guard, Boston?" he asked softly as he reached into the pack behind his saddle for his gun.

"Not someone who thinks I don't belong here," she countered coldly.

"I was wrong."

Burn watched her eyes widen with surprise at his blunt admission. She appeared to weigh it. She might hold out and make him crawl the way he no doubt deserved to. Two weeks ago he had no doubt that's what she would have done. But a lot of things had changed since then. He'd changed and so had Allie, and he wasn't surprised when she nodded, accepting his contrition with the same simplicity it had been offered with.

"I suppose a man with a gun might come in handy," she allowed.

"For a lot of things," Burn told her, letting his gaze drift lazily to the enticing, pale shadow of her body beneath the water.

"So far you've talked a good game. The question is, can you really shoot that thing?"

Her smoky drawl cranked his racing pulse up another notch.

"I never draw it unless I plan to shoot." Swinging his leg over the saddle, he dismounted. "Only thing wrong right now is my aim."

"What's wrong with your aim?" she asked, watching as he sat on a rock and tugged off his boots, his socks with them.

"The angle. In order to protect you properly I really ought to be coming from a different angle."

"Such as?"

He strode into the warm water still clad in his jeans and shirt, stopping with the gun in his hand when he was directly in front of her, with only inches separating them. "This feels about right. For starters."

He watched Allie's eyes grow wide with understanding and a reassuring flicker of excitement. She wanted this. He wanted it. How could it be wrong?

Her lips parted.

"Burn," she said. It was a warning, clearly a warning, issued as he put his hand on her shoulder and let it slide down her arm, then under it and through the water to rest on her hip.

"Burn," she said again, not quite as firmly as the first time, and Burn dared to move his hand from her hip to her fanny, caressing her lightly, pulling her against him, his fingers playing so close to the heat of her that the desire inside him was like a flash fire he wasn't sure he could control.

"I like the way my name sounds when you say it, Boston," he said, his lips in her hair.

She said it again. "Burn."

It was a caressing sound now, as the need for warnings slipped away along with reality. What chance did caution or reality have in this place of silence and eerie light and warm water? Burn felt it, too, felt his own demons taking flight, his own good reasons for not touching this woman drifting out of reach.

Being very careful with the gun, he closed his arms around her, pressing her to him, tipping her hips into his, the motion part demand, part declaration. Even through the heavy, wet fabric of his jeans, he felt her softness and heat, and he stiffened with desire, wanting, waiting.

He just about stopped breathing as he paused, braced for another rebuff, prepared to use everything short of force to change her mind. No, not change her mind. Her mind wanted what her body did, the same thing his body wanted and had been wanting ever since that first day. What he was prepared to do was whatever it took to override her silly notion that all the heated looks and the surreptitious touches and the unspoken fantasies didn't matter, that simply because they didn't make love, their relationship was somehow strictly professional. And safe.

There was no safety here, for either of them. Burn understood that—he had from the beginning—and it was best that she understand it, too.

Still prepared for her protest, he felt her relax instead. Her head tipped back and her eyes, a dark, smoky green in the shadows, met his.

"Oh, what the hell," she murmured.

It wasn't exactly a consent, never mind an invitation, but Burn chuckled, knowing it was as close to one as he was likely to get from Allie.

Checking to be sure the safety was secure, he tossed his gun the short distance to the bank and took her into his arms. She felt small and fragile, and it felt so good to hold her that for a moment that's all he wanted to do—hold her against him and run his hands along the delicate arch of her back.

Soon that wasn't enough, however, not for either of them. Allie clung to his shoulders, the restless movements of her legs reflecting his own mounting impatience. Wrapping one hand in her hair, he tipped her face up to his and kissed her, long and hard and deep. His tongue swirled against hers, seeking, demanding, receiving.

Still kissing her, he slid his other hand to her breast, cupping her beneath the water. She was small and firm, her nipple already pebbled. At his touch she arched, swelling to fill his hand, and a jolt of excitement shot through Burn's body. She was as aroused as he was; he was sure of that even before he slid his hand lower, seeking the dewy heat between her legs. The confirmation that she wanted him as much as he wanted her pushed him perilously close to the edge of control.

The first time ought to be slow and easy for a woman. Burn was a firm believer in "ladies first," but right then he wasn't sure that slow and easy was within the realm of possibility. Allie wasn't making it any easier. She had wrapped her legs around his hips, the water helping to support her weight so that he was free to kiss the silky skin at the base of her throat and play his tongue over her breasts, sipping drops of water that beaded there and drawing on one hardened tip until she cried out in a sharp exclamation of pleasure.

Coming upright in his arms, she tore impatiently at the buttons of his shirt, baring his chest and turning the tables on him, nibbling and licking, her hot tongue finding the tiny pebbles of his nipples and working them over until Burn thought he would explode from the pulsing pressure of his need for her.

"Hell, Allie," he said, dragging her head up so that he could kiss her mouth. "I can't take much more of this."

"Then don't," she said, her tone husky and dripping with passion, fueling his urgency. She slid her hand down his chest and inside his jeans. "Take me."

It was a miracle he didn't finish right then, before he was able to work his belt loose and his jeans open, giving Allie a little more freedom to caress him with long, slow strokes just firm enough to make him crazy.

She was incredible, open and giving and making no secret of the fact that she was eager to feel him inside her.

He wanted that, too. Throwing his head back, eyes squeezed tightly closed, he struggled to savor her sweet ministrations without surrendering to them prematurely. He felt her fingertips on the inside of his thighs, making him tremble as she had trembled when he touched her intimately. Then he felt her other hand at his pocket, inside. Puzzled, he opened his eyes enough to catch her gaze.

"I was looking for..." she began dazedly. "Damn, Burn, don't you carry a wallet?"

"Not into the water," he countered. "I left it with my boots. Why? Are you trying to pick my pocket?"

"No, I was trying to find out if you had protection. Because I don't."

"Oh, hell." He dropped his head so his forehead touched hers. "I can't believe I forgot all about it."

"I can," she whispered provocatively. "I've never felt a man get so hot so fast."

"You noticed, huh?"

She swayed against him, the buoyancy of the water keeping the contact frustratingly light. "It would have been hard not to notice...no pun intended. I'm glad," she added, pressing closer, "because I've never gotten so hot so fast for a man, either."

"Don't do that," he groaned, even as he pulled her more tightly between his spread thighs. "Not if you're serious about needing protection."

"I'm serious," she replied, suddenly solemn.

"Then let's head back to the ranch and take care of it. And fast."

He took her hand to lead her from the water, faced with a dilemma as they reached the bank and climbed out. Part of him wanted to ogle Allie as if she was a centerfold come to life; a more grown-up part warned that he ought to try and appear a little more sensitive and sophisticated. Unfortunately, the immature part of him won out. As she reached for her shirt, he spun her around to face him and let his heated gaze caress the curves and valleys he had just explored so freely.

"I was right the last time we were up here." His voice was revealingly hoarse. "You are the most beautiful sight I've ever seen. You're pretty all over, and I don't want to let you away from me for a minute," he said, reaching purposely for her, "never mind how long it takes to ride back."

Allie laughed softly, her cheeks colored from his intimate inspection and praise, and held him at arm's length. "But just think—the sooner we get back, the sooner—"

"I get the idea," he said, releasing her. "Get dressed."

The promise of her words spurred him on as he yanked on his boots and helped her mount before retrieving his gun and swinging into the saddle himself. He'd ridden Vagabond hard on the way up, desperate to escape his own guilt by finding Allie and making amends with her. Now he rode him just as hard, but with a different demon chasing him. Desire.

They left the horses in the corral and headed for the house together, reaching the front-porch steps just as a beat-up black pickup truck tore down the gravel drive.

Burn muttered an oath that drew a quizzical look from Allie.

"Rhonda Sue," he said as the woman slammed the truck into Park and jumped from the cab.

"What on earth—" Allie asked.

"Later," Burn interrupted. "What's up, Rhonda?" he asked, a knot forming in his belly as he noted the frantic look on her face. He knew better than anyone that Rhonda wasn't the type to come running to him or any man without damn good reason.

"It's Rory," she said, panic in her voice and eyes. "He's been arrested."

"Arrested?" he countered, stricken. "What for?"

"Stealing a car. He and his friends took one of their father's cars and went joyriding."

"But I just left him . . ." Burn stopped, a glance at his watch telling him that it had been a couple of hours since he'd left Rory. Plenty of time for a kid with a major chip on his shoulder to find trouble to get into. "Damn."

"The police called and said I've got to go down there, talk to them and pick him up. I wanted Keith to come, but he just said to let him sit there, that this would teach him a good lesson. I told him he could go to hell and I'd go down there and get him myself. But the truth is, I'm scared, Burn."

"Rory's the one who ought to be scared."

"Maybe he is and maybe he's not. He's just been so moody and silent lately, it's like I don't even know him anymore. I've got a bad feeling, Burn, and I'm just about scared out of my wits."

"Did he take off right after I left?"

Rhonda nodded. "He must have. I went to call him in for supper and he was nowhere to be found. I figured he was off doing his chores, but Keith says that'll be the day he does chores without being told a half-dozen times. Keith's a good man, but he has no patience for this sort of thing."

"Who's Keith?" Allie asked.

Burn sighed wearily. He'd wondered how long she could continue to stand by in silence.

"My husband," Rhonda Sue replied.

"Wait here, Rhonda," he said. "Have a cup of coffee or something. I'll go get Rory."

"Who's Rory?" Allie asked next, as he had known she would.

Burn turned to answer her before Rhonda could.

"My son," he said.

Chapter Seven

Allie did her best to mask her shock as Burn took off in his Jeep at breakneck speed. Rhonda stood by with her arms wrapped around herself as if she were freezing. In freshly ironed blue jeans and a pale pink jersey, the other woman didn't look nearly as brassy to Allie as she had the other night. And in spite of what she'd just learned and everything it implied about Burn's relationship with Rhonda, at that moment Allie felt more sympathy for her than anything else.

"Come on inside and I'll make some coffee," she offered, thankful she'd recently mastered the art of making coffee along with acquiring a rudimentary knowledge of simple cooking.

"No, really, I shouldn't be bothering Burn at his workplace to begin with, and I surely shouldn't be imposing on his boss because of my troubles. Just tell Burn I—"

"Don't be silly. You're not imposing at all. I was just—" The sudden memory of what she and Burn had been about to do when Rhonda Sue's arrival intervened made her break off abruptly. "I was just going to have a cup of coffee myself. And a sandwich. Now that Burn's gone I'd be glad for the company if you stayed."

Talk about sublimating your desires, Allie thought, recalling the appetite she had so recently worked up. A sandwich instead of a roll in the hay with Burn seemed a pretty paltry trade-off.

Rhonda Sue considered the invitation and nodded tentatively. "Well, if you're sure it's no trouble..."

"No trouble at all," Allie assured her, leading the way into the house and to the kitchen. She quickly measured coffee and water for the coffeemaker and took a loaf of bread from the bread box. "I hope you like ham and cheese. It's Burn's favorite and I've found it's simpler to stock up on one thing."

"Swiss cheese, right?" Rhonda Sue countered with a small smile. "I remember how that was his favorite. Ham and Swiss cheese with just the tiniest trace of hot mustard."

She said it in a dreamy tone, as if she were recalling something as precious as her wedding day instead of a man's preference in sandwich meat. Just the same, Allie's lips puckered as she slapped the package of ham on the counter. She hadn't known about the hot mustard.

"So," she said, assembling the sandwiches with a degree of culinary competence most people who knew her would have found astounding, "I take it you and Burn go back a long way."

"I guess you could say that."

"I didn't know he had a son," Allie stated, deciding on the direct approach.

"I'm not surprised," the other woman replied. "He didn't know himself until a few months ago."

Allie turned to her in amazement. "What?"

"I said he didn't know about Rory himself until a few months ago. I never told him. I know, I know," she added hurriedly, "I was dead wrong in what I did, but at the time I thought it was all for the best."

"Then you are Rory's mother?" Allie asked, seeking confirmation for what she already knew in her heart.

Rhonda Sue nodded. "Burn and I lived together for a while years ago. We'd already split up when I found out I was having his baby. Burn was still new on the circuit then . . . the rodeo, that is," she added for Allie's benefit.

Allie nodded.

"Anyway, he was new and rising fast, and he'd made it clear he didn't intend to be dragging a wife around the way some guys on the circuit do, never mind a baby."

"And so you just didn't tell him?" Allie asked, unable to keep the disbelief from her voice.

"I couldn't. I knew that if I told him about the baby, he'd quit in a second and do what he thought was right. Burn's just that way. But deep down inside he would have hated it, hated being tied to a life he didn't want any part of and maybe hated me for tying him. I loved him too much for that."

"You still love him." Once more Allie was simply seeking confirmation for what she'd already deduced from the woman's tone and expression as she talked about him.

"In a way, I guess. He is Rory's father and all, and there were never any hard feelings between us. But Keith's my husband now," she said, her eyes becoming clear and bright in a way that sent relief streaming through Allie. "And I love Keith more than anything. I just hope we can survive all this trouble with Rory."

She took a bite of the sandwich Allie had placed before her. "Do you have kids?" she asked Allie.

Allie shook her head. "No, I don't. Is Rory your only child?"

"Yes. Keith and I planned to have a couple of our own, but it hasn't happened in the two years we've been married, and sometimes, when Rory's acting up this way, I think Keith is just as pleased."

"How old is Rory?"

"Fourteen. He'll be fifteen in a few weeks."

"That's a tough age." Hadn't she just said that same thing to Burn about his own youth?

"You're telling me," Rhonda agreed. "When he was younger, everything was fine. It was always him and me against the world, you know?" she said, her expression wistful. "Then I married Keith and Rory turned thirteen. He had a new house, new school, new friends, and suddenly he was like a different kid. Fresh mouthed, disobedient, flunking in school. It shocked poor Keith, I can tell you." She shook her head. "I'm ashamed to say that's part of the reason I finally changed my mind about telling Burn. I was just flat-out desperate for help."

"Because Rory was giving you and your husband so much trouble?"

"Yes, and because he was forever throwing it up to us that Keith wasn't his real father. I suddenly got the bright idea that maybe getting to know his real father would straighten him out. Plus my own dad died about a year ago and I got all mushy and sentimental about family and how short life really is and... I don't know, one day I just decided to see if I could track Burn down, and I found out he was working at the Double D, not an hour away from our place. So I called and arranged to get together."

"He must have been... surprised."

Rhonda Sue laughed out loud. "Not quite the right word. Shocked... and mad as hell at me when it all finally sank in—I mean, about him being a daddy and all. It was rough at first, but Burn and I finally worked things out." She sighed. "I just wish I could say the same for him and Rory."

"They don't get along?" Allie asked, intensely interested in Burn's relationship with his son.

"Not really. Not so far, anyway. Of course, it doesn't help that Rory is at war with the whole world. Deep down they're more alike than Rory will admit, and I think he's a little in awe of Burn—you know, his reputation on the circuit and all.''

''Burn doesn't say much about his past, but I've gathered he was pretty successful?''

''A legend is more like it, an out-and-out legend. Of course, it almost killed him in the end.''

''He told me he quit because of a lot of little injuries.''

''I guess that's how Burn would put it,'' she responded dryly. ''He quit because the doctors told him if he got thrown one more time he might not get up.''

Allie shivered and took a sip of her coffee. ''He said he'd been advised to quit, but he made light of it.''

''That's Burn. But believe me, his last fall was a bone crusher, and it was a big deal when Burn Monroe walked away from the rodeo. It was written up in all the papers. 'Course, he was always being written up for one thing or another. I saved all the clippings over the years and made a big thick scrapbook for Rory.''

''That's nice. I'm sure that helps him to know more about his father.''

''It would if he ever bothered to look at it. Rory's so busy resenting Burn for not being around all those years that he hasn't got time to get to know him.''

''But that wasn't Burn's fault!'' Allie exclaimed, instantly defensive on his behalf. She caught herself and shrugged apologetically. ''Not that I'm blaming you....''

''You'd be right to. I know the blame is all mine. I just wish I knew how to repair the damage I've done.''

''I'm sure once Rory has had more time to adjust, he'll come around.''

''Maybe. If he doesn't break his neck or end up in prison first.'' Rhonda Sue shuddered, a mother's anguish pinching her face. ''Until now the trouble he's gotten into has all been kid's stuff—cutting school, that kind of thing. Nothing that would involve the police.'' She twisted her napkin, pushing aside the plate with half of her sandwich untouched. ''Between dealing with Rory and trying to help

Keith keep our place going, I'm about at the end of my rope.''

"Do you and Keith own a ranch?"

"Well, the bank owns most of it," she countered with a harsh laugh. "More every month, in fact. It's not easy to keep a place going these days, but then, you'd know all about that."

Allie nodded, instinctively aware that sacrificing tile for pipe was minor compared to what the woman across from her was facing every day. "I'm learning, that's for sure."

"You're from back East, right? Boston, I think Burn said."

"That's right."

"No offense, but what on earth made you move way out here? I asked Burn, but he's real closemouthed where you're concerned. Protective like. I think he's sweet on you, too."

"Really?" Allie said, too intrigued to feign disinterest. "What makes you think so?"

"The way the back of his neck gets all pink when I tease him about it," she replied with an easy laugh that told Allie the idea of Burn being interested in her didn't bother Rhonda Sue in the least.

"And," the other woman continued, "the fact that the man is as happy as a clam working here as your foreman when he swore on a stack of Bibles that he'd never work a ranch in his life."

"He really said that?"

She nodded vigorously. "And meant it. He never did, either. The Double D doesn't count, since that's more Disneyland than ranch. The toughest thing he ever did around there was teach city women which end of a horse was which. Sorry," she added quickly, lifting her hands. "I didn't mean any offense."

"None taken. But I think you're wrong about Burn's reason for working here. He applied for the job before he ever met me."

"I don't know anything about that," she replied with a shrug. "But I do know Burn Monroe, and I know that either you're paying him a small fortune or he's got some other powerful reason for changing his mind about ranching after all these years."

Allie certainly wasn't paying him a fortune. But she didn't have a chance to ponder whether Rhonda Sue was right and what his other reasons for working here might be, as the other woman peppered her with questions about her decision to move west and buy the Circle Rose. Without planning to, she found herself telling Rhonda Sue all about her aunt Verdy and her inheritance. She braced herself for the usual reaction, but Rhonda Sue neither laughed nor looked incredulous. She simply nodded understandingly, as if following a pipe dream was as sensible and ordinary as getting out of bed in the morning, and Allie's affection for her surged.

For the next hour they talked freely, about dreams and ranching and men and the way the three had become entangled in each of their lives. Allie felt at ease with Rhonda Sue in a way she had never expected to feel with the woman who was the mother of Burn's child. Rhonda also seemed to relax and forget the trouble that had brought her there, until the sound of tires on the gravel out front made her shoulders tense and her fingers knot.

"He's back. I just hope he's got Rory with him."

"I'm sure he does," Allie told her as they stood. "The police would never hold a juvenile overnight for stealing a car."

"But maybe Rory wouldn't go with Burn. Maybe he—"

But by then they had reached the front door and could both see that Burn had someone in the passenger seat beside him. As they watched, Burn hopped from the Jeep and went around to yank open the passenger-side door.

"Get out," the two women heard him say from where they stood on the porch steps. He didn't sound happy.

The figure inside the Jeep sat stiffly still.

Burn reached inside and grabbed him by the shirt. "I said get out."

He dragged his passenger from the Jeep as if he were a sack of feathers, depositing him on the ground, and Allie was amazed to see that when he scrambled to his feet, the boy was nearly as tall as Burn was, only much more wiry. He also had the same dark, wavy hair and intensely blue eyes. Even the hot, angry look in them at that moment was one that Allie had seen in his father's eyes at times. She had no doubt that the youth looked an awful lot like Burn had looked at his age, and she wondered what kind of memories were evoked when Burn stared into those fierce young eyes.

Whatever those memories might be, they certainly didn't seem to inspire feelings of commiseration or patience. Burn grabbed the boy by the back of the black silk shirt he was wearing with black jeans and boots and led him unwillingly to stand before Allie and his mother. With his hand still firmly on the back of his neck, as if Rory might bolt at any second—which seemed a pretty legitimate concern considering the hostility emanating from every pore of the kid's very tense body—Burn looked directly at Rhonda.

"Rory has decided to stay here with me for a while." Allie saw her own shock at the announcement reflected in the sudden widening of Rhonda's eyes. Burn gave his son a prodding nudge. "Isn't that right, Rory?"

"No," Rory spat, also looking at Rhonda. "I don't want to stay anywhere with him. Don't let him make me, please, Mom."

Rhonda laced and unlaced her fingers. "Burn, maybe we ought to talk this over before—"

"No." Burn's tone was adamant. "The time for talking has passed. I've talked to you, I've talked to the police, God knows I've tried talking to him." He tipped his head toward Rory. "I've talked until I'm sick of the sound of my own voice."

"That makes two of us," Rory muttered.

"That's too bad, kid," Burn continued, slanting him a narrow-eyed glare. His tone was soft and dangerous. "Because I've got a hunch you're going to be a lot sicker of me before we settle this."

"There's nothing to settle," Rory insisted hotly. "The police told you there'd be no charges pressed if I stayed out of trouble for—"

"The police are the least of your worries right now," Burn interrupted. "And you're going to stay out of trouble because when I'm done with you you're going to be too tired to go looking for it, too tired to go joyriding with your unfortunate choice of friends."

"Hey, my friends are—"

"History," Burn interjected. "You won't have time for friends. You won't have time for anything but work and school."

"But how will he get to school?" asked Rhonda, her loyalties obviously torn between her son and the man who'd fathered him, the man she herself had turned to for help. Allie could understand how Burn's harshness might give any mother second thoughts. As an uninvolved observer, she could also understand the rationale for his tough stance.

"I don't think the bus will pick him up way out here," Rhonda went on. "In fact, I know it won't."

"I'll take him to school," Burn told her, adding pointedly, "and I'll make sure he goes inside."

"You can't make me stay there," Rory told him.

Burn smiled nastily. "Maybe not. But I can make you damn sorry if you don't."

Rory twisted and tried in vain to break free. "Mom, please..."

"Go home, Rhonda," Burn ordered over Rory's desperate entreaty. "Pack enough clothes for him for a week or so and bring them back here."

"A week," she echoed with relief. "So he'll only be here a week."

"No. He'll be here indefinitely. But once a week he can do his own laundry."

"But he never—"

"Then he'll have to learn. And don't bring any of this stuff," Burn added, fingering the silk shirt. "Does he have any normal clothes?"

Rory snorted, quickly reverting from entreating little boy to surly adolescent. "Who gets to decide what's normal? You?"

"You got that right," Burn replied. "In fact, I'm going to be making all your decisions for you, Rory. When you go to bed, when you get up, who you see, what you do with your time."

"That's not fair," Rory shouted.

"No, but it's life. Think of this as a reality check."

Now the boy struggled in earnest. "Screw you," he cried. "I don't want any part of your reality . . . or you, either. So you can just take your reality and your macho, Wild West routine and stuff it. You think I want to end up a washed-up has-been of a rodeo cowboy like you?"

"Nah," Burn countered, holding him effortlessly. "I think right now you want to end up breaking your mother's heart by being a low-life, drop-out punk." He grinned. "But I'm not going to let you."

"How can you stop me? You're nothing to me."

"Wrong," Burn snapped, jerking him around so they were face-to-face. "Like it or not, I'm your father. That's another piece of reality for you. Start dealing with it. And starting right this minute you're also going to treat me with the respect I deserve as your father."

"My father?" Rory drawled contemptuously. "Not so I'd notice. A father is someone who's there when you need him—like when you're learning to ride a bike and throw a baseball and—"

"Sorry, Rory. That stuff sounds great on those soft-touch greeting cards, but real life isn't always that picturesque. Now, for the last time I'm going to tell you that no matter how much I wish things had been different for us, I can't change the past—"

"You can't change the future, either," Rory broke in.

"You don't think so? Watch me. I'm your father, Rory, and that's a biological fact. Blood is thicker than anger. If it wasn't, I would have walked away from you the first time we met."

"I wish you had."

"I know you do, son," he said, his tone turning gentle briefly. "I also know that you need my help now more than you ever did learning to ride a bike."

Their gazes locked, both narrowed and steely eyed.

"I don't need anything from you," Rory uttered.

"Yeah, you do. For starters, you need to borrow a shirt. You can't work on a ranch dressed up like a gigolo, and there's still an hour or so of sunlight to work in."

"You can't make me work here. I hate ranching."

"Me, too."

"Keith tried to make me and—"

"I'm not Keith. I can and I will make you work... provided that's all right with the boss."

For the first time Burn directed his attention toward Allie. Rory automatically followed suit, the resentment in his eyes being replaced by surprise and a brief glimmer of adolescent interest before a sneer once more claimed his mouth.

"You work for a woman?" he said, his tone suggesting that such a fate was only slightly preferable to being publicly flogged.

"*We* work for a woman," Burn corrected. "That is, if she'll have you. What do you say, Allie? Any objection to making Rory our first official hand?"

Allie shook her head, her emotions roiling on behalf of Burn and Rory and Rhonda.

"That's fine with me," she said, turning to Rory. "Welcome to the Circle Rose, Rory. I'll fix up one of the spare rooms for you and—"

"Forget it," Burn said. "He'll stay in the bunkhouse. We both will."

His gaze met Allie's, and an awareness of lost moments and unspoken wishes passed between them. As the moment stretched, she felt Rory as well as Rhonda staring at them quizzically, and she knew they had to be wondering why Burn had felt it necessary to include himself in announcing the move to the bunkhouse.

"It will give us a chance for a little father-son bonding," Burn added.

Allie nodded. She couldn't help wondering what the move would mean for the prospect of another sort of bonding entirely, one between her and Burn. She didn't have time to fret about it now, however, as Burn finally managed to convince an uneasy Rhonda to drive home and pack Rory's things. He then led Rory inside the house to get supplies so they could both get settled in the bunkhouse. Allie helped them locate sheets and towels. Her offer to pitch in and make the beds for them was politely but firmly declined by Burn.

"It's time the kid started looking after himself," he told her, nudging Rory ahead of him out the back door.

Allie caught his arm and hesitated until Rory was out of earshot.

"I know what you're trying to do," she said, "but he's still just a boy. Why don't you let me—"

"Stay out of it, Allie," Burn said, his eyes shuttered. In spite of the intimate glimpse into his life that the afternoon had afforded, she felt as cut off from him at that instant as she ever had. "As far as you're concerned, Rory is just another hired hand."

"And how about you? Am I supposed to think of you as just another hired hand, too?" she demanded, the memory of that afternoon blazing in her mind.

She was shattered by his grim nod.

"I think that would probably be best," he agreed. "Considering."

"But—"

"Look, I've got to go."

Allie watched him catch up to Rory and head for the bunkhouse.

Considering?

She felt as if her head was going to explode with unasked questions.

Considering what? Considering that his son would now be staying there and any physical relationship on their part would have to be discreet? Which shouldn't be a problem if they didn't want it to be. After all, Rory would be away at school five days a week. Or did Burn really mean considering that he'd had second thoughts since this afternoon?

What kind of second thoughts could he have had? Not very elaborate ones, she thought peevishly. Between talking to the police and lecturing Rory, he simply hadn't had time. But then, how complicated did a man have to get when deciding that he didn't want a woman after all?

Damn him, she fumed, slamming the kitchen door, wishing she could close her mind as effectively. She'd spent weeks trying to convince him and herself that it wasn't wise for them to become emotionally involved, that it would only complicate matters unnecessarily. But had he listened? Of course not. The man was unbelievably stubborn. And she was embarrassingly vulnerable where he was concerned.

And so she had finally tossed caution to the wind, accepted the fact that she was wildly attracted to him and resigned herself to letting nature take its course. Which it would have, with a vengeance, Allie had no doubt, if it hadn't been for Rhonda's untimely arrival. Now, suddenly, Burn had done this mysterious about-face and was saying she'd been right all along. That it would be wrong for them to become personally involved with each other. Considering.

So she was back to square one, she thought, impulsively deciding to cool off with a shower before starting dinner. If she even bothered with dinner. The sandwich she'd picked at earlier had taken the edge off her hunger, and she really didn't care if Burn Monroe starved to death. She paused as she reached to turn on the water. Of course, there was Rory to consider as well, she reflected, wavering briefly and then turning the water on full blast. Let Burn handle it. After all, he seemed to be a master at making decisions.

He didn't want to make love, he did want to make love, he didn't want to make love.

One thing was certain. The next time he changed his mind, he was going to find her a whole lot less amenable. Indomitable, in fact. She had to be, she told herself as the cool water rushed over her. She was facing the biggest challenge of her life in trying to salvage the Circle Rose and she meant to succeed.

She had moved here to simplify her life and make it her own, not take on new complications. The last thing she needed was to fall for the wrong man. And if anything, she was now more convinced than ever that Burn was the wrong man. Not simply because he worked for her, but because he was too headstrong, too moody and had too many secrets. Not to mention he had his hands full with a rebellious teenage son. Such a man definitely constituted a complication.

From now on she would simply be cordial. She could see that Rory's arrival had been a blessing, after all. There would be no more cozy house sharing, no more hours spent alone with only each other for company and definitely no more fantasizing about the impossible.

Burn had told her to stay out of his life, and she would.

Chapter Eight

"**Y**ou want to toss me that extra rope?" Burn called to Allie, who was sitting on the corral fence watching as he and Rory unloaded the newest addition to the Circle Rose family, Traveler, an Angus bull. He caught the rope without looking at her. Not a simple feat, but a necessary one.

Traveler was a formidable bull and worth a small fortune. He and Rory had driven six hours to pick him up, hauling him home with the utmost TLC in a trailer hitched to the back of the Jeep. He'd missed Allie the whole time he was away, much more than he would ever admit, and he would have liked nothing more now that he was back than to just stand and look at her. That's why he didn't dare cast even a quick glance her way. He couldn't afford to be distracted by those long legs framed by cut-off jeans and allow the frustrated bull to hurt himself in his hurry to escape from his cramped traveling quarters.

Traveler would eventually be leased to stud, and if Burn and the two neighboring ranchers who'd kicked in to buy him were right, he would chalk up some impressive statistics before he was done. Technically, Allie and the other ranchers each owned one-third of the bull and would take turns availing themselves of his services. For the time being he would be staying here.

Buying the bull had been Burn's idea, and since the neighboring ranchers remembered him and his father well enough to know they could trust a Monroe, it hadn't been difficult to convince them to join him in the deal. Allie had been a different story.

"Sounds like an awful lot of money for a cow," she had grumbled when he first broached the idea.

"Bull," he corrected.

"It's still a lot of money."

"Traveler's a lot of bull," he had assured her. "Just wait till you see him."

Now he secured the corral gate and turned to her, wiping the sweat from his forehead with the handkerchief he'd pulled from his back pocket.

"So what do you think?" he asked.

"I think he looks mean," Allie replied, staring at Traveler, who strode across the corral as if he owned it. "More like a fighter than a lover."

"Nah, he's really a pussycat. That macho look is just an act."

"It better not be," she retorted. "I paid plenty for that macho look and it better be more than skin-deep."

"Don't worry. He'll have all the cows swooning."

"Dumb cows."

He laughed as he hooked one boot heel onto the fence rail beside her, bracing himself on his elbows. "What's the matter? Don't you go for the macho type?"

She ran her gaze over him slowly and consideringly before replying, and Burn instantly felt his body stir in response. He suddenly felt more foolish than macho and cursed himself for letting this get started. Again. Then he reminded himself that you couldn't restart something that had never really ended.

There hadn't been a night since Rory's arrival at the ranch that Burn hadn't climbed into that single bed in the bunkhouse damning himself for being a fool. Far from putting an end to anything, his move to the bunkhouse had simply forced this thing between him and Allie to go underground, where it simmered hotter and hotter all the time, like a volcano fated to erupt.

"Oh, I can take or leave the macho type," Allie replied at last, her provocatively lazy drawl making him even warier. "It's studs who talk a good game and then never deliver who bother me."

Burn winced as the carefully aimed and well-deserved dart hit home. He struggled to resist the urge to shrug and walk away, his usual method of dealing with troublesome women. He couldn't bring himself to treat Allie that way.

"Look, Allie," he said, "we've never really talked about this, but I'm sorry about the way things turned out between us."

"It's rather difficult to talk about anything when you spend most of your time avoiding me."

"I haven't been avoiding you."

Silence.

Burn reluctantly turned his head and met her sardonic gaze. He shrugged sheepishly.

"All right, maybe I have been avoiding you some of the time," he conceded, "but I've also been busy. I've gotten more accomplished in the last two weeks than I expected to in ten. This place is actually beginning to look like a ranch again."

"I know," she agreed, a flash of pleasure replacing the tense glitter in her eyes. "I can't believe it's the same place I bought."

"Just goes to show that you have good judgment."

"Thanks, but I think it was more a matter of Cal Rosen's good judgment than mine. He was right about the Circle Rose and about hiring you."

Burn nodded noncommittally, the mention of Rosen making him suddenly uneasy. Although for long stretches of time he completely forgot about the circumstances of his being here, whenever he was reminded, it was like a time bomb ticking away in his gut. One of these days, he promised himself, when the time was right, he was going to have to tell Allie the truth. About everything.

Now wasn't the time, however. Not when she was still obviously chafing over the way things stood between them.

"Anyway, I've been meaning all along to apologize to you for that afternoon," he told her.

"No apology necessary. I'm a consenting adult."

"Still, I could have handled things better if I'd had time to think straight."

"I don't think either one of us was doing much straight thinking that afternoon. If we had been, things wouldn't have gotten so out of hand."

"You're probably right," he agreed, trying to appear unruffled, while a big part of him wanted to grab her and shake her for being so damn amenable to the barricades he was putting between them . . . that he was forced to put between them.

"In fact," Allie continued, "it's a good thing Rhonda showed up when she did."

"Yeah, right." Burn could feel the pulse in his throat throbbing.

"And that Rory is staying here," she added.

"I have to hand it to you, you've been real decent about having Rory here," he said, hoping for a change of subject. "A lot of women wouldn't have been so understanding about having him dumped on them that way."

"I have no problem with Rory being here," she replied. "On the contrary, I think he's been a big help."

"He's coming along," Burn agreed, glancing briefly toward where Rory was feeding the horses, just one of the daily chores that kept him busy and out of trouble.

"How did the trip go?"

"Fine. Not much traffic and the directions were perfect."

Her sigh held an edge of impatience. "I'm not talking about the traffic, Burn. I mean how did it go with Rory? You two were alone in that Jeep for hours, and I know things between you have been a little strained—to put it mildly. I was just wondering if you had a chance to talk at all."

"We talked whenever he didn't have his headphones on. Or rather, I talked. I'm not even sure Rory's listening most of the time."

"He's listening, believe me."

"Maybe. At lunch today he asked me for some change for the jukebox, and I thought that if he was instigating conversation at all, we must be making progress. Then he didn't say another word all the way home. Sometimes I don't even know what the hell I'm doing keeping him here," he said, removing his hat and dragging his fingers through his hair as an increasingly familiar surge of frustration ripped through him.

"You're doing the right thing," Allie said softly. "I'm no expert on parenting, but I did take a course or two in child psychology and I am an unbiased observer. I think it's obvious that Rory was on the wrong path and needed a strong hand to stop him. And in spite of his attitude, I have a hunch that he knows it, too, and that he's grateful."

Burn snorted.

"All right, make that as grateful as a fourteen-year-old who's not getting his own way can be," she amended with a laugh that seemed to Burn to be the sweetest sound he had heard in days. Maybe ever. It gave rise to a sharp longing inside him.

"I noticed you two have been getting pretty chummy," he remarked.

Allie shrugged. "We talk. He helps with the roses sometimes."

"Doesn't look to me like you need any help. You've turned out to be quite a gardener."

She smiled broadly. "Thanks. That's quite a turnaround from your original reaction."

"I was wrong. I've been meaning to tell you that, too."

"Thanks."

"I can't help wondering, though—how come you don't have to twist Rory's arm to get him to help?"

"Because I'm not his father. He doesn't have to prove anything to me."

"Did you ever think that maybe it's because you walk around with one too many shirt buttons unbuttoned?" he inquired, his offhand tone at total odds with the frustrated way he was feeling at that moment, standing so close to her, wanting to touch her and not being able to.

Allie's sitting position on the fence put her breasts level with his gaze, and now he purposely let it linger on the enticing shadow that began at the base of her throat and arrowed down inside her faded work shirt, which was so softened from many washings that it made his fingertips burn with wanting to reach out and caress her through it. The view inside her open collar was one he'd been studiously avoiding as they talked, and now, as desire mingled with the memory of how her breasts had felt and tasted, he wished to hell he'd had the sense to keep avoiding it.

"No, I didn't," she retorted, immediately sliding from the fence to land lightly on her feet. "It never even occurred to me to think such a thing, since Rory always treats me courteously. Which is a hell of a lot more than I can say for his father."

"Allie, wait," he said, catching her hand to stop her from walking away. "There was no call for that and I'm sorry.

Again. Hell, why do I seem to be saying that to you all the time lately?''

"Good question," she countered, her tone dry. "Think about it, Cowboy."

"I don't need to think about it. I'm always apologizing because I'm always acting like a jerk around you."

"I won't argue with that."

He squinted, more because of tension than the late-day sun. "Look, I know I'm hard to be around these days. Believe it or not, that's one reason I try to stay away. It's just that I want so much for things to work out with Rory. I feel as if I'm his last hope."

"I think it's wonderful that you're so concerned."

"You do?" he asked, surprised by her response and her obvious sincerity. He'd expected her to resent Rory or at least resent his presence here.

Allie nodded. "Of course I do. Especially considering how you were left out of his life completely for so many years."

"That's just it," he told her, encouraged by even a small suggestion that someone understood what he was going through. "None of that was his fault, and I feel like I have to make up to him for all the times I wasn't there."

"I can understand why you feel that way. I'm sure it's normal. But don't you see, Burn? You don't have to give up your own life in order to do that." Now she was the one gripping his arm, while he once more fought the impulse to withdraw, physically and emotionally. "You can be a father to Rory and have a life of your own."

"Maybe," he said, knowing he sounded unconvinced because he felt that way. "Maybe someday."

And maybe with some other woman, he refrained from adding. He knew that when Allie talked about his having a life of his own she was really talking about his having a relationship with a woman. More specifically she was talking about him and her. But she was wasting her breath.

Ever since Rhonda had first come to him and told him about Rory, he had been struggling with his feelings and trying to figure out just what his role as a father should be. He'd been feeling his way until Rory's brush with serious trouble shocked him into facing up to his responsibility full-time. Until then he'd lived his entire life answering to no one, living for the moment and for himself. That had to change. It was time to think of someone beside himself.

Driving to pick up Rory at the police station that afternoon two weeks ago, he'd had plenty of time to think things through and he'd come to some important decisions. First, he'd decided that for now, at least, he owed Rory his undivided attention and everything he had to give, physically and emotionally. He was determined to do whatever it took to convince the kid that he mattered to someone, that someone gave a damn what happened to him.

Not that Rhonda didn't care about him. She was a good mother. But somehow, when she'd married Keith, Rory had decided it meant there was no longer a place in her life for him. He'd never come right out and admitted this to Burn, of course, but Burn knew enough about being fourteen and about losing a mother to understand without being told just what that felt like and all the crazy things it could make you feel like doing to get back at the world. He figured that, in time, Rory would come to terms with Rhonda's marriage, but by then it might be too late. In his mind he'd had no choice but to step in and provide what Rory needed.

And the last thing Rory needed right now was to lose another parent—especially one he'd just found—to a relationship with someone else. Allie could say what she wanted about having a life of his own. Right now Rory needed to believe that he came first with someone, and no matter what Burn might feel like doing with the woman gazing up at him so beseechingly, he was going to make sure his son got that message. Like he'd said a minute ago, maybe someday the time would be right to find a woman he could share his life with, but that time wasn't now.

What's more, every instinct he possessed warned him that Allie wasn't the right woman and never would be. Even if Rory didn't outright resent her the way he did Keith, right now the boy needed stability and security. Hell, for all he knew, maybe that's what they both needed. And while Allie Halston's sweet mouth and enticing body promised a lot of things, stability and security weren't among them.

"You know, Burn," Allie said, quietly breaking the silence that had grown between them, "I spent a lot of years telling myself that someday I would do this or try that. And I can tell you from firsthand experience that life feels a whole lot better when you don't keep putting it on hold."

"I'll keep that in mind," he countered lightly. "In the meantime, I ought to go and check on—"

He was going to say he ought to go and check on Rory, but at that moment his excuse for making a graceful exit came loping around the corner of the stable, heading directly for them. Dressed in jeans and a dark blue cotton shirt, Rory looked as if he belonged on a ranch, and though he made a point of frowning whenever he was around his father, Burn had a hunch the kid didn't hate being here as much as he claimed. He did his best to be fair with the boy, balancing discipline with attention, treating him the way he would have liked to be treated in the days after his mother's death and his father's retreat into some place deep inside himself.

"I finished feeding the horses," Rory announced, coming to a halt a safe distance from where Burn and Allie were standing. Burn had noticed that after the first couple of times he had placed a hand on his son's shoulder or ruffled his hair, Rory had taken to standing out of arm's reach. "Can I go watch TV now?"

"Did you use that ointment on Fortune the way I showed you?"

"Yeah," Rory replied, then quickly jerked his gaze up to meet Burn's. "I mean, yes, sir, I used the ointment on her. She looks a whole lot better, too."

"Good. You're doing a good job with her," Burn told him. He had a feeling it was more for Allie than him, but he was still pleased by Rory's attempt at civility after the weeks of sullen silence and monosyllables. So pleased he felt generous. "In fact, I was thinking maybe you'd like a horse of your own."

The flare of excitement in Rory's eyes was so brief that Burn wondered if he'd imagined it. Almost instantly the kid's mouth curled into the familiar sneer.

"Horses are dumb," he said. "I'd rather have a dirt bike."

Burn swallowed his disappointment and said, "I didn't offer you a dirt bike."

"Fine," Rory said. "Can I watch TV now?"

"Is your homework done?"

Rory nodded.

"Including the make-up work for the day you missed?"

"It's not due till Monday. I've got the whole weekend."

"Not if you want to watch TV, you don't. No homework, no privileges."

"Since when is TV a privilege?"

"Since it's something you want and I don't have to give it to you."

"Fine. I'll do the stinking make-up work. It's only a chapter outline and some math. Then can I watch TV?"

"If you get your work done, then the time between now and dinner is your own. If you want to spend it cooped up inside watching TV, go right ahead."

"I do," Rory said as he turned to go.

Burn waited until he was out of earshot, then released a disgusted sigh. "The kid won't give an inch."

"Maybe you have to learn to give, too."

"I do," he said hotly. "At least I try. He doesn't even try."

"He's not the parent," Allie returned, her tone a blend of amusement and gentle rebuff. Burn wasn't sure he liked either.

"Don't remind me," he muttered. "If it's this hard when he's fourteen, I can't imagine how tough it is to be a parent of a two-year-old."

"I suspect it's tough in an entirely different way."

"Well, I'm not in any hurry to find out, believe me. I hate to admit it, but I'm looking forward to dropping him at his mother's tomorrow."

She looked surprised. "Rory is going back to live with Rhonda?"

"Just for the weekend," Burn explained. "I know you have friends coming to stay, and I thought it might be easier all around."

"You didn't have to do that. Rory wouldn't be a problem."

"Rory can be a major problem when he chooses to be," he corrected. "I know how much it means to you to have the ranch look good and everything go smoothly when your friends are here. I didn't want to take any chances."

"Thank you. That was really very sweet of you."

Burn shrugged off her smile of surprise and pleasure, though he decided he liked that reaction a whole lot better than her amusement of a moment ago.

"The kid misses his mother anyway," he told her, "and he's worked hard. He's earned a furlough."

"You make it sound as if this is a prison."

"I'm sure that's pretty much how Rory thinks of it."

"Well, maybe we ought to try and change that."

"You mean by coddling him more?" Burn shook his head. "That's what got us into this mess."

"I don't consider it coddling him to make him feel at home."

"And just how do you propose we do that?" he asked warily.

"For starters, I was thinking of having a birthday party for him. Rhonda mentioned he'll be turning fifteen shortly...."

"Next week," Burn confirmed.

"Fine. Why don't we plan on next Saturday? And don't worry, I'll handle everything. I like throwing parties."

"Somehow that doesn't surprise me," Burn responded, his mouth curving into a wry smile. "But I don't know about this, Allie. Who will you invite?"

"How about his friends?" she countered; now it was her turn to smile wryly. "Call me wild and unconventional, but I think friends ought to be invited to birthday parties."

"Very funny. Problem is, I don't even know his friends . . . or want to, judging from what I've heard."

"For heaven's sake, they're kids, Burn, just like Rory. Kids make dumb mistakes all the time. Lord knows, I did. This will give you a chance to meet Rory's friends and make up your own mind about them. And it's a way of reaching out to him, of showing him you're willing to meet him halfway."

"Halfway to the penitentiary," Burn grumbled.

"You're jumping to conclusions again. Come on, Burn, give them a chance. Give Rory a chance," she added.

When she put it like that, in that soft, cajoling tone that made shivers race up and down his spine, what choice did he have?

He nodded. "All right. I'll ask him who he wants—"

"No," she said, cutting in. "Let's keep the party a surprise. Ask Rhonda to call me when she has a chance and I'll get the names of Rory's friends from her."

"All right. I'll mention it to her tomorrow morning. Now I suppose I ought to go tell Rory that he's being sprung for the weekend. He'll probably be even more thrilled than I am. I think we can both use a little break from each other."

"Speaking of breaks," Allie said, clasping her hands together a bit apprehensively, not a gesture she used often. "I was wondering how you would feel about taking one this weekend as well."

He gave a short, biting laugh. "Sure thing, Boston. Do you want me off the ranch entirely or should I just stay out of sight in the bunkhouse for the duration? After all, someone has to be around to tend to the—''

"That's not what I meant at all," she interrupted, an angry flush on her cheeks. "How can you even think I would want you out of sight?"

"I'm never quite sure what you're thinking or why you do the things you do. Fact is, I'm still wrestling with why you came here and why you stayed."

"Do we have to rehash this again? I came on impulse, I've already admitted that. I stayed to prove something. And now..."

"And now?" Burn prodded quietly, curiously as her words trailed off and she gazed across the fields that stretched all the way to the hills in the distance.

"And now I love it here," she said softly, shrugging. "I can't explain it, so don't ask. *I* don't even really understand it, I just feel it. I love having something to do when I wake up in the morning and I love going to bed at night feeling like I accomplished something. I know that must sound foolish and like no big deal to you, but—''

Burn shook his head and broke in. "It doesn't sound foolish at all, actually. And it is a big deal. I know because I feel pretty much the same way. Building something a little piece at a time gives you a better feeling than proving you can hang onto the back of a horse a second longer than the next fool."

Allie laughed, her smile reaching her eyes in a way that told him the moment of shared confidences made her feel as good as it did him.

"Okay," he said, returning her smile, "so I won't hide in the bunkhouse all weekend. I'll still try to stay out of your way."

"No, you've still got it all wrong. When I asked if you'd mind taking a break, I meant a break from any work that can be put on hold for a few days. You see," she continued, clasping her hands once again, "I sort of wondered if you'd come with me to pick up my friends at the airport tomorrow and join us for dinner and..."

"And?"

"And just sort of be around."

"Around for what?"

"Oh, I don't know. Just around. The fact is, I haven't made a single friend since I've been here, and my friends from home aren't going to understand that. You see, they're very social minded. I was, too, actually, before I came here. And they're not going to understand how a person can be so busy working that she doesn't have time to makes friends or go to dinner or have parties. It will just make everything easier if they think you're..."

She paused.

"Your man," Burn supplied, his eyes crinkling at the corners as understanding settled on him. "You want me to pretend that we're—"

"Ha!" she interrupted. "That'll be the day! I hardly need to prove to my friends that I can find a date."

"Then why the charade?"

"I'm not suggesting a charade," she countered, her voice rising slightly. "I'm merely asking you to spend some time with me and a few old friends this weekend so that they'll see I do indeed have a life here and—"

"A man in that life."

"Friends. I was going to say so they'll see I have friends. We are friends, aren't we? I mean, more or less."

"More or less," Burn drawled, thinking it felt like a lot more than less.

"Good. Then as a friend, do you think you could do me a favor and help me entertain my guests this weekend?"

Burn thought it over. He thought about spending a whole weekend with Allie—going out to dinner, maybe dancing afterward, holding her in his arms, pretending to be her man...which he was certain was what she was asking for, no matter what she said to the contrary. He thought about all that and knew that if he wanted to remain sane and in control of his feelings, he had to refuse.

"All right," he said. "I'll do it."

"Don't sound so enthusiastic," she said dryly. "If it's such a chore, I can pay you overtime."

"That won't be necessary."

"Good. After all, I'm not exactly asking you to face the guillotine. They're very nice people."

He wasn't so sure of that, but it wasn't Allie's friends he was worried about.

"All right," he said again, a little less grimly this time. "I'll do it. Just tell me what time we have to be at the airport."

Chapter Nine

Allie was in a great mood. She'd discovered that she was
looking forward to her friends' visit with a great deal more
enthusiasm ever since yesterday, when she had persuaded
Burn to join them. She didn't have to waste any time wondering why that should be so. The explanation was as ap-
parent to her as the fact that her pulse raced and an army of
butterflies invaded her stomach whenever she so much as
thought about Burn Monroe.

In fact, her feelings toward him and her mood were directly related, and as she dressed to go to the airport on
Saturday, she couldn't help recalling how Burn had inter-
preted her invitation, insisting that what she really wanted
was for him to act the part of her man this weekend. And
she couldn't help admitting—strictly to herself, of course—
that there had been a bit of truth in his assessment of the
situation. She just wasn't sure whether the charade, as he'd
described it, was intended more for the benefit of her friends

or herself. But then, lately she wasn't sure of much of anything where her feelings for Burn were concerned.

Allie liked men, and in her rather colorful past, she'd liked several particular men a whole lot. The distinctive and pleasurable little tingles and rushes associated with falling in love were not exactly foreign to her. Some of the men—all right, *all* of the men—for whom she'd fallen had proven to be spectacularly poor risks. It took a bit longer for her to be convinced of that with some than with others, but looking back, she had to concede that her father's disapproving appraisal of her choice in men invariably proved to be accurate. Depressingly accurate.

So she was experienced at falling in love and at falling in love with the wrong man. But usually she didn't know he was the wrong man while she was still falling. There was no doubt in her mind what her father, mother, sisters and everyone else who knew her would think of her becoming seriously involved with Burn. And she had only slightly more doubt about the fact that they would all inevitably be proven right. Again.

She and Burn were from different backgrounds; their individual life-styles and expectations were too much at odds for them to ever be happy together once the heady rush of passion had subsided. Her friends, particularly Liz, one of the four friends visiting this weekend, would probably tell her to enjoy that first rush and be satisfied.

To be truthful, the idea had crossed Allie's mind. More than once, in fact. After all, the prospect of a fling with a genuine cowboy was one of the exciting, though unspoken, fantasies that had led her here in the first place. And there was no denying that Burn was about as genuine a cowboy as she was ever likely to come across.

She was no longer sure, however, that a fling with Burn was what she wanted. Or even if anything as casual as a fling was possible for the two of them. At least not without a high price being paid. She was conveniently overlooking the pertinent fact that he no longer seemed interested in her as anything other than his boss; her feelings were confused and contradictory and getting more so all the time. She was as guilty as Burn in that area. She wanted him, she didn't want him, she wanted him so much she was afraid she'd scream if he didn't reach out and touch her just once more the way he'd touched her and held her that day at Antelope Basin.

The fact that she knew he was all wrong yet wanted him anyway was dumb. And a little scary. Even scarier was the growing awareness that, deep down, what she wanted from Burn was more than a little pleasure and an honest day's work. She, who had never cared much what others thought of her, wanted his approval and his respect. She wanted to prove to him that she wasn't at all what he'd first thought— a flighty, spoiled brat from back East who thought of nothing and no one except herself.

Allie tossed her hairbrush onto the counter beside the bathroom sink and gave her reflection in the mirror one final glance. The simple, sleeveless white dress she was wearing with high-heeled white sandals was cool and flattering and would take her comfortably through an afternoon of sightseeing and shopping in San Antonio and on to dinner, before they all returned to the ranch later that evening. Allie was proud of the Circle Rose, but she wasn't at all sure her friends would share her affection for its undeniably simple charms, and so she had planned a full array of activities to keep them busy throughout the two-and-a-half days they would be here.

They'd visit San Antonio on Saturday and take an outing on horseback on Sunday, arranged by Burn, who had also managed to come up with some additional horses in time for their visit. She planned a barbecue for Sunday night, a relatively safe way to show off her new cooking skills, and then, first thing Monday morning, they would be returning to Boston.

The thought that they would be returning there without her brought Allie not a flicker of the homesickness she had felt when she'd first arrived in Bandera. Probably, she mused as she ran her hands through her hair, because she had already come to think of this as her home. She tossed her head, letting the shoulder-length waves settle loosely into place, and adjusted the gold clips on her ears.

She looked good, she decided. Tan and trim and happy. Why shouldn't she? She *was* happy. Happier than she'd been in a long while. For the first time in her life she felt involved and productive, and she had discovered it was a wonderful and addictive feeling. And one, she suspected, that would not be easy to explain to Liz and the others. It would be difficult to convince them that her glow was the result of hard work and plenty of fresh air. Like it or not, she had a hunch that with just one glance, they were going to draw exactly the conclusion Burn had predicted—namely, that the two of them were involved in something a lot more hot and heavy than resurrecting an old ranch.

What would her friends think of Burn? she mused. And what would he think of them? She had asked him to join them, hoping he would provide moral support and add a specter of credence to the new life she'd adopted. Now, as her new world and the one she'd left behind were about to collide, she wondered if it had been such a good idea after all.

Fortunately, she didn't have much opportunity to worry about it. Burn returned from driving Rory to Rhonda's just in time to leave for the airport. As usual, his eyes were hidden behind his sunglasses as she emerged from the house, but he looked at her long and hard enough to give Allie a pretty good idea what he was thinking, and she was suddenly glad she'd decided on a dress instead of slacks. He saw her in boots and jeans all the time, and it wouldn't hurt to remind him that she was a woman.

Not that she wanted to seduce him. She didn't. At least she didn't think she did. But she also didn't want him to make the mistake of thinking she was just one of the guys.

En route to the airport to meet the twelve-thirty flight from Boston, Burn told her that he'd discussed the birthday party with Rhonda, who thought it was a wonderful idea. She'd promised to phone Allie as soon as possible with the names of a few of Rory's friends, and she had also offered to help any way she could.

Allie was grateful for the offer, not to mention being greatly relieved. In spite of what she'd told Burn about her knack for parties, the truth was that most of her experience had been as a guest, not a hostess. She'd certainly never thrown a party for a teenager before, nor for that matter ever hosted one without lots of professional help with food and entertainment. Rhonda, on the other hand, probably had at least some experience entertaining kids Rory's age, and her advice would be appreciated.

It was odd, Allie thought as they drove along. The mother of the son of a man to whom she was wildly attracted was hardly a likely candidate for friendship, but right then Allie felt she shared as many common interests with Rhonda as she did with the old friends she would soon be seeing. Had she changed even more than she'd realized?

The unanswered question prompted some apprehensive feelings as they parked the Jeep and located the right gate. Allie sensed that, beneath Burn's habitual ease, he was also a bit apprehensive at the prospect of meeting her friends, and she was thankful they had only a short wait before the plane was scheduled to arrive. The flight was on time, and for Allie, at least, all nervousness vanished the instant she caught sight of Liz, tall and slender, her long, dark brown hair caught back in a ponytail, which—like everything she wore—managed to look elegant.

Liz came hurrying toward her and they caught each other in a hug, laughing and talking as the other friends she'd invited gathered around and took turns hugging her as well.

"Sherry, you look terrific," Allie said. "You cut your hair. I love it."

"My Peter Pan phase revisited," quipped Sherry, a petite blonde whose pixielike features were enhanced by the short, feathered hairstyle. "Oh, Roger, be quiet," she admonished the tall, handsome man who stood beside her chuckling. He had dark hair and tortoiseshell glasses and an Ivy League air discernible at a hundred paces. "You're just miffed because you have to stand in line for a hug from Allie. Didn't anyone ever tell you that patience is a virtue?"

"*You* never did," Roger retorted, gently elbowing Sherry aside as he grinned at Allie. "That's for sure. As I recall, you were always saying, 'Hurry, Roger, hurry...'"

"I never...ooh." Sherry colored and glared prettily at him. "As if you could even remember back that far."

"All the way back to last summer?" Roger countered, an eyebrow cocked. "Surely you haven't forgotten the boathouse and—"

"All right, all right," Sherry said, cutting him off. "This is no time for dredging up bad memories." She turned to Allie, who was smiling at the familiar exchange. "It's so great to see you again."

"You, too," Allie said. She glanced around. "All of you."

It was true. Now that they were there, she couldn't imagine why she had ever been uneasy about this visit. They were the same old friends and she was the same old Allie. It was silly to think that anything substantial could have changed in so brief a time. She grinned happily. They were a tangible reminder of home, and she was suddenly struck by how much a part of her missed all she'd left behind.

They were also a very attractive group—young and well dressed and successful looking, although the truth was that except for Chris, who was a lawyer and, besides Roger, the only other man in the group, they were mostly successful at having a good time and living off their trust funds.

"Chris, I'm glad you could get away," she said, going up on tiptoe to give him a quick hug as well. "Was the trial you mentioned cancelled?"

"Postponed," he explained, running his fingers through his sandy-colored hair. "Although for, uh, personal reasons, it was still touch and go for a while there as to whether

I'd be able to make it. I hope you don't mind an extra mouth to feed."

He smiled at her with the absolute confidence of someone accustomed to doing exactly as he pleased and not running into any opposition.

For the first time Allie noticed the woman next to him, half-hidden by his large frame. Buffy Winchester. Gorgeous, difficult, back-stabbing Buffy. For years Chris and Buffy had been an on-again, off-again twosome, and Allie detested the woman.

"Of course not," she replied, managing a polite smile. "Hello, Buffy. Welcome to San Antonio."

"Is it always this hot?" Buffy asked by way of greeting as she lifted her long silky mane of auburn hair off her neck and let it drop. Every move Buffy made was dramatic and calculated.

"For heaven's sake, Buffy, it's air-conditioned in here," Sherry snapped.

"Really?" countered Buffy. "It doesn't seem to be."

"Try taking off your sweater," Sherry suggested, turning her head so that Buffy couldn't see her roll her eyes in disgust.

Chris could, however. "Sherry, really—"

"Shouldn't we get our luggage or something?" Liz, the peacemaker, interrupted.

"Good idea," Roger agreed, glancing around. "Where's a porter when you need one?"

"Who needs one? We only have one bag each," Liz reminded him.

"Speak for yourself," Roger said. "As it so happens, I brought two. I can't stand for my jackets to get crushed."

"Who needs a jacket?" Buffy asked, fanning herself with her hand. "It's so damn hot here."

"Then take off your sweater," Sherry ordered. "Or aren't you wearing anything under it?"

Chris shook his head. "For heaven's sake, Sherry. Will you lay off?"

"I'm just saying that if she's going to constantly complain about the heat, then—"

"Who's complaining? I'm simply remarking. Can't a person remark about the weather without being crucified?"

"Crucified? Give me a break."

"Do you have to be so picky?"

"Do you all have to start bickering the minute we get here?"

"Why not? Never put off until tomorrow and all that..."

"I give up," Liz said, shaking her head and grinning at Allie. "Sorry you invited us yet?"

"Not a bit," Allie insisted, although that thought had begun to sprout. She didn't have time for regrets as she went through mental gymnastics, juggling beds and bodies, wondering how she was going to accommodate the unexpected Buffy. She'd intended to ask Roger and Chris to share a room, but that was out now. Chris and Buffy would want to sleep together, of course, which meant Roger would need his own room. She'd worry about that later. Perhaps Roger would even agree to sleeping in the bunkhouse. She'd try to convince him it was an adventure, and Burn could...

Burn.

In all the excitement and verbal sparring, she'd completely forgotten he was there. Now she turned to find him standing off to the side, his face expressionless except for the cynically amused gleam in his dark eyes, which Allie had become expert at discerning. She motioned to include him in the circle of her friends.

"There's someone I want you all to meet," she said, letting her fingers rest lightly on the sleeve of the khaki shirt he wore with black jeans and boots. "This is Burn Monroe. Burn's the foreman of the Circle Rose and a friend. Burn, you'll never remember all these names and faces right away, but here goes anyway."

She quickly ran through the introductions, providing for Burn's benefit such helpful background details as the fact that she and Liz had attended first grade together and that Roger's family summered near her own on Martha's Vineyard. The only one she didn't have some affectionate comment about was Buffy. Operating on the theory that if you can't say something nice it's better to say nothing at all, Allie decided that everything she knew about Buffy Winchester was best left unsaid.

After collecting the baggage, they arranged for a rental car to supplement the seating space in Burn's Jeep. They wasted only a little more time bickering before they all agreed on visiting the Alamo first and then driving to Oliver Square in the northeast section of the city, where, Allie explained, there were a number of specialty shops she was sure Liz and Sherry would enjoy. Chris wanted new boots and expressed an interest in visiting Lucchese Boots on Broadway.

"Do you know where that is?" Allie asked Burn several hours later, after they had made the requisite tourist trek to the Alamo and done some shopping, stuffing still more bags and packages into the Jeep and rented car.

"I know where Broadway is," he replied. "I'll find Lucchese's."

"It shouldn't be too hard to find," Allie remarked. "They're famous for their custom-made boots."

"They're also expensive."

"Then you've been there?"

"Not exactly. I don't care to spend as much on my feet as I do on a car. But some of the other guys on the circuit were really into all that showy western gear and they were regulars at Lucchese's."

"What circuit?" asked Buffy from the back seat. They'd been playing a game of musical cars throughout the afternoon as Allie took turns catching up with her friends, and this time Chris and Buffy had elected to ride with them.

"Burn's talking about the rodeo circuit," Allie explained when he suddenly seemed to find it necessary to focus all his attention on the road ahead.

Burn wasn't overly talkative at the best of times, and judging from the way his jaw had hardened back at the Alamo as he'd endured Buffy's snide remarks about the memorial and the general difference in quality of cultural life between East and West, Allie had a hunch this wasn't turning out to be the best of times for him. She did have to credit him for his patience, however, as he trailed her and the others through one trendy boutique after another, when all the time she was sure he was thinking of what he could have been accomplishing back at the ranch. To her amazement, several times Allie caught herself thinking the very same thing.

"Rodeo?" Buffy echoed, a thread of laughter in her voice. "You're kidding, right?"

"No, I'm not," Allie answered, aware her tone had cooled dramatically and hoping Buffy would take the warning. "Burn competed in rodeos professionally and he was very good."

"How fascinatingly quaint," Buffy said, her husky voice amused. "A veritable slice of Americana. Burn will just have to give us a demonstration of his skills, won't he, Chris?"

"Sure. That would be great," Chris agreed, sounding about as interested as if Buffy had suggested watching Burn sleep.

"As silly—and I might add, politically incorrect—as all that rodeo nonsense is, I have to admit there is something rather compelling about the idea of pitting a man against a wild animal," Buffy remarked. "Something raw and primitive. Although I have a hunch the animals aren't really all that wild, that it's mostly for show, like professional wrestling. Is that correct, Burn?"

"No."

Allie tried to think of a graceful way to change the subject, but before she had a chance to, Buffy laughed smugly.

"Oh, come now, you don't really expect me to believe that you'd risk breaking your neck on the back of some bull or wild stallion simply to win a little prize money?'' she demanded.

''It's not about money,'' Burn replied, meeting Buffy's gaze in the rearview mirror as he steered the Jeep into a parking place near Lucchese Boots. ''It's about courage. And no, I really wouldn't expect you to believe it.''

''Well, here we are,'' Allie announced brightly.

Buffy looked slightly bewildered, as if she knew she'd just been lampooned by a master but couldn't quite figure out how. Allie doubted she ever would. Over the past few weeks she herself had had several opportunities to listen to Burn talk about the rodeo and the kind of courage it took for a man to challenge fate on the back of something so much bigger and stronger and meaner than himself.

She'd heard him talk about the passion and respect he'd felt each time he competed, and about the fear. He'd tried to explain how the feelings would consume him, driving him on, and about how those men who were in it solely for the prize money often made disastrous mistakes. Thinking with their heads and not their hearts, was how he put it. It wasn't something she'd expected to hear Burn say, since it was so at odds with the practical and levelheaded side of him that she usually saw. Clearly he had a reckless and passionate side as well, another part of the mystery and paradox of the man. And something that Allie doubted Buffy would ever be able to comprehend.

Inside the store they fanned out and examined the wide array of boots on display, boots crafted out of everything from purple fringed suede to hand-painted ostrich skin. The price tags were, as Burn predicted, equally outlandish. Not surprisingly, the expense involved didn't deter Chris or Liz from each ordering two pairs of custom-made boots. While they were being measured and fitted, Burn idly inspected a case of silver belt buckles and then dropped into the chair closest to the door to wait. Watching him from across the store, Allie had a feeling he was doing his best not to look bored stiff.

It was an understandable reaction on his part, and she was increasingly sorry she had twisted his arm to get him to come along. Not for her sake. She loved having him there, and she had to admit that, silly as it was, she enjoyed the pointedly speculative looks she'd gotten from Liz and Sherry after they'd checked him out. Later, when they were alone, they would want to know everything. Unfortunately, there wasn't much to tell.

Her regrets about pressing Burn to join them were entirely on his behalf. She'd always considered her friends to be extremely friendly and gregarious, and had blithely assumed that in no time he would mesh with them and become one of the gang. They'd been together hours now, however, and Burn wasn't meshing. What's more, she understood belatedly that if the others hung around for a month instead of just a weekend, he would remain as much an outsider as he was at that moment.

It wasn't due to rudeness or a lack of effort on either side. Well, she supposed some of Buffy's remarks bordered on rudeness, and Burn's effort could be described as minimal. Allie didn't have the heart to fault him, however. Boutique hopping and the brand of witty, utterly pointless one-upmanship her friends practiced so relentlessly were hardly his style. He and the others were like water and oil in the same bottle—close enough to touch, but with characteristics that made it impossible for them to ever blend completely. She clung to the thought that tomorrow had to be better, that Burn would be more at home outdoors and on horseback.

Finally Chris and Liz were through, and they were on their way out of the shop when Sherry spotted a pair of black eel-skin boots she absolutely had to try on.

"They call to me," she insisted when the others groaned. Roger had been complaining of being hungry for nearly an hour.

"What do you think?" Sherry asked, turning in front of the angled mirror to check out the rear view.

"I think they look just like the black boots you already own," Liz told her.

"No, the toes of these are much narrower. See?" She turned again.

Liz examined them and nodded. "Now I see. Buy them."

"Don't humor me," Sherry returned, pouting slightly. "Tell me what you really think."

"I told you what I really thought and you didn't like it, so I figured I'd tell you what you want to hear instead."

"I hate when you do that." Sherry glanced at Allie. "Allie, what do you think?"

"I think they look great. Very Texas."

"Texas?" Sherry frowned. "I thought they looked sort of Russian."

"Russian Texas," Chris offered. "Can you hurry up and make up your mind? I'm hungry."

"Really, Chris, I didn't rush you."

"But when he was ordering his boots we weren't already late for dinner," Buffy pointed out. She looked at Allie. "Didn't you say our reservations were for eight sharp?"

"Well, I said eight," Allie acknowledged. "But it's only a few minutes after that now."

Buffy raised her eyebrows. "I detest being late."

"Then go on without me," Sherry snapped, glancing in the mirror once again. "I can't decide." She turned sideways. "I wish they had metal tips like that pair over there." She turned a little more. "And spurs."

"I didn't know you were looking for boots to wear to bed," Roger remarked, meeting Sherry's irritated glare with a smile.

"I have some black leather boots with steel tips," the saleslady offered. "They're not eel skin, but they're real soft. Would you like to see them?"

"Yes," Sherry replied, ignoring another round of groans that followed. Chris and Roger joined Burn on the chairs as the young clerk returned with the boots. Sherry tried them on, pirouetting several times before deciding she'd rather try them in gray, then taupe, then red and finally without the steel tips after all. The floor around her was strewn with discarded boots, tissue paper and empty boxes when she finally sighed wearily and reached for her own shoes.

"I can't make up my mind," she announced. "And now I'm just too hungry to even think."

"I knew it," Liz said, throwing up her hands. "I knew it would end this way."

"At least it's ending," said Chris. "Let's get out of here before anything else calls to her."

"Like sanity, perhaps," Buffy added, shaking her head. "I cannot believe she kept us waiting all this time for nothing."

They had already filed out when Burn got to his feet. Allie purposely lagged behind the others, hoping to have a word with him privately and reassure him that his ordeal was almost over. But instead of joining her at the door, he bent and helped the salesclerk toss the boots back into the empty boxes. As Allie watched, he piled them in a stack and smiled as he stood and handed the stack to the young woman.

"Sorry about that," he said, and Allie knew without a doubt that he was referring to Sherry's cavalier behavior.

"No problem," the clerk replied with a shrug. "I'm used to it."

His smile became twisted. "I'm not."

He turned toward the door, looking surprised when he saw Allie waiting for him. As if, she thought, he had assumed she'd traipsed out with her friends and left him there. As if there were sides being subtly, silently drawn, and she wasn't on his.

At one time that might have been true, she thought, but no longer. Not only did she want to be on Burn's side, but she knew in her heart that she *was*. As much as she liked Sherry, watching her performance had made Allie uncomfortable in a way it never would have back home. Not merely impatient or irritated, as the others had been, but conscious of her thoughtlessness toward the salesclerk, who'd had to ferry boots to and from the storeroom on Sherry's whim and clean up the mess afterward.

Allie was honest enough to admit that at one time she wouldn't have seen the episode this way, the way Burn saw it, and she had a hunch that right this minute he was thinking she was more like Sherry than not. That left her feeling the same way she had that night he'd questioned her about the housekeeper at home picking up the messes she'd created. She longed for a way to make him see that she wasn't the same woman she had been back in Boston. Not by a long shot.

Since coming here, she'd worked harder than she'd ever worked before and she'd experienced firsthand both the physical aches and the tremendous pride that result from a tough job well done. She'd sweated and she'd struggled and she'd changed. She suddenly understood that the time period involved didn't matter. If an overgrown, neglected old ranch could be so transformed in a matter of weeks, then surely a woman could be. And that's exactly what had happened. She'd been so busy helping to change the Circle Rose that she hadn't paid much attention to how much the Circle Rose was changing her.

"Burn," she began as he drew next to her, "I'm sorry about today. It hasn't turned out quite the way I expected."

"Really?" His expression was wry. "That's funny. It's turned out exactly as I expected."

"So you were prepared to dislike my friends?" she demanded, suddenly feeling tired and angry and frustrated.

"Not exactly prepared. Maybe *braced* would be a better word."

"That's not fair. You obviously judged them before you even met them."

Burn shrugged. "Before or after, what's the difference? The way I see it the result's just the same."

"So it's true. You don't like them."

"I don't even know them, Allie. And it's hard to get to know them running from one shop to another while they take turns roasting each other. A better question might be do they like each other?''

"Of course they do. We've all been friends for years. Well, except for Buffy. They just like to tease each other.''

He nodded, his smile forced. "Whatever you say.''

"Would you rather skip dinner? I'm sure we can all squeeze into one car if you want to take off.''

"No. I told you I'd do this for you and I will.''

"Even if it kills you?''

"I've been through worse," he told her. This time his smile was real and Allie's heart lifted in response.

"Thanks," she said. "It means a lot to me.''

"I know. There is one thing, though," he added as he held the door for her.

"What's that?''

His smile broadened. "Is that offer of overtime still good?''

Chapter Ten

They had dinner at The Cypress Grill, a casually elegant restaurant overlooking the San Antonio River. As is usually the case when old friends get together, the conversation turned toward memorable incidents from their shared past. Allie did her best to include Burn, filling him in on those names and places he wouldn't recognize, but it wasn't easy.

Finally he reached for her hand under the table and squeezed it firmly.

"Relax," he said softly, leaning close so that the others, engrossed in their reminiscing, couldn't hear. "You don't have to worry about me."

"I don't want you to feel left out," she admitted.

His smile suggested that being left out of this particular group was not a major crisis in his life, but he simply squeezed her hand again. "Left out? Are you kidding? This is the most fun I've had all day."

"Sure. I'll bet you just love hearing all these embarrassing stories from my youth."

"I do like hearing about you, it's true. But when I said I was having fun, I was actually referring to holding your hand."

It was a harmless comment, not particularly eloquent or passionate, and there was certainly no reason it should leave Allie breathless and struggling to concentrate on the conversation around her. But it did.

The fact that Burn was holding her hand and willing to admit he was enjoying it overrode the stoic professionalism with which he'd been treating her for the past couple of weeks. She wasn't sure exactly what it might mean, but just the touch of his hand had her carefully constructed resolve not to get emotionally involved with him trembling like beach sand in an earthquake.

After dinner they stopped by a popular local club called The Farmer's Daughter, which featured a western band. Burn refused to dance anything more elaborate than the two-step, ride the mechanical bull in the bar or respond to the goading he received because of it, particularly from Buffy. Allie marveled at his relaxed self-control, but she wasn't particularly surprised by it.

During the time she'd known him, she'd seen him deal with stubborn cattle, sick horses and the sullen fourteen-year-old son whom he loved and was stymied by in about equal parts. Almost always, his mood remained the same: calm and persistent. He had a firm hand underscored by gentleness, and the same unswerving self-assurance that proclaimed that here was a man who understood what mattered and what didn't, who knew what he wanted and didn't want out of life.

One thing was certain. He didn't want to ride a mechanical bull just to indulge a passing whim of Buffy Winchester's. And no matter what he might think of the woman or her razor-edged comments, he was too much of a gentle-

man to respond in kind. To Allie there was something solid
and reassuring and very appealing about that.

As she watched him sip his beer and walk a fine line between being polite and ignoring Buffy outright, she suddenly realized that she'd been wrong earlier when she'd
anticipated that today might bring about a collision of her
two worlds, Boston and Bandera. She saw now that it wasn't
going to happen. First, because Burn would never let it
happen. And second, because planets in different orbits
never collide. That's what she was watching here, she
thought. Concentric orbits, train tracks running side by side
and never touching.

There would be no collision, no outburst, no fireworks,
because when you came right down to it, Burn wasn't interested enough to be bothered. Buffy and the others—their
life-style, their pastimes and their private little jokes—were
outside his sphere of interest. He was here because she'd
asked him to come and he'd given his word that he would,
period. And his word mattered to him more than custom-
made boots or fancy restaurants ever would.

What else mattered to Burn was back at the ranch—the
field that needed clearing, the section of fence he'd intended to complete this weekend. Traveler, too, she thought,
smiling as she pictured the huge bull that represented the
future of the Circle Rose. And Rory, of course, despite the
fact that Rory let his dad know in every way possible that he
wished he would just get lost.

She doubted that any of it—livestock, back-breaking
work or an ungrateful kid—would interest her friends any
more than their world interested Burn. It was a case of mutual indifference. They didn't want what Burn had, and as
far as she could tell, he didn't covet anything associated with
them—not their social standing or their whirlwind life-style
or their freedom to do anything or nothing at all as they
pleased.

Nor would he covet a woman who came from that world,
she realized with a sudden catch in her throat. No matter

how rich or beautiful that woman might be. Burn was interested in something else, something more, and in a flash Allie understood why from the start things between them had never proceeded as she expected. It was because money and beauty, perhaps her greatest assets and definitely those that other men found most appealing, were not all that important to Burn.

It was strangely ironic, she thought, since that's what she'd always claimed she wanted: a man who would value her for herself rather than for what she owned or how she would look on his arm.

She glanced around the table, almost oblivious to the laughter and teasing of the others. There might not be a collision here tonight, but there was clearly a choice to be made, if she had the courage to make it. A choice between a life she knew and a life she'd only dreamed of, a choice between the past and the future. Suddenly the differences between her and Burn didn't seem so much a detriment as a blessing, a wake-up call.... An opportunity.

Tonight had proved to her that those differences would mean disaster if she ever tried to force Burn to live in the world she'd left behind. But she had no intention of doing that. The gradual changes that had been occurring in her since she'd arrived here had been brought into focus for her today, as she was reminded time and again of how she used to spend her days, of the restlessness she used to feel so much of the time. She hadn't felt that in weeks—not since she'd moved to Bandera, not since she'd found a reason for getting up in the morning. Not since she'd met Burn.

Burn and the ranch and her newfound sense of purpose and satisfaction were so entwined that Allie wasn't sure she could separate them even if she wanted to. Which she didn't. It was a package deal and she wanted it all. She loved her friends and they would always be her friends, although she knew they thought she was crazy for coming here in the first place and expected her to tire of the whole venture very soon. They were in for a surprise. Everyone was, because this time the choice was hers alone to make, and she chose the future. She chose the Circle Rose. She chose Burn.

He might have been the wrong man for her six months ago, when she was floundering through life back in Boston, but he was the right man for her now. He was the right man for the woman she had become, the right man for the woman she wanted to be. Now all she had to do, Allie thought, with a surge of the same indomitable spirit that had led her and a great many others to pull up stakes and move west, was convince Burn that she was the right woman for him.

It was late when they finally arrived back at the ranch. Allie had dreamed that her friends would be awestruck by the mere sight of the house, especially with moonlight spilling over its sturdy low roof, with the cypress trees standing as dramatic black outlines against a paler sky. She'd dreamed of such a reaction, but of course she hadn't seriously expected it. So she wasn't disappointed when she received a round of modest praise, punctuated by stifled yawns. It had been a long day for all of them.

"Did it come with real cows?" Sherry asked.

Allie laughed, catching Burn's eye as they climbed from the Jeep, knowing he was thinking the same thing she was. That it wasn't so long ago when she might have asked just such a question.

"It didn't come with any livestock. We added that ourselves," she explained.

"Livestock," echoed Roger. "Don't we sound professional?"

"A month or so and already she thinks she's Annie Oakley."

"Miss Kitty."

"Ma Barker."

"Ma Barker?"

"Wrong era?"

"Wrong era and wrong profession, you idiot." Liz shook her head and yawned. "I don't care if the cows are real as long as the beds are…and as long as I get one. Allie, do you really have room for all of us?''

"Sure. If not in the house, there's always the bunkhouse.'' She pointed in that direction.

"The bunkhouse?'' Buffy's brow furrowed. "How bizarre.''

Allie ignored her. "In fact, I figured that Chris and Buffy could take my room, Liz and Sherry could share the largest of the two guest rooms and maybe Roger would like to rough it?''

Roger adjusted his glasses and peered steadily at her. "Me? In the bunkhouse? Surely you jest!''

Allie managed a laugh, her best hope crushed. "Of course I am. I have the other guest room all set up for you. Come on, you can have the grand tour in the morning. I'm sure right now you're all as tired as I am.''

"Amen,'' Liz said, following her onto the porch.

They gathered around, waiting for Allie to unlock the front door. She was very aware that Burn hadn't headed for the bunkhouse as soon as they arrived, but was holding the screen door open to make it easier for her to use her key. It was service above and beyond the call of duty to be sure, and it was typically, wonderfully Burn. At that moment Allie would have liked nothing better than to rest her head on his strong shoulder and close her eyes to everything and everyone else in the world.

"Oh, look,'' Sherry said, drawing Allie's attention from the lock as she pointed at an old watering trough for the horses. "Just like on 'Bonanza.'''

"What's 'Bonanza'?'' Buffy asked.

"You've never seen 'Bonanza'?'' Sherry demanded. "Pa, Adam, Little Joe?''

"It's an old television series,'' Chris explained.

Buffy shrugged. "Must be very old. I've never even heard of it.''

"Well, I guess some people are just more well rounded than others,'' Sherry retorted.

"Yes." Buffy gave the sweetly cutting smile that was her forte. "And some people have better things to do than while away the lonely hours watching reruns . . . reruns of old cowboy shows, of all things."

"You have something against cowboys?" Sherry inquired, a gleam in her eyes at the thought that she had the other woman cornered between her own quick tongue and Burn.

Buffy arched her brows. "Well, I don't consider them to be the most challenging or stimulating form of life. . . ." She swung her gaze toward Burn. "Present company excluded, of course."

Allie had had it. She froze with her hand on the doorknob and glared at her. "Buffy, why the hell don't you—"

But Burn silenced her with a glance and a smile. "That's perfectly all right, ma'am," he said, cranking his drawl up a notch, "no need to exclude me. Fact is, I do my best to be as unstimulating and unchallenging as I can. Life's a lot easier that way.

"Just think," he went on softly, his gaze steady on Buffy, who was beginning to look a bit like a deer caught in headlights as he slowly crossed the porch in her direction. "If I were less primitive and uncivilized, and more challenging and stimulating and politically correct, I just might attract me a woman like you."

Buffy made a huffing noise that was barely audible over the collective chuckle. The group appreciated nothing more than subtlety.

"And now," Burn went on, "since you all seem to be squared away with your sleeping arrangements, I think I'll say good-night."

It was much later, after Allie had shown them all to their rooms and explained where extra blankets and towels could be found, that she stopped and thought about the fact that no one, not even Burn, had bothered to ask where the hell she was going to sleep.

After this brief, eye-opening reunion with her old friends, she wasn't particularly surprised that none of them had given any thought to anyone's comfort but their own. But she would have thought that Burn, who had seen fit, after all, to help a total stranger stack shoe boxes, might have at least wondered where in this house of too many guests and too few beds she was going to park her pillow. Correction—make that her rolled-up parka stuffed into a pillowcase. Since Buffy couldn't breathe correctly without extra pillows to support her neck, Allie was going to do without a pillow tonight.

Unless she went out to the bunkhouse and got one, she thought, weighing the idea. The house had been noisy as everyone got ready for bed and, though they were rarely required to wait for anything, were forced to take turns in the bathroom. Now all was quiet. There wasn't even a sound from the room Chris and Buffy were sharing. Her room, thought Allie, longing for its big, comfortable bed and smooth, cool sheets. Either Chris and Buffy were exhausted or feuding, or the walls of this house really were as solid as Burn claimed they were.

Allie turned out the lights, except for one in the bathroom in case anyone should get up to use it during the night. She stretched out on the sofa, her makeshift pillow beneath her head. The new sofa was gorgeous, but it wasn't a bed, and the rolled-up jacket wasn't a pillow. She at least needed a comfortable pillow if she was going to get any sleep at all. She groaned silently, thinking of the morning, just a few short hours away.

Sitting up abruptly, she swung her feet to the floor.

This was ridiculous. She needed a pillow, and there were at least a half dozen of them going unused in the bunkhouse, all soft, all comfortable and all hers. There was no reason she shouldn't march out there and get one, even if she was dressed for bed and even if Burn was liable to attribute some sort of ulterior motive to her visit, the way he had when she'd asked him to come along today. Well, let him. She was tired and mixed-up and ready to take him on.

She used the back door and had crossed the porch to the top step when she heard the rocking chair behind her creak. She whirled, frightened, and saw a tall shadow unfolding from the chair.

"What took you so long?" Burn asked softly.

It was several seconds before Allie's heart stopped pounding and she could speak.

"Burn! You scared me half to death! What on earth are you doing out here?"

"Waiting for you. Only you," he added. "So will you please keep your voice down? Unless, of course, you'd like for a few of your house guests to join us."

Allie hurriedly shook her head. "No, please, I love my friends dearly, but enough is enough. And twelve hours straight is enough."

"Twelve-and-a-half hours, but who's counting?"

"You, obviously, and I can't blame you," she said with a quiet chuckle. "A better question is, why are you waiting out here for me? Didn't you think I'd gone to bed already?"

"Where?" He moved closer, stepping out of the shadow cast by the roof so that the moonlight allowed her to see his face clearly. "I may not be especially stimulating, but I can count. I counted bodies and beds and came up one short. And I knew that if anyone in that bunch was going to do without, it was going to be you."

"How did you know that?"

"Let's just say none of the others struck me as the self-sacrificing type."

"And I do?" Allie countered. "That's quite a turn-around. Here I thought you thought I was just a spoiled brat from back East who didn't know one end of a cow from the other. I thought you thought I was too impulsive and self-centered and never put anyone else's—"

"You know," Burn interrupted, silencing her more by resting his hands on her shoulders than with his words, "if you'd be quiet for half a minute you wouldn't have to worry about thinking about what I'm thinking about you, because I'd go ahead and tell you myself."

"By all means," Allie replied, vividly aware of his touch and of the tiny shivers it sent racing down her spine. "Tell me what you think of me."

"I think you're all right," he said with predictable restraint, and then shrugged, swallowing hard as he moved one hand from her shoulder to curl around the back of her neck. "Hell, I think you're a walking, breathing miracle, Allie, and beautiful. So beautiful that sometimes it makes my eyes hurt just to look at you."

He smiled as he delivered a compliment that could have come only from him and that meant more to Allie than having her name emblazoned in diamonds by any other man in the world.

"Oh yeah?" she said, lifting her chin to gaze at him as awareness and anticipation slowly uncurled inside her.

Burn squeezed the back of her neck, smiling. "Yeah."

"Does it make anything else hurt when you look at me?"

His smile turned dangerous. "Why do you ask?"

"I was thinking maybe I could..."

"Kiss it and make it better?"

"Yeah."

"Oh yeah. Please."

"If you're interested, that is."

"Interested? Lady, I'm going into overdrive just standing here. But just one warning..."

Allie looked at him quizzically.

"This time I'm prepared. This time there won't be any interruptions... or reprieves."

She reached up and looped her arms around his neck as she murmured, "Promise?"

"You really want this?" he asked, his words barely more than a warm breath against her face as he brought his mouth tantalizingly close. "You really want me?"

Allie was struck by the note of incredulity in his rough voice.

"I've been wanting you for weeks," she declared in a whisper, "as if you didn't know."

"I guess knowing and believing are two different things."

"Why wouldn't you believe it?"

He shook his head, shifting his gaze from hers as his mouth tightened.

"I'd have thought it was all pretty obvious that day up at Antelope Basin," she prodded.

She saw his eyes darken at the memory.

"I believed you wanted me that day, all right," he told her, "nearly as badly as I wanted you."

"So what changed?"

"I did," he said, meeting her troubled gaze. "At least, I figured I had changed in your eyes, once you found out I had a kid. A kid I hadn't even known about for fourteen years."

"But that wasn't your fault."

"Result's the same for Rory. And it still doesn't exactly feel like a merit badge. If I'd been a different kind of man back then, maybe Rhonda would have felt she could tell me... who knows? I just know that I've learned not to believe in miracles, and it seems to me that's what it would take for someone like you to want to get mixed up with someone like me. A miracle."

"Someone like me?" Allie echoed, stiffening. "You mean someone rich and spoiled, someone like Buffy and Sherry, someone who—"

"No." He cut her off, shaking her lightly. "You've got it all wrong. Maybe I thought that once. I jumped to a few conclusions about you, the same as you jumped to a few about me, I'll bet."

He paused and Allie offered a noncommittal shrug.

"I guess we've both had a few surprises along the way. The fact is, I've known for a while that you aren't what I thought at first, that you're not like Buffy or the others now, if you ever were. I saw how you helped Rhonda through that afternoon when Rory was in trouble and she needed a friend to talk to. And I've seen you reach out to Rory time and again when more often than not the kid's about as pleasant as sitting bare butt in a pricker bush."

Allie smiled faintly. "Rory's my buddy."

"Because you took time to get him to trust you. You didn't have to do that. Just like you didn't have to pitch in and help around here, working harder than I'll bet you've ever dreamed of working."

"I didn't have much choice," she groused, "once you explained to me how I couldn't afford to get the job done any other way."

"You didn't have to listen. You didn't have to put the future of the ranch first. If you'd really been as headstrong and self-centered as I once thought, we'd have a lot more skylights and a lot fewer cows around here right now."

"You can't herd skylights," she said, recalling what he'd once said to her.

"No, and you can't change a bad risk into a good one. A woman like you deserves the best. You deserve a man with a clean slate and a bright future, not some washed up cowboy with a kid who's like a powder keg waiting to explode. Face it, Allie, any way you look at it, that adds up to a bad risk for a woman."

"You're probably right," she said, seeing the pain etched on his face as he prepared to let her go. She moved her hands to his arms, holding them in place. "All in all, I'd say you're probably almost as bad a risk for me as a woman with a history of self-indulgence and a short attention span is for you."

His eyes narrowed. "So you're saying that we're all wrong for each other?"

"No, I'm saying it sure looks that way." She leaned closer, pressing against him as she let her mouth hover within a whisper of his. "But that's sure not how it feels."

Just the slightest lift of her chin brought their lips together, and a lifetime of waiting and wanting turned the kiss into an explosion of passion. Allie hadn't known she was waiting, hadn't known what she was searching for; she only knew she'd found it and that at this moment she didn't care about odds or risks, only about Burn and being with him tonight.

"How does it feel to you, Cowboy?" she asked when they finally paused to catch their breath.

"Good," he murmured, his mouth hot and damp and demanding at the side of her throat. "Too good to stop."

"Then don't," Allie pleaded, running her hands over his broad back as she surrendered to the currents of delight his lips sent shooting through her. "Don't stop."

"Come on," he said, his tone rough and impatient as he reached for her hand and pulled her after him toward the bunkhouse. Glancing at her over his shoulder with eyes that glittered like sapphires in the night, he vowed, "One of these days, lady, I'm going to start making love to you in a place I can finish it."

He opened the door and led her quickly through the main room with its row of single beds to one of the two rooms at the end, rooms he and Rory had claimed. It was not exactly a classic scene for seduction. There was no satin and lace, no candlelight, no scent of lavender.

Instead the heat from the day hung in the air like another presence. The scent of cedar from the paneled walls was thick and sweet and the feel of cotton caressed her legs as Burn lay her on his quilt-covered bed. Allie couldn't think of any place she'd rather be.

Through the window at the head of the bed she saw the moon and she smiled. A faint breeze came from out of nowhere to ruffle the simple white cotton curtains she'd hung despite Burn's protests, and somewhere far away there was a faint rumble of thunder.

"Rain," she said, as he knelt beside her on the bed, gazing at her as reverently as if she'd been dropped there from heaven just for him. "We need it."

He smiled at that. "You really have turned into a rancher."

"You moved the horses inside, right?"

"Yes, ma'am, and even if I hadn't, they'd just have to get wet. There's nothing short of a natural disaster that could drag me out of this bed tonight."

"Shh," Allie whispered, covering his mouth with her fingertips. "With our track record, you probably shouldn't tempt fate."

"You're right," he agreed, licking her fingers playfully. "Especially when I'd much rather spend my time tempting you."

Allie could have told him he tempted her just by breathing, but she didn't. She smiled to herself as he stretched out on top of her, bracing his weight on his side even as he covered her.

She wasn't quite sure how he managed that, but as his fingers traced lightly over her face, followed slowly by his lips, she quickly moved beyond caring. Her arms opened to welcome him as his slow, gentle caresses drew her into a world of warm, lazy sensation.

From her face he moved lower, indulging her throat in the same lavish, unhurried treatment. Allie closed her eyes and gave herself up to the shifting currents of pleasure he was creating. Time stopped as she heard the rustle of the curtain overhead caught in the rising wind and the intermittent roll of thunder as the storm moved east.

Then even that receded as Burn's touch became all-consuming, until there was only the deliciously rough scrape of his fingertips against her soft skin and the warm pressure of his mouth, licking, nibbling, caressing. Arousing and soothing at once. And hypnotizing.

"Oh, yes," she breathed as he found and lightly bit the most sensitive spot at the side of her throat. Goose bumps danced across her skin.

"You're shivering," he noted. "Let me warm you up."

"By taking off my clothes?" she asked with hazy amusement as he dragged the oversize T-shirt she wore to sleep in over her head.

Burn grinned and tossed it aside, leaving her in only her panties, high-cut white lace panties that he clearly found fascinating. Allie shivered again under the intensity of his gaze.

"Exactly," he said, lifting his eyes to meet hers. "It's my own secret recipe for imparting warmth. Instead of a hot-water bottle," he explained, pressing himself to her intimately, "you get me."

"Mmm." Allie arched her back and sighed. "Definitely an improvement over the hot-water bottle. I think it might work even better if we took your clothes off, too."

"Help me."

It was more than a request. His husky tone and the heat in his dark eyes transformed the words into one more assault on her senses.

Allie's fingers trembled as she reached for his shirt and slowly began to unfasten the buttons. Peeling it open, she pressed her palms flat against his chest, savoring the heat and strength and uniquely male alignment of muscle over bone. She lifted her head to kiss him there, inhaling the heady blend of soap and man that clung to his skin. She caressed his chest with her lips the way he had caressed her with his own. The wiry mat of dark hair there tickled sexily. She was intoxicated by his nearness, excited by the revealing quickness of his breathing.

"Ah, Allie," he murmured softly, his lips in her hair, his hands sliding between their warm bodies to cover her breasts.

Allie felt her nipples tighten in response, and suddenly desire changed from a sweet flicker of sensation in her belly to something hotter and more urgent. She wanted more of him . . . all of him.

Eagerly she slipped his shirt over his shoulders, grateful for his help as he shrugged it off. Impatience made her clumsy. She ran her hands over his shoulders, exploring his different textures, smooth and rough, hard and resilient. She gloried in his maleness, in the way he felt and smelled. In his gritty rasp when she briefly slid her fingers lower and inside the waist of his jeans.

Burn retaliated by rolling so that he lay on top of her once more, a subtle, exciting reminder of his physical dominance. Allie caught her breath, struck by the primitive beauty of the way his body molded perfectly with hers, an enticing foreshadow of the complete joining that lay ahead.

The sheer anticipation of feeling him inside her heated her senses beyond control. Reaching for the silver buckle on his belt, she worked it loose, her progress slowed only by the assault of Burn's mouth. He pressed her head back into the pillow, her shoulders to the mattress, his tongue deep inside her, searching, demanding, thrilling in a way Allie had never before been thrilled by the rougher edge of a man's possession. She'd thought she liked sex only when it was swathed in silk and romance. She was wrong.

She had seen Burn's tender side, but what was happening between them now was stark and raw and hungry, and it struck deep at her core, unleashing something in her that was wild and elemental and had never before been touched. Burn said nothing as she pushed him to his knees, straddling her waist, and worked the button on his jeans open and his zipper down. She didn't expect or want him to say anything. Their choppy breaths and avid caresses and the fiery lock of their gazes expressed better than words ever could exactly what they wanted and how badly.

Sliding her hands inside his briefs, she dragged them down along with his jeans, freeing the swollen proof of Burn's need. He was hot and hard, and Allie was sure she must look as awestruck as he had when he'd undressed her a minute ago. She touched him, running her fingers along his velvet length, stroking lightly as his breathing grew slow and heavy, and she felt him throbbing with desire.

His need fueled her own, overwhelming all restraint, and she rose to capture him intimately with her mouth, her fingers curled around him as she teased and caressed with her tongue and lips and the lightest pressure of her teeth, until Burn muttered a sharp oath and tugged her head away.

"Enough," he said as a fierce clap of thunder exploded overhead. "I hope you're ready, sweetheart, because you've got me feeling like I have to be inside you or die."

"I'm ready," she whispered even as Burn slid his hand along her thighs and between them, discovering that for himself.

"You're so warm," he whispered, "so wet." He brought his fingers to his mouth. "So sweet. Next time I'll taste you slow and proper, the way you deserve to be appreciated, but tonight…" He trailed off as he ripped her panties from her with a sexual recklessness Allie had never witnessed before now. "Tonight I need you hard and fast and right away."

Far from being alarmed by the power of his need, Allie was thrilled and excited by it. Never had she felt so wanted by a man, or so sure that he wanted her for all the right reasons. And never before had she ever wanted a man the way she wanted Burn at that instant…more than she wanted her next breath.

She shifted beneath him, opening to him and moaning softly as she felt the blunt tip of his arousal at the soft gate to her femininity. A quickening began deep within her as soon as he pushed inside, a sensation hotter and fiercer than anything she had ever felt. It grew stronger as Burn rocked against her, his possession becoming harder and deeper with each thrust.

Allie wrapped her legs around his lean hips and clung to his shoulders, feeling herself being pushed along by the feverish craving inside, feeling Burn with her all the way, reaching, straining, grinding. The fractured sounds of their hunger blended with the fury of the storm now raging full force outside the open window as the need they shared built and built until it overtook them and sent them hurtling together into a world of dark secret pleasures that belong only to lovers and hot, stormy summer nights.

It wasn't until they lay side by side on the narrow bed, sweaty and satisfied and dazed, their hearts still pounding, that they realized the rain was coming through the open window, soaking them and the sheets.

"What the—" Burn began, then quickly reached for the window and slammed it shut.

When he looked down at Allie, she was smiling. "I told you," she said. "Rain."

"I know, I know." He smiled back at her in spite of the wet sheets. "We needed it, right?"

Allie nodded and reached for him. "Desperately."

Chapter Eleven

The following day was a beauty, the sky a dazzling blue and everything beneath it scrubbed clean by the storm that had passed overnight.

Even Burn felt new, scrubbed clean of all the doubts and second thoughts that had been plaguing him for weeks now, doubts about himself and Allie and what he was doing there. He hadn't looked forward to this visit from Allie's friends, but he sure thanked God for it now. Yesterday had been an eye-opener for him, helping him to see Allie in a new way, and to see how she just might fit into the new life he was determined to make for himself.

Allie was convinced that she'd changed since coming to the Circle Rose. She'd told him so during one of the quiet moments they'd shared last night between all the not-so-quiet moments of lovemaking. Burn wasn't so sure about that. He had a hunch she hadn't changed so much out here as much as she'd found herself, the real Allie who had been lost back in Boston.

Fate. He'd never thought much about it, but he'd become a believer overnight. He credited fate with bringing him back to the Circle Rose the same day Allie arrived and with all the seeming mistakes and missteps that had somehow led up to last night. It had been the greatest night of his life and he'd gladly suffer through a dozen times as many weeks of frustration and doubt if it meant having Allie in his arms in the end.

Yep, he thought, whistling as he saddled the final horse for their ride, today was going to be a great day. They were all going to be great days from today on. Not even the sight of Buffy Winchester approaching the corral could dim his mood this morning. Buffy, Rory, the new seed that had probably been washed down Pebble Creek in last night's rainstorm—he could handle anything that came his way as long as he knew Allie was his.

Only one small thing interfered with his feeling of contentment, lying there at the back of his mind all the time, like a burr caught under a saddle—out of sight, but impossible to ignore. Actually, it wasn't such a small thing. It was monumental...the lies that still stood between him and Allie. He had to tell her the truth, about everything. That was more important than ever after last night.

He rationalized that he wasn't the world's biggest bastard for not coming clean before he made love to her by telling himself that his feelings for Allie were what counted most, and his feelings for her were as honest as he knew how to be. Nothing he had to tell her would change the way he felt even the slightest bit. He just prayed that it wouldn't change the way Allie felt about him.

She would be plenty angry when she found out he'd never even applied for the job of foreman here, much less been selected for the position. That much was certain. But he was counting on the fact that he'd done the job as well as anyone could have to stand in his favor. That and the little matter of the real foreman, whoever the hell he was, never even showing up. Imposter or not, Allie ought to be thankful he hung around. And she would be, Burn assured himself. As soon as she got over being mad as hell.

As for the rest of it, it could all be explained, and knowing Allie as he'd come to know her, her compassion and generosity, he was sure that she would understand why it was something that had been hard for him to talk about before now. As it was, it wasn't going to be easy to drag all those murky old memories into the light of day. That was bound to happen. Allie would have questions, and Rory, too, and answering them would mean remembering things he'd sworn to forget.

But easy or not, he was going to tell her everything. And soon, Burn thought, checking a strap here, adjusting a saddle blanket there. As soon as possible, in fact, which meant that today was definitely out. It just wasn't possible—not to mention sane—for him to attempt to explain any of this to Allie while she had a houseful of guests to worry about. The truth would just have to wait until tomorrow.

Burn made it through the ride and the barbecue afterward, spending most of his time avoiding Buffy and fantasizing about another night in the bunkhouse with Allie.

It was even better this time, without the rain and wet sheets. Hot steamy sex like none he'd ever had before, and Burn knew that had less to do with hormones or positions than the fact that this was Allie he was holding and touching and loving, and she was like no other woman in the world. She was his. Special. With all the pleasure and risk that implied.

It was an all-new feeling for Burn, and he found it both satisfying and terrifying. Always for him, the thought of possessing something was linked intricately and painfully with the thought of losing it without warning and forever. The way his mother had been lost to his father . . . to all of them. It was a feeling he'd chosen to live without until now, or thought he had. This thing with Allie had taught him what his father had tried to—that choice has nothing to do with it. He could no more choose to let Allie go now than he could choose not to be Rory's father. She was his. That's just the way it was.

He was still reluctant to explore his feelings too closely or put a name to them. It was like the model plane his mother had helped him build when he was a kid, the only physical reminder of her he'd had left after she died. It was so fragile he'd never played with it and was almost too afraid to even hold it. Then one day he came home from school to find it had fallen from the shelf above his bed and was broken beyond repair. Maybe someone had slammed a door too hard or bumped the wall from the other side. He'd never figured out how it happened. And, crazy as it was, he couldn't shake the feeling that if he tried too hard to dissect his feelings for Allie, they would shatter like that toy plane.

After a great deal of thought he decided the drive home from the airport Monday afternoon would be the perfect opportunity to talk to Allie. He waited until they were on the highway and away from the airport traffic. *Coward,* chided his conscience, even as he told himself he wasn't stalling, just being cautious.

"So," he said finally, "did I pass muster with your friends?"

His brilliant strategy was to back into the whole thing—more caution and not his usual style at all. He was accustomed to speaking his mind without much thought of whether or not anyone else liked what he had to say. Where Allie was concerned, however, he wasn't nearly that cavalier. Every man has his price, his father used to say, and his weakness. Burn had a feeling he'd found his.

Allie had been sitting with her head back on the headrest, eyes closed. At Burn's question she opened her eyes and shot him a wry look.

"Counting Buffy?" she asked.

"I asked if I passed muster with your friends," he replied. "Somehow I don't see Buffy as being a close friend of yours."

"Thank you. I'll take that as a compliment."

"Can't think of any other way it could be taken," he said dryly.

"True. Poor Chris, but then, he's been down this road with Buffy often enough to know better."

"He seems a decent-enough guy. What does she have that interests him?"

"Money."

Burn turned his head briefly to see if she was joking. She didn't seem to be.

"Pardon my lack of expertise in this area, but don't all your friends have money?"

"They all have some. Buffy has lots. And lots. Chris has considerably less family money and very expensive tastes. An awkward combination," she added, the dryness back in her tone.

"Come on, Allie. The guy's a lawyer. He must make decent money."

"Decent, sure, but decent doesn't even approach what it takes to support the life-style Chris prefers. Don't get me wrong," she continued quickly. "I don't think that money is the only reason Chris is interested in Buffy. They've had this strange sort of love-hate thing going for years. But love aside, if Buffy wasn't also a very lucrative marriage prospect, I think Chris would move on to someone who was. That's life."

"No, that's just plain weird. Seems to me there's about a million easier ways to make money than marrying for it . . . especially marrying Buffy Winchester."

Allie laughed and reached over to rub his shoulder. Burn felt her touch like a flash fire ripping through him, making him want to put off what had to be said until tomorrow and step on the gas to get them back to the ranch. They still had a few hours before Rory returned, a few hours to spend enjoying each other in a real bed with plenty of room for all the things he wanted to do to her.

Only a wellspring of self-control, probably developed from all those years of climbing on the backs of angry bulls when every fiber of his body was telling him to walk away, enabled him to drive slowly and keep his mind on the unpleasant task ahead.

"You don't know how happy it makes me to hear you say that," Allie told him, grinning at him as if he'd just delivered a statement of Pulitzer Prize-winning importance.

Lost in his own troublesome thoughts, Burn had to stop and try to remember what he said that could have made her beam at him with such approval. Whatever it was, maybe he ought to say it a few more times to build up a reservoir of goodwill before telling her how he'd been lying to her from day one.

"About marrying for money," Allie explained when she saw he was puzzled. "And how you can think of a million ways you'd rather earn it. I knew you'd feel that way, of course—I even told Liz—but it was still nice to hear you say it."

"You talked to Liz about me?" Burn asked. "I mean about me marrying for money? Who was the potential bride in this scenario, you or Liz?" He shot her a look. "Not Buffy. Don't even kid about that. It's too scary."

Allie laughed. "There was no potential bride. It was a very hypothetical discussion. You're not angry, are you?"

"No," he said, shrugging. "Just curious, I guess."

"Well, you asked about passing muster and that's actually how it came up in the first place," she explained.

"Is that supposed to make sense?"

"Not unless you know Liz and me and our methods of ... shall we say, cataloguing the male of the species."

"This I've got to hear."

"Not on your life. It's a girl thing. Suffice it to say that you did well. Very, very well. That's all you have to know."

"I'm not sure, Boss, but I think maybe this falls into the category of sexual harassment."

"Definitely not. Sexual harassment is more what I have in mind for when we get back to the ranch ... if we ever get back there," she added, leaning over to check the speed-ometer. "Why are you driving so slowly?"

"So we can have a chance to talk."

"Is this the same man who was so very uninterested in talking with me last night?"

"You're damn right I'm the same man," he said, grabbing her hand and holding on to it. "Nothing you or I say will change that or change what happened between us this weekend."

"Who wants to change anything?" she asked, her soft tone jarring him from his overreaction. He loosened his grip on her hand, bringing it to his lips to kiss it gently.

"Sorry." He forced a smile. "I guess I'm a little more tired and cranky than I thought."

"You have a right to be. This was probably the roughest weekend off you've ever suffered through."

"I'd hardly call it suffering." He dragged his fingers through his hair, searching for the right words. "Damn it, Allie, you don't know how I feel. I feel as if this weekend has changed my life."

"I think I know exactly how you feel."

He shook his head. "No... it's changed everything."

"You sound so serious."

"This is serious. And I think we should talk. Seriously."

"And here I thought you just wanted to hear all the flattering things my friends said about you."

Her dry humor was infectious and Burn was open to any and all stalling maneuvers. There was still a lot of road between there and the ranch, he told himself, plenty of time to say what had to be said.

"Roger and Chris said flattering things about me?" he countered, poker-faced.

Allie swatted his shoulder. "Very funny... although, come to think of it, Roger did say he wondered if you used a weight machine to develop your pecs. I told him I believed the closest you ever got was wielding a post-hole digger."

"Smart girl," he said, chuckling.

"Sherry just kept saying how much you reminded her of Clint Eastwood . . . or rather, Rowdy Yates—you know, his character on 'Rawhide'."

He laughed and nodded. "Yeah, I heard that line a time or two at the Double D."

"I'll just bet you did," Allie retorted, glowering.

Burn shot her a grin. "Don't worry, sweetheart, the only trail I'm interested in riding is yours."

She groaned. "And here I told Liz you had the body of a Greek god and the soul of a poet. I'll have to write her and take the poet part back."

"That's all right, I like the other part better anyway— even if that would have to be a slightly stiff and battle-scarred Greek god. You really told her that?"

"Of course not. What I really told her was that you were the man of my dreams, the real thing. And that I was in love with you."

The humor was gone from her voice, leaving it stark and riveting, and even without meeting her eyes, Burn knew that the words came straight from her heart and that she meant them with everything that was in her. He swallowed hard before he dared to glance her way. His muscles tensed from head to toe.

"Allie, please . . ."

"No, stop. You don't have to say you love me, Burn. Truthfully, I'd rather you didn't. I would always think I forced it out of you. You know, the old I-love-you, I-love-you-too routine. I just wanted you to know how I feel."

He nodded, eyes fixed on the road ahead, the words he needed to say to her before he had the right to even think about saying he loved her suddenly more out of reach than ever.

"So," he said, flailing desperately for safer ground so he could collect his thoughts, "did Liz tell you that you were crazy to think you were in love with a battered, broken-down cowboy with a bad attitude?"

Allie laughed. "No, as a matter of fact she said she understood exactly what I was talking about when I told her I'd finally found a man who wants me for me."

"What does that mean?" he asked, eyes narrowing. "Why else would I want you if not for... oh, wait a minute. You mean I want you for you as opposed to the way Chris wants Buffy?"

"Something like that. Let's just say that my romantic past has been filled with men who proved more interested in the Halston part of my name or the way I enhanced their image walking into a party than in the way I make chili."

"Speaking as one who's experienced your chili, that's probably a good thing for you—ouch!"

"You said my chili made you drool."

"Weep. I said your chili made me want to weep."

"Drool, weep—I was close."

Burn laughed.

"You see," Allie cried, "you even laugh at my jokes. Really laugh, with your head thrown back. Not all of my former loves had the grace to even chuckle politely."

"What a way to choose a lover."

"Go ahead and laugh," she said, sounding smug and contented. "You have no idea how it feels to be with a man who can laugh at all this, a man who doesn't care about my family or how I look in a Scaasi original or for that matter if I even own a Scaasi original."

"Hell, sweetheart, I don't even know what a Scaasi original is, but with you inside it, I guarantee you I'd like the way it looked."

"Oh, I love you," she cried, leaning over to hug him hard. "I love you so much, Burn."

Burn winced. Those were the words he wanted most and least to hear at that moment. He gently eased her back to her side of the car.

"There's just one thing that confuses me," he said. "If it was so important to you to find a man who wasn't interested only in your family's money or all the glamorou trappings that go along with it, why not hide the fact? Use your mother's maiden name, go around in burlap." He turned and ran his gaze over her appreciatively. "Make that baggy burlap... very baggy burlap. What I'm getting at is, why not—"

"Lie?" she interjected. "Why not pretend to be someone or something I'm not?" She shook her head. "That might solve the problem for a while, but it's just not my style. Besides, how could I expect someone to want me for me when from the start I was lying to him and hiding who I really was?"

She shook her head again, even more vehemently, and something inside Burn collapsed like a balloon pierced with a pin.

"I know how I'd feel if I met someone and developed feelings for him and then found out he was lying or hiding things from me," she declared. "That from the start he didn't trust me with the truth."

"How would you feel?" Burn asked, amazed he could force the words past the knot that had formed in his chest.

"Used," Allie replied, the finality in her tone clear even before she added, "and finished."

Chapter Twelve

Finished was not a difficult word to decipher. Especially not when it was combined with Allie's tone and the determined set of her fragile jaw as she uttered it.

She meant finished as in complete, done, over with, the end. It was clear that where men were concerned, honesty was her Achilles' heel, and Burn was dangerously close to treading on it. Dying inside, he continued to drive, doing his best not to succumb to frustration and rip the steering wheel from the drive shaft. With that one word she'd managed to freeze him in his tracks, stifle all his honorable intentions to tell her the truth about himself and the Circle Rose.

He needed more time, he decided. Time for Allie's feelings for him to become more firmly rooted. True, she had told him she loved him, and Burn believed her wholeheartedly. It was easy for him to accept that she had fallen in love with him in such a relatively short period of time and with little or none of the traditional courtship rituals being observed, because he had fallen in love with her the same way,

ompletely and forever. He just didn't have the right to tell
er that yet.

He believed that she loved him, and the part of him that
ad embraced the mysterious workings of fate believed that
ltimately their love would see them through whatever
ough spots lay ahead. That didn't mean he wasn't deter-
ined to do everything in his power to smooth out this par-
cular rough spot before they had to hit it.

At the moment, the only way he could think of to do that
as to give it time, to give them time. He wasn't exactly sure
ow much time, but he would know when the moment was
ght to tell Allie the truth.

The week following her friends' visit was a busy one for
ll of them. Burn had to repair some minor damage caused
y the storm in addition to his regular work, Allie was at-
mpting to wallpaper the bathroom and devise a book-
eeping system for the ranch, and Rory had a science project
ue the following Monday.

For his project Burn had talked him into building a small-
ale version of the solar pump he planned to install on the
nch next year. He even offered to help, hopeful it might
ring them closer together, envisioning nights spent con-
lting over blueprints and discussing ways to translate the
ll-size dimensions and materials into a working model that
uld be displayed in the three-by-five-foot space the offi-
al science-fair rules allowed each student.

Unfortunately, it hadn't turned out quite that way. Rory
ossessed neither a gift for mathematical conversions nor
e slightest interest in solar power. The nights of father-son
onding that Burn had hoped for turned into battles to get
ory to finish his chores and homework early enough to
ave extra time for the project. These would be followed by
series of minor skirmishes to get him to remove his head-
hones and say more than "Sure" to everything Burn pro-
osed.

Eventually Burn, too, began finding excuses not to work on the project, so that now, with less than a week until it was due, the model was still only half-completed.

"We're going to have to decide on something to use for the hose running from the pump to the simulated field," Burn reminded Rory on Wednesday night as they sat together in the bunkhouse, trying to cram several weeks' worth of work into a few nights. "Have you given any thought to it?"

"Sure."

Burn mentally counted to ten and kept his gaze fixed on the worktable covered with bits and pieces of sheet metal and plastic.

"Good," he said, when he felt back in control. "What did you come up with?"

"Nothing."

"Nothing?" He looked from the cable he was trying to work into place to his son, who was rapping his fingers on the table in a way that reminded Burn of Indian war drums. "I thought you said you gave it some thought."

"I did," Rory replied. "I thought about it a lot. I just didn't think of anything."

"How could you think about it without thinking of anything?"

Rory shrugged and Burn's temper climbed.

"That's not an answer."

"I don't know. Is that an answer?"

Their gazes clashed and locked.

"Yeah," Burn said, "that's an answer. It's just not the right one . . . and it's not complete. How many times do I have to tell you to use a respectful form of address when you're talking to an adult? You can either call me Dad or call me sir—it's up to you."

"Sure . . . sir."

Burn remained expressionless. In fact, he hardly ever flinched inside. He was getting used to these minor rejections that added up to one big frustrating hurdle he couldn't seem to get over no matter how hard he tried. When he wasn't worrying about the future of his relationship with Allie, he was worrying about the past relationship he owed his son.

"What I don't understand," he said to Rory, "is how you could think about a problem like this and not come up with a solution. You shouldn't have stopped thinking about it until you had an answer."

Rory laughed, and Burn lost it even before the boy followed his laughter with a muttered "Far out."

"What did you say?"

"Oh, sorry," Rory replied, a smirk lurking at his lips. "Far out, sir."

"Exactly what is that supposed to mean?"

"It means far out," Rory replied, his sharp tone suggesting he was as tired and frustrated with this whole venture as Burn was. "It means maybe that's how you would have done it, thinking about it until you had a solution, but not me. I have other things to think about—"

"Such as?" Burn broke in.

"Such as my music and my friends—not that I have many left, since you won't ever let me out of this prison to see them. And girls . . . although I suppose that's a crime, too. I suppose I'm not supposed to think about anything but work, the way you do."

"If you did think more about your own work, maybe you wouldn't be flunking math and coming close to flunking science."

"Well, I happen to think there are more important things in life than math and science and some stupid solar pump . . . and ranching," he said, getting to his feet, his whole body tense, poised for confrontation. Burn recognized the stance as a mirror image of his own. "I thought Keith was a jerk for living and breathing that stupid ranch, but you're even worse. At least old Keith owned the piece of dirt he was sweating over. You're just busting your butt here for something that's not yours and never will be."

"That's enough."

Both Burn and Rory spun to look behind them at the sound of Allie's angry voice. Burn hadn't heard the bunkhouse door open and wondered how much she'd heard. Enough, it was soon evident. He'd never seen her look so ferocious.

"Rory, how dare you talk to your father that way?" she demanded.

"He's not—"

"Shut up."

Rory looked shocked by Allie's outburst. Burn folded his arms across his chest and watched.

"I don't ever again want to hear you say that he isn't your father—not around here. He is your father and there's nothing either of you can do but come to terms with the fact...and each other. Your father's trying, although Lord knows you don't make it easy for him. Why don't you give him a break?"

"Why doesn't he give me a break?" Rory shot back, although Burn noted that the fire was gone from his eyes and his voice cracked midway through, making him sound awfully young and vulnerable. Burn felt his own tension drain away. "He's worse than Attila the Hun. All he ever thinks about is this stupid ranch, and it's not even—"

"Not even his?" Allie finished when he broke off uneasily. "I'd say there's a lesson to be learned there, if you're willing to learn it. A man who does the very best work he can even if he doesn't own his own conglomerate or earn a million dollars a year has something money can't buy. He has pride and a very rare kind of contentment. Your father sees a value in his accomplishments here that goes beyond whose name is on the deed."

Oh Lord, thought Burn, shifting uneasily in his chair. He had to wonder if Allie would still think him so honorable if she knew the truth.

Rory shrugged awkwardly. "Yeah, maybe...but he still won't let me out of his sight. He still treats me like a baby, wanting to see my homework all the time, calling school to check up on me. Why can't he just trust me?"

"Maybe because you refuse to give him any reason to think he can," Allie replied quietly. "And maybe because he's as new at being a father as you are at having one around. You're both learning the hard way."

Rory shrugged. "He's making it hard."

"Then give him a chance to ease up."

"How?" Rory asked, more plea than demand this time. "How am I supposed to do that?"

Burn took a deep breath as he watched Allie search for an answer to his son's question. Damn, he thought, she was as much a novice at this as he was, even more, but she'd come out swinging in his defense just the same. And she wasn't simply taking sides, because she'd thrown herself into planning the upcoming party for Rory the same way. At that moment, as fraught with tension as the situation was, he felt like a very lucky man.

"You can start by not fighting him every step of the way," she said at last. "Start right here, with this." She swept her arm toward the half-finished project. "He's doing all this for you, you know, because he wants you to be the best at everything you do. He wants you to take pride in your accomplishments. Don't you see, Rory, he wants you to be the best because he knows you can be?"

"Yeah, right, but I don't know anything about this solar stuff."

"A couple of weeks ago you didn't know anything about roses, either." She shot him a wry smile. "Neither did I, actually, but we learned. And you can learn this, too, if you listen... if you try... if you really want things to get better around here for all of us."

Rory stared at the toe of his sneaker as he dragged it back and forth across the floor in front of him.

"Of course," Allie continued, "maybe you're content to leave things as they are for the next three years or so, until you're eighteen and on your own. Maybe you don't want to

spend time with your friends or borrow the Jeep for a date
or—''

''No, I do,'' Rory interrupted, looking up in a hurry. ''I
do want all that...and I want things to be better.'' He darted
a quick look at Burn, then back at Allie. ''I really do.''

''Then what does that ad say.... 'Just do it'?''

Rory smiled and nodded. ''Yeah, just do it.'' He turned
to Burn, who still sat at the table. ''How about straws?''

Burn's brow furrowed. ''What?''

''Straws, you know, like the ones you drink through. How
about using straws for the hose? That's really what I thought
of, but I didn't say it before because I figured you'd think it
was, you know, stupid or something.''

''No, I don't think it's stupid at all,'' Burn told him,
turning the idea over in his mind. ''I think it's pretty inge-
nious, actually. We'll have to find a way to join them without leakage....''

''Duct tape?''

Burn nodded, excited not so much by the breakthrough
on the project as by Rory's willingness to contribute. ''Duct
tape just might do it. We'll give it a try tomorrow, okay? I
think we've both had enough for one night.''

''Sure...I mean okay,'' Rory replied. ''I guess I am sort
of beat. 'Night, Allie. Good night...'' He hesitated, staring at Burn, and for just a split second Burn thought,
hoped, wished... ''Sir.''

''Good night, son,'' Burn replied, swallowing his disappointment.

Allie said good-night and squeezed Rory's shoulder as he
passed her on his way to his room.

They heard his door shut.

''Don't worry,'' Allie said, ''he'll come around.''

''Hey, that was more progress than I've made in weeks.''
He smiled at her. ''Thanks. I think I owe you a big one.''

Allie raised her brows. ''A big one, hmm? I wasn't aware
you knew any other kind.''

"Now I owe you twice," he said, chuckling as he stood and took her in his arms. "Once for talking to Rory and once for the flattery."

"And where will flattery get me?" she drawled, winding her arms around his neck, the feel of her against him starting his heart pounding with anticipation the way it always did.

"A fast roll in my bunk if you're not careful," he replied, taking her mouth in a long, hard kiss that almost, but not quite, eradicated the uneasiness that was always at the edge of his mind these days. The lies he had put between them were like a permanent shadow, and he knew the only way to get rid of it was to turn on the lights.

"A fast roll in your bunk sounds good to me," Allie told him.

"Me, too. The problem is how it would sound to Rory... assuming he doesn't have his headphones on and the volume at max."

"No problem. How about a leisurely roll in my bed instead?"

"Deal," he said, reaching for her hands and bringing them to his mouth to kiss. It was then that he noticed for the first time that she was holding something. "What have you got there?" he asked.

She glanced down as if she'd forgotten she was holding anything. "The mail," she explained. "I forgot to pick it up earlier, so I walked down to get it now.... That's how I happened to overhear you and Rory, shall we say, exchanging solar theories."

"I suppose that's one way of putting it. Anything interesting in the mail?"

She shook her head. "Not really. A supermarket flyer and a few bills about covers it. One of the bills is from Cal Rosen. I was wondering when he'd get around to collecting for services rendered."

Burn froze, doing his best to let his arms fall to his sides nonchalantly instead of as if he'd just been zapped by the postal equivalent of fifty thousand volts. The moment he'd been waiting for just might be about to hit him broadside.

"Did you open it?" he asked.

"No." She yawned. "I open all bills on Friday. It's part of my new system."

"That's crazy."

"Do I tell you how to mend fences?"

"Point taken. I guess we'll have to wait until Friday to see what Rosen's services are worth."

"I already know. They're priceless," Allie retorted, stretching up to kiss his lips. "They brought me you, remember? See you in a while," she said, heading for the door.

"Yeah, see you in a while," Burn echoed, thinking that if he was smart—if he was honorable—he would plead exhaustion or a sudden headache or anything else that would get him out of doing the one thing he wanted to do more than anything else, the thing he spent his days fantasizing about and his nights reliving—making love to Allie. He had no more right to make love to her than he had to say the words *I love you,* not until he was able to be completely honest with her.

The really honorable thing to do, of course, would be to be honest...to just walk into the house and tell her the truth. Before Rosen's itemized bill did the dirty work for him, making it even dirtier and more bitter for Allie to have to hear. The time bomb inside him had suddenly kicked into overdrive in anticipation of her opening that bill on Friday.

Why couldn't her system call for her to open bills on Monday, he thought, or Tuesday or any day after Saturday, the day of Rory's party? He'd decided not to tell her before the party, not after she'd worked so hard on it. The truth was going to pull the rug out from under her in a big way. To do that now wouldn't be fair to Allie, who was really looking forward to surprising Rory, or to Rhonda, who was helping her with the preparations, or to Rory, for that matter.

No matter how many mistakes he'd made, the kid deserved to have his birthday acknowledged in style, and Allie was going all-out to see that it was. Her plans involved dozens of his friends, a disk jockey to provide music for dancing and junk food galore. It was guaranteed to be a fifteen-year-old's dream party, right down to the gift Allie had talked Burn into buying for him. He couldn't take a chance on ruining all that for Rory... or for Allie.

Especially not simply to relieve his own increasingly guilty conscience a few days sooner. He wished he'd told her the truth weeks ago, before he'd made love to her, before he'd fallen in love with her. Hell, he wished he'd never lied to her or hid anything from her in the first place. But he wouldn't make a second mistake by telling her now. Even if the guilt was killing him.

No, now he would have to wait until after the party. But that was it, Burn swore. Rosen's bill had thrown a major scare into him, but maybe it wouldn't be an itemized bill and he would have the time he needed. If fate would just stay in his corner until after Saturday night, he vowed, he would talk to Allie and put an end to all this the very first thing Sunday morning.

Allie couldn't recall ever being so nervous before a party as she was all day Saturday. She worried whether Rory's friends would show up. Nearly everyone who'd been invited had RSVP'd to Rhonda that they would be coming, but as the other woman warned her, kids that age were incredibly fickle. She worried whether the music, the decorations and the food would meet with Rory's approval or if something would cross that dreaded line into teenage nerddom. She worried that he would somehow guess what was happening beforehand and not be surprised, or else that he would be so surprised he'd be embarrassed and wish he'd never been thrown a party in the first place.

It wasn't easy being the mother of a teenager.

Allie stepped back from checking out the birthday cake she'd picked up from the bakery earlier and wondered where the heck that thought had come from. She was far from being Rory's mother.

True, she was wildly, ecstatically in love with his father, but Burn had yet to say that he loved her in return or to mention anything further in the future than the following day...unless it involved the ranch, of course. He seemed to have plans for the care and improvement of the Circle Rose laid out into the next century. Allie drew comfort and hope from that. If he planned to be here, so did she. She had a good feeling about their future, good enough that she was willing to take it and enjoy it one day at a time.

Her instincts told her that was the best approach for Burn as well. It was clear that deep emotional attachment was new to him, and Allie could tell he was still coming to terms with his feelings for her much the way he was still adjusting to being a father. She had no intention of rushing him or pressuring him in any way.

From time to time this past week, ever since they had become lovers, he had seemed especially moody and preoccupied. She could understand that. Burn had led a pretty freewheeling life for a lot of years. No doubt the idea of being tied down to family responsibilities, to one place and one woman, was a little overwhelming. One day at a time, she reminded herself. It seemed to be working for Burn and Rory, and it was good enough for her.

If the day ever arrived when she in fact became Rory's stepmother, she would be proud to have him in her family. But Rory had a mother and his first loyalty would always be to Rhonda. Allie adored him all the more because of it. Working so closely with Rhonda on the party preparations had only confirmed Allie's impression of her as a wonderful mother and a good person. She and Keith would be coming over later, and Allie was looking forward to meeting him. Rhonda was such a talker that in some ways she felt as if she already knew the man. She admired his hard work and determination in the face of all the bad luck they were having hanging on to their own ranch.

At the sound of footsteps on the porch, Allie hurriedly moved to peek through the kitchen window, relieved to see that it was Burn and not Rory approaching. She didn't know how in the world she would have hidden a cake this size in a hurry if it had been Rory. Burn had promised to keep him busy away from the house for most of the day, but she still wasn't taking any chances. Later Burn would ask Rory to get cleaned up and help him with an errand in town, bringing him back after the guests had arrived.

"Hi," she said as Burn stepped through the back door. "I'm glad you're here. I have to ask you something very important."

"What?"

Allie glanced at him quickly. "Nothing so earth-shattering that you have to snap at me that way."

"I'm sorry." He rubbed his temple, still frowning.

"Headache?" Allie inquired sympathetically, moving closer. She could feel the tension in him as she wrapped her arms around his neck, and she wished she could magically make it all go away, could tell him that he didn't have to worry so much about Rory or the ranch or her... that everything was going to be all right. Instead, she kneaded the muscles at the back of his neck.

"What did you want to ask me?" he said.

"Oh... about the candles for the cake. I bought some of those trick ones that you can't blow out. Do you think Rory will get a kick out of them or is he too old for that kind of thing?"

"Hell, Allie, is that your idea of important?"

"Well, yes. It just so happens that today it is. Is that a problem? I mean, it's not as if I called you all the way in here to ask you about the candles. You were here, so I asked. Is that such a big deal?"

He shook his head, smiling and drawing her back against him. "No, it's not a big deal or a problem. I'm the problem.... Just bear with me, all right?"

"You've got it. Forever."

"Ah, Allie," he murmured, resting his head against hers as he rubbed her back. "It won't be that long, I promise. Just...bear with me." He held her like that for a moment that Allie wished could last forever, then straightened, releasing her.

"Now about the candles," he said. "Use the trick ones. Rory might think he's too old, but he's not."

"That's what I thought, too. The trick ones it is." She crossed candles off her list on the counter. "Let's see, what's next?" she said mostly to herself. "Ah, yes, two gallons of sangria coming up."

"Sangria? For kids?"

"Mock sangria," she clarified. "To go with the make-your-own-taco bar. Rhonda gave me the recipe for it. Did I tell you that I think she's really nice?"

"Once or twice. Did I tell you that I think you're really sexy?" he asked, lifting her hair to kiss the back of her neck. "Really, really, really sexy?"

"No," Allie replied, shivering as his light touch sent tingles through her. "But I'd much rather have you show me, anyway. Later."

"You've got it," Burn promised, then was gone.

The party was to be from seven until eleven, and by the time guests began arriving, Allie was worn-out. She had barely had the energy to drag herself into the shower after Burn and Rory left around six, and she might have tried to sneak a nap afterward if she wasn't afraid she'd never wake up in time. Instead she dressed in clean white jeans and a black knit top that showed off the new silver-and-turquoise jewelry she'd bought last weekend.

She became reenergized when Rhonda and the first guests arrived, everyone pitching in to set up the tables and carry the food outside. It was too beautiful a night to have so many kids cooped up inside. One on one, Rory's friends all seemed polite and friendly. If they got a little loud when they were all together, Allie was young enough to remember that her crowd had been a little loud at fifteen, too. She reminded herself to tell Burn he could also stop worrying so much about the company Rory kept.

By the time Burn's Jeep pulled into the drive around seven-thirty, anticipation had crowded out any trace of weariness she'd felt. Since most of Rory's friends were too young to drive and had been dropped off, there were few cars to hide. When Allie flipped on the outdoor spotlights and the deejay she'd hired let loose with "Birthday" by the Beatles, there was no question that Rory was surprised. *Shocked* might be a better word for the expression on his face.

And happy. Any doubt Allie might have had about the party fled instantly as he broke into the biggest smile she'd ever seen on anyone, a smile of utter amazement that all this hoopla could possibly be just for him. She bit her lip as she watched him become swallowed up by his friends, and from her position on the front porch she caught Burn's gaze. He grinned and gave her a thumbs-up sign, and Allie didn't have to wait until eleven o'clock to know the party was a complete success.

Eventually Rory dragged himself away from his friends long enough to find the four adults sitting on the porch steps.

"I can't believe it," he said. "This is the greatest party ever."

"You can thank Allie and your mother for it," Burn told him. "They did everything."

"Well, not quite everything," Allie corrected. "I seem to recall needing a hand with those two-hundred-pound speakers."

"And Keith shredded all the cheese for the tacos," added Rhonda.

"Thanks, Allie," Rory said. "And thanks, Mom. Thanks..." His grin flickered as he ran his excited gaze over the four of them. "Thanks, everyone."

If Burn was hurt at being lumped under the heading of "everyone" along with Keith, he didn't let it show.

"I'm just relieved it all meets with your approval," Allie told him.

"Are you kidding? It's great—perfect."

"Good. I didn't want to do anything...dorky. Is that the right word?"

"It'll do," Rory replied, grinning. "And don't worry, you didn't."

"Then go have fun. In fact, why don't you open your presents now so you can have fun with your friends and we can go inside where it's quiet?"

"All right," Rory cried enthusiastically.

His friends gathered around as, one by one, he opened a pile of CDs, which Allie was sure were exactly what he wanted. He also received several rock posters and T-shirts with obnoxious slogans on the front. There was a new denim jacket from his mom and Keith and state-of-the-art headphones for his stereo from Allie. Finally Rhonda handed him the final gift, a two-inch-square box from Burn, who had made an exit as Rory neared the bottom of the pile of gifts.

"It's a key," Rory said, looking bewildered as he held it up and searched the crowd for Burn. "To the house?" he asked.

"Not quite," said Burn, coming around the corner, pushing something.

There were a few hoots of approval from the guys in the crowd as they cleared a path for him to reach Rory.

"Try using it on this," he suggested.

"A dirt bike!" Rory cried, leaping to his feet in excitement.

"You got it," Burn confirmed. "Happy birthday, Rory."

Rory stared at the chrome-and-black bike as if mesmerized, reaching out to stroke the gleaming handlebars as if uncertain whether it was real or just a dream. Reassured it was really there and really his, he looked up at Burn, and Allie saw him swallow hard, the very same way his father did when he was fighting back emotions that frightened him.

Let it go, Rory, she urged silently, *just let go.*

As she watched, the boy broke into a slow smile and looked straight into Burn's eyes as he said, "Thanks... thanks, Dad."

From the corner of her eye Allie saw Rhonda clutch Keith's hand, and she felt her own throat tighten as Burn reached out with one arm and hugged his son for just a second, then urged him onto the dirt bike for a trial run. His face looked young and relaxed as he watched Rory careening around the yard, as if the burden he'd been lugging around had disappeared. Allie hoped so, hoped that this magic would last, for all of their sakes. There was, she thought, as she sprinted for the door to answer the telephone, nothing more thrilling in the whole world than watching the man you loved smile with utter happiness.

"Hello," she said as she lifted the receiver on what must be the tenth ring.

"Allie... you are there."

The music had started again and she had to turn away from the door and strain to hear the man's voice. "Yes, this is Allie."

"This is Cal Rosen."

"Oh, hello, Cal." What timing, she thought.

"Sorry I didn't get back to you yesterday. I was in court all day."

"No problem. I told your secretary it was no big deal... that you didn't even need to call back. I just wanted to let you know that the bill you sent didn't include charges for the hiring you did for me."

"That's just it, Allie. I felt terrible when she gave me the message. You see, I know we talked about my handling the hiring of someone to run the ranch for you, but either I didn't think the matter was settled or I just completely forgot, but I never even placed the ads.''

"I'm sorry, Cal, could you repeat that last part? There's a lot of noise here tonight."

"I can tell. Sounds like a party."

"As a matter of fact, it is."

"Good. You must be settled in and doing all right then. It makes me feel slightly less guilty about my oversight. What I said was that I didn't bill you for hiring someone because I never did it...never even started the process. Why the heck didn't you call and remind me before now?"

"Because..." Allie was struggling to string her thoughts together, never mind answer his question. "Because I—I... But Cal, if you never even placed the ad, then how—who—"

"I'm sorry, Allie, now I can hardly hear *you*. What did you say?"

"Nothing," she said, staring through the window at the party going on outside and feeling as if the fifty-ton weight Burn seemed to have shaken loose had just landed in the pit of her stomach. "It's not important. I'll mail you a check right away... and thanks, Cal."

She replaced the receiver in slow motion; at least it felt that way. Everything seemed to have slowed and dulled to a blur around her, everything but her thoughts, which were jumping and sizzling like live electrical wires held together.

She still wanted answers to the questions she'd started to ask Cal. She'd just realized he wasn't the right man to provide those answers. That man—the man she loved, the man she had trusted with her ranch, her life, her heart—was outside, grinning and having a ball.

All Allie's instincts were to go charging out there, stop the music and demand the answers that she wanted and had a right to. It wasn't love or even fear of what she might find out that held her back. It was concern for Rory. At one time she might have thoughtlessly put her own needs before anyone else's, but she couldn't do that to him. This was his night, and nothing and no one was going to spoil it. Her business with his father would have to wait.

And so she waited. She smiled and she waited and she laughed and she waited and she waited and waited and waited through the longest hours of her life.

Finally the party was over, the last guest gone. Rhonda and Keith left after helping to clean up, and even Rory had said a final, yawning thank-you and gone off to bed, his new dirt bike parked right outside the window of his room where he could see it first thing in the morning, a reminder that this night hadn't been a dream.

If only it had been, Allie thought as she went inside the house and closed the door behind her. It was only a matter of minutes before Burn followed, as she knew he would. He found her sitting alone in the dark living room. He switched on the light and met her eyes, his face no longer looking either young or relaxed.

"You know" was all he said.

Chapter Thirteen

"If you're referring to the little matter of your not being who you say you are and being here on my property under false pretenses...which, by the way, I'm sure there's a legal name for. Trespassing at the very least, perhaps fraud, perhaps something worse. If that's what you're referring to, then yes, Mr. Monroe or whoever the hell you are, I know."

Allie was amazed that she succeeded in keeping her voice quiet and controlled until near the end of her little speech.

Burn answered in kind. "I can explain."

"Then you damn well better start," she said, "before I call the police."

He looked stunned. "The police? Come on, Allie, I know I have some explaining to do, but do you really think I—"

"At this instant," she cut in, "I'm not ruling out anything. Now, if you intend to explain, get started."

Burn heaved a sigh, tossing his hat aside and dragging his fingers through his hair. His expression reminded Allie so much of Rory at his most lost and vulnerable that her heart twisted in her chest. Closing her mind to the image, she sat with her arms stiffly folded and waited.

"For starters," Burn said, "my name really is Burn Monroe. I told you the truth about that. For that matter, I've told you the truth about mostly everything. I did work the rodeo circuit, and the Double D, Rory is my son and I did just find that out for the first time a few months ago. But I lied to you when I said I'd been hired and sent here by Rosen...and I've regretted it just about every minute since. Standing here right now, I regret it more than anything I've done in my whole life and... I'm sorry. I don't know what else to say."

His eyes reflected his sorrow, and beneath Allie's anger ran a thread of longing to go to him and offer comfort. Feeling the way she did, it wasn't hard to resist acting on it.

"Then you'd better think of something fast," she said, "because 'I'm sorry' just doesn't cover it. Why don't you try telling me why you lied to begin with? Because I just don't understand why..." She trailed off with a bewildered shrug, her voice turning hollow. "I don't understand any of it. Why, Burn?"

"Good question," he replied, his short laugh bitter, his expression full of self-recrimination. "Impulse, stupidity, an old habit of taking foolish risks just because they're put in front of me. Probably all of the above and more."

"But did you plan it? How did you even know I'd made arrangements with Cal to do the hiring or that I was expecting someone?"

"You told me."

"Me?" she scoffed. "Try again, Cowboy. I never even set eyes on you before you came poking around down at the pond that day."

"That's when you told me. I'd already figured out that you were here alone and didn't know what the hell you were doing...."

"I beg your—"

"You wanted the truth, I'm giving it to you. I swore to myself that once this was all out in the open I'd never lie to you again about anything, and I won't. It might not seem like my word is worth much right now, but it is, and I intend to spend the rest of my life proving that to you, Allie...if you'll give me the chance."

"I'm still a long way from thinking about second chances," she retorted. "So go on...you figured out I was a woman here alone and you saw a perfect chance to take advantage of me, is that it?"

He grimaced. "Why don't you tell me? I lived here alone with you for weeks...slept right here in this house, just a few feet away. Hell, we slept a lot closer than that the night we spent outside. Believe me, if I'd wanted to take advantage of you, I had plenty of opportunity. That was never part of it."

"Then what was part of it? Why did you want to work here so badly you lied to get the job?"

"I can't explain it...not to you, not even to myself. I was just passing through, on my way back to the Double D from spending the afternoon with Rory. I was sick to death of the work I did there, sick of the people. I hated the whole idea of going back, and maybe that set me up for it. That and Rory, wondering what he thought of finally having a dad and having that dad turn out to be me—a man who'd gone from a rodeo has-been to marking time on a dude ranch."

He crossed the room, shoving his fingers into the back pockets of his jeans as he stood staring at the night-blackened window, which reflected the anguish on his face back to Allie.

"I'd been doing a lot of thinking and wishing that I was different, that I'd chosen to lead a different sort of life and had more to offer him—a home, maybe even some sort of family. I don't know...." He broke off and spun back to face her.

"But if any of that mattered, it wasn't consciously. I won't try and tell you that I was thinking of Rory first that day, or that my motives were at all lofty or righteous. They weren't. The bald truth is that I saw you there in the water. . . through the water," he added, his eyes darkening, "and I wanted you. . . the same way I want you now."

"Oh, please," exclaimed Allie, getting to her feet. "Are you trying to sell this as a case of love at first sight? If so, forget it. I was there, remember? And—"

Burn was shaking his head, moving closer.

"No, it wasn't love at first sight. . . and I wouldn't have known it if it was. I didn't know much about love back then."

"And now you do?" she said, fighting the instinct to back away.

"I'm learning. What happened at the pond that day wasn't love at first sight, it was lust. . . and you damn well know it, because you felt it the same as I did."

"I did not."

"Who's lying now, Allie?" he taunted softly, reaching for her. "I can prove it to you. . . prove to you that there's been something there from the start between us. . . since the moment you walked naked out of that pond. Before that, even. It's there and it's real and it's powerful enough to make a man lose his head, make him tell a stupid lie, make him do a lot of things."

He ran his hands over her as he spoke, his touch familiar and soothing to Allie's jangled nerves. She drew a deep breath, resisting the sensual pressure of his caress and her own body's instinctive response.

"I'm hoping it's enough to make a woman willing to forgive," he continued, his touch and tone both coaxing now. "And forget. Allie, I can make it up to you if—"

"No." Allie shrugged off his hands and sidestepped away from him. "I don't want to forget. That's how you end up making the same mistakes twice and I have no intention of doing that. I also have no intention of forgiving anything until I understand exactly what it is I'm forgiving you for. So far all I know is that you were riding by that day and saw me there, and on some sort of crazy impulse you claim you don't even understand, decided to pass yourself off as the new foreman of the Circle Rose.''

''That about covers it.''

''What did you plan to do when the real foreman showed up?'' she demanded.

Burn's mouth slanted into a wry smile. ''Cross that bridge when I came to it. I like to think I'd have told you the truth and hoped my record by then was enough to convince you that I was the best man for the job.''

''But why didn't you just do that anyway and avoid all this?''

''Lady, you don't know how I wish I had.''

''That's not an answer.''

He exhaled wearily. ''You sound like me talking to Rory.''

''Except Rory eventually comes up with an answer.''

''Okay, if you want an explanation, I'll do my best. I thought about telling you a million times, I can tell you that much. I even planned out the words I would say, but in the end I was always...afraid.'' He glanced down, suggesting the admission had cost him heavily.

''I was afraid you would send me packing, and with each day I spent here with you, I hated the thought of leaving more and more. Then Rory ended up staying here and somehow I saw this as some kind of last chance for him...for us. I mean, it wasn't a real home or anything, but it was the best I had to offer him, and I didn't want to blow it. Now maybe I ended up blowing it anyway.''

Allie avoided his gaze as she wrapped her arms around herself, hurt by him and hurting for him in about equal parts. Maybe that was what love did to you, she thought—made you feel someone else's pain over and through your own.

''Okay, maybe at first it was a crazy impulse, just as you said,'' she ventured after thinking it over, ''and I can even understand why you would put Rory's welfare ahead of the woman you worked for. But what about after that all changed for us...after last weekend? Burn, I just don't understand how you could make love to me the way you did, knowing our relationship was built on a lie from the start."

"I didn't plan to make love to you that night. It just... happened. I wanted it to happen, of course. I'd been fighting it for weeks, because I knew it was wrong with this lie between us, but that night..." He stopped, his jaw hardening. "I just wanted it too much to keep fighting."

Allie, recalling the growing frustration she, too, had felt over the past few weeks and his attempt to resist even that night as they stood together on the back porch, was willing to accept the truth of what he said.

"Afterward," he went on, "I fully intended to tell you everything. But I didn't want to do it while your friends were here, and then driving home from the airport that day we somehow got to talking about men who lie to women and use them for what they can get from them, and I got cold feet all over again. I—"

"But—"

"No. This is hard for me, Allie. I'm into it now. Please let me keep going to the end."

She nodded.

"I never felt so good and so rotten and slimy all at the same time as when you told me you loved me. I felt good just thinking a woman as beautiful and special as you could ever fall in love with me, and rotten because a big part of how we came together in the first place was a lie and I knew it and you didn't."

He drew a deep breath, his chest shuddering with its release. "I wanted more than anything to tell you I loved you, too...."

"Oh, Burn..."

He shook his head, halting her move to touch him. "I wanted to tell you because it's true—I love you, Allie, more than I ever thought I could love anyone. But I told myself I had no right to say it until I came clean with you. I finally decided I would tell you as soon as Rory's party was over, so I wouldn't spoil it for him or you after all the work you put into it. When I heard that Rosen had sent you a bill, I knew that this time I couldn't put it off no matter how scared I was of what might happen. You might not believe it, but I planned to tell you first thing in the morning.

"For a while," he concluded grimly, "it even seemed that that bill hadn't blown my cover after all, that I was going to make it."

"Actually, the bill didn't," Allie said. "I did. I phoned to find out why there was no charge for hiring you. Cal called back tonight to say he hadn't charged because he hadn't done it. He'd completely forgotten we had agreed on it."

Burn laughed mirthlessly and shook his head. "Fate."

"Looks that way." Allie felt a small smile claim her lips. "Burn Monroe, you are the most confusing, challenging and utterly infuriating man I have ever had the good fortune of falling madly, head over heels in love with." She tipped her head and studied his unexpectedly glum response. "In case you need a prompt, that sort of means I forgive you. You shouldn't have lied, but I have to admit it was the sort of reckless thing I might be tempted to try myself under the right conditions. And," she concluded, "I sure can't complain about the end result."

Burn wasn't smiling.

"There's more," he said, sounding as if the words had been dragged from deep in his gut.

Allie's smile faded. "More?"

Burn closed his eyes briefly, nodding. Never had he been so tempted to take the easy way out of a tough situation. Maybe, if he just kept his mouth shut and accepted Allie's forgiveness for having lied to her about being the legitimate foreman, he would never have to tell her the rest and she would never find out. While this part wasn't a lie, exactly, he had come to know Allie well enough to know that its repercussions would be far more devastating to her than the fact that he had twisted the truth to get a job here because he had the hots for her.

"What is it?" she asked, her posture as rigid as her tone.

"You remember that I told you I'd grown up on a ranch?"

Her expression relaxed. "And you didn't? You mean you also lied about your experience? Believe me, that's no big deal . . . I can't imagine anyone doing a better job around here."

"No, I didn't lie about my experience . . . and you're right, I'd say there's probably not another man alive who could have walked onto this land and known just how to work it the way I did. You see, I did grow up on a ranch—this ranch, to be exact. I was raised right here on the Circle Rose."

Allie frowned, laughed softly and frowned again, as if struggling to absorb what he had just told her and fit it into some sort of context.

"You grew up here . . ." she gestured with her arm ". . . on the Circle Rose?"

Burn nodded. "That's right. The room I slept in when I first got here was my old room. That rocking chair on the back porch was re-covered by my mother after the dog chewed through the old seat. The rose garden you rescued was hers, too," he said softly.

"This was the only home I ever had," he told her, "until my mother died and my father lost it, piece by piece. I hated watching that happen to him, to all of us, and not being able to do anything to stop it. I learned a lot about hate in those days, and by the time we had to leave here, I hated the Circle Rose along with the rest of the world." He gave a bitter laugh. "Probably more. I guess I came to blame the land somehow, and I swore I'd never set foot on it again, much less break my back trying to make it what it once was."

Allie turned away, and Burn knew that her silence meant she was still struggling to come to grips with his revelation, make some sort of sense out of it. Maybe she would just chalk up his coming here as a case of nostalgia and dismiss it as interesting, but unimportant. Maybe, but Burn didn't think so, and dread was like something scratching at his insides.

"But you did come back," she said at last. "After all those years, you finally did come back. I wonder why." She whirled around and met his gaze, hers a clear cool green that instantly turned the dread gnawing at Burn into something else, something worse. "And I also wonder what else you've lied to me about."

"I didn't lie to you about this," he countered. "I never said I didn't grow up on the Circle Rose."

"Oh, please," she cried, "don't insult me with a game of semantics. Call it a lie of omission if it eases your conscience, but it's the same in the end. You kept the truth from me."

"You're right," he conceded grimly. "I did."

"I suppose that was just one more wild and crazy impulse?"

Burn winced at her tone, which had moved past anger to icy wrath. "No, it wasn't an impulse so much as something I didn't talk about . . . something I couldn't talk about."

"Oh, really? And why is that?"

"Because it hurt too damn much, that's why. It still does."

Silence. Then she tossed back her hair and faced him. "Look, maybe you think I should feel sorry for you, and I am sorry that your mother died when you were so young and that your family lost their home, but—"

"No." Burn cut her off harshly, incensed by her suggestion. "I don't want you or anyone else to feel sorry for me. Ever. I got a few rough breaks back then, sure, but life is full of rough breaks—ask Rory. I came to terms with the hand I was dealt a long time ago . . . at least I thought I had."

He paced across the room, struggling for control, and when he spoke, his voice had lost its edge. "I thought I had outgrown all those old feelings of rage and wanting back something that was gone forever. Then I came here and a lot of old ghosts surfaced all at once. Bad feelings and good ones came flooding back, and I didn't know what to do with any of them.''

"You might have tried a little honesty."

He shrugged. "I'm not used to talking about my feelings, not to anyone, and for damn sure not to a woman who thinks I was hired out of the blue to run her ranch for her. I was afraid that if you knew of my ties to this place, it would only raise new questions about why I wanted the job and whether Rosen knew about my situation, and raising more questions was the last thing I wanted to do.''

"I can see why. After all, you were counting on one lie to cover the other."

"No. That's not it at all. It was never anything that... calculated."

"Well, it sure couldn't have been as spur-of-the-moment innocent as you led me to believe a few minutes ago," she charged. "After all, the Circle Rose isn't exactly in the center of town. No one ends up here accidentally. There was a reason you were on this property that afternoon. What was it?"

"Nothing momentous, I swear," Burn replied. "I was driving near here on my way back and I just decided to come take a look at the place."

"For old times' sake?" she prodded, her skepticism lethal.

Burn told himself he deserved everything she threw at him, and more. He just didn't deserve to lose her. He couldn't, not after discovering all that his life could be like with Allie in it.

"Probably not so much for old times' sake as for Rory's. I think that getting to know him started me thinking about being his age, about how I might have lost a home, but how at least when I was growing up I had one. All Rory ever had was a series of crummy apartments and then a move to a ranch owned by the man his mother married.''

"Rhonda and Keith have tried hard to—''

"I know that," he said with an impatient gesture. "I'm talking about the way things looked to Rory. I'd heard the Circle Rose was on the market again and I guess I just wanted to take a look and see how it felt to be back here."

"And how did it feel?"

"Strange. Like I told you, good and bad."

"So you admit that you came with the idea that it was for sale and you might be interested?"

"No," he told her vehemently. And honestly. "I came without any ideas at all. I came without a clue. Then I saw you and . . ." He shrugged, a sad half smile forming at the memory. "You know the rest."

Allie wrapped her arms around herself as if she was cold. "Then why do I suddenly feel like I don't know anything at all about you?"

"Don't say that," he ordered, stepping toward her and stopping when she quickly moved out of reach. "I'm the same man I was yesterday. The same man I was last weekend."

"I'm sure you are. I just don't think I ever knew that man."

"Please, Allie, I know you have a right to be angry, and I am sorry for hurting you. That was never my intention, you have to believe me."

Her expression remained stony.

"But please don't make more of this than it is," he pleaded softly. "None of it has anything to do with the way I feel about you, or with the fact that I love you and I want to spend the rest of my life with you."

"Are you serious?" she retorted, her eyes glazed with disbelief. "Because this has everything to do with the way I feel about you."

Burn went cold with fear. "Are you saying you could stop loving me just like that?"

"No."

His heart lifted, then froze again as she continued.

"It takes time to stop loving someone . . . I know because I've had some practice in that area. But trust is another matter."

"What are you saying? That you can never trust me again?"

"I'm saying that I think you came here that first day because you were looking for a way to make up to Rory for all the years you weren't there for him. You heard the ranch was for sale, and when you found I had already bought it, you did whatever you had to do to hang around. Not because you wanted me, but because you wanted the Circle Rose."

"That's not how it was."

"That's how it looks. Maybe you thought I'd get tired of roughing it and you'd be right here on the spot to get a good deal when I decided to sell. You certainly made no secret of the fact that you never thought I'd last here."

"I didn't think you would . . . at first. But you proved me wrong and no one could be prouder of you for that than I am. Or happier about it."

She shrugged off his praise. "Once it became obvious I wasn't going to bail out anytime soon, you had to find another, faster way to make the ranch your own . . . to provide a stable home for Rory. His coming here must have put even more pressure on you. It must have really irked you that you and your son were relegated to the bunkhouse while some stranger lived in your family home."

"I was the one who insisted we stay in the bunkhouse," he reminded her.

Allie arched her brows. "And you say it wasn't calculated."

Burn had gone from cold inside to very very warm. "I don't think I like the sound of this . . . or where it's leading."

"That makes two of us, Cowboy."

"Are you trying to say that I came on to you as part of some sort of scheme to get my hands on the ranch?"

"Gold-star time again," she drawled.

"That's garbage," Burn snapped, grabbing her by the arms before she could sidestep him again. "I told you that day in the car what I thought of men who marry for money. I would never do that."

"I don't believe you ever would—marry for money, that is. Money just isn't important enough to you. But the Circle Rose is." Burn was so stunned she was able to pull free of him easily. "I guess I had something you wanted, after all, just not what I expected."

She turned toward the door.

"Allie, wait . . ."

She shook off his arm, only half turning back to face him. "No, I've had enough for one night."

"All right. Tomorrow we can—"

"Tomorrow I'll be gone."

"No, I—"

"You were right all along . . . I don't belong here. And your gamble paid off, because now I'm the one who doesn't want to set foot on this place again. It's yours, Burn . . . yours and Rory's. The paperwork is all in the file cabinet. I'm sure you can find a lawyer to handle the details—I can even recommend one," she added harshly.

"I don't need a lawyer. And I don't want this place. Not if—"

"Well, you sure wanted it badly enough a few weeks ago," she cried. "Badly enough to lie for it. Badly enough to . . ." She stopped and closed her eyes tightly. The sight of tears glimmering on her lashes when she opened them again ripped Burn in two.

"You can't just walk away," he said. "Not after all you've put into this place, not after all that's happened."

"Watch me. The terms of my loan call for a balloon payment in a few weeks and I have no intention of making it now. As for what I've already put in, let's just call it payment in full for being taught a lesson I thought I'd already learned."

"Allie, please don't—"

She continued to speak over his attempt to reason with her. "You can make that final payment and I'll sign whatever I have to, saying the ranch is yours free and clear. Or else just sit back and let the bank foreclose and snap it up at a bargain price. Either way, you win."

She was gone before Burn could stop her, leaving him feeling like anything but a winner.

Chapter Fourteen

Burn didn't sleep all night. He could barely lie still, much less sleep. The scene with Allie played over and over in his thoughts until his head ached from the accumulated pressure of all the things he could and should have said. He was just no good with words. Still, it was physical torture to keep from charging back into the house and into her bedroom and waking her so that he could try to say all the right things to her now.

That's if she was even able to sleep, which Burn doubted. She might not be plagued with regrets as he was, but anger alone was probably keeping her awake tonight. He'd seen Allie grumpy and had witnessed quick flashes of temper, but he'd never seen her so coldly angry. But then, she'd probably never before had so much reason to be.

No, he thought, that wasn't entirely true. She'd had this very same reason dealt to her in the past. In her own self-deprecating way she had gradually told him about the other men she had thought herself in love with. Men, it turned out, who were interested in her for their own selfish reasons. And knowing all that, he had still gone ahead and let matters drift to the point where it probably looked to Allie as if he was guilty of the same thing—wanting her for what she had to offer him instead of just plain wanting her because she had become as much a part of him as the steel pins holding him together.

Through the years the doctors had done a terrific job of patching him back up after each fall, but for so long it had felt to him that even though his body endured, he had lost pieces of his soul along the way. Finding out about Rory had given him the courage to start searching for some of those missing pieces, but he hadn't had any luck at it until he met Allie and fell in love with her. She had showed him how to look in places inside himself that he'd long ago forgotten existed. Crazy as it sounded, it was as if Allie was holding his heart together the same way those steel pins were holding his body.

He needed her, and over and over throughout the night his thoughts brought him back to the same place: he couldn't let her go and he had no idea how to make her stay.

Sometime around sunrise he fell asleep, still wrestling with the problem of how to keep Allie around long enough for her to cool off and give him another chance to explain. Eventually even he would have to hit on the right words to make her understand what was in his heart. He woke to the sounds of Rory tearing around outside the bunkhouse on his dirt bike.

He immediately gripped his head to stop it from throbbing, the way he recalled doing a time or two in the past, usually after a particularly rowdy night of celebrating. It wasn't possible to have a hangover from drinking mock sangria, he told himself, but that's sure how it felt.

He opened one eye, startled to see it was full daylight outside his window, and quickly swung out of bed. Come to think of it, *hangover* was a fitting word to describe his state this morning. He felt as if the night before, along with the weight of every stupid mistake he'd ever made with Allie, was hanging over his head, just waiting to crush him.

Hurriedly grabbing a clean shirt from his closet, he headed outside as he pulled it on.

"Morning," he called to Rory, who skidded to a stop nearby. If Rory was up and dressed without being prodded, it must be even later than he thought.

"Dad, this bike is great, totally the best. I can't believe it's really mine."

"It's yours, all right," Burn assured him, managing a smile for his son even as his gaze and his thoughts wandered to the house. "How does it ride?"

"Super...perfect." His eyes gleamed with more enthusiasm than Burn had ever seen in them. "You want to give it a try?"

"Maybe later. You enjoy it this morning."

"I know I'm supposed to finish my chores before I do any fooling around, but—"

"But the day after your birthday is a special occasion," Burn told him and was rewarded by a major grin. "Just don't forget to get them done sometime today."

"I won't. Does that mean I can ride up into the hills for a while?"

Burn scanned the horizon in that direction. "As far as that crest I can see from here," he decided.

"But—"

"But nothing, Rory. That bike comes with some responsibilities and some restrictions. Later we'll get together and talk about the specifics. Right now I have some things to work out with Allie."

"All right."

To Burn's amazement there was no argument, no smirk, no ditching the bike and stomping off in anger. Rory simply nodded. He even looked happy as he wheeled the bike around and pointed it toward the low-lying hills to the west.

"Allie's pretty cool, huh?" he said.

"I think so," Burn agreed.

"Me, too. Later, Dad," he called over his shoulder as he pulled away in a cloud of dust.

Right. Later, thought Burn, a small flicker of satisfaction penetrating his otherwise dark mood.

It looked as if there was going to be a later for him and Rory after all. For weeks he'd doubted there was even a slight possibility they could form any kind of normal father-son relationship. He hadn't even known how to begin until Allie had helped point out the way to reach Rory.

Yesterday, the simple exchange they had just shared about Allie would have left him walking on air for a lot of reasons. This morning it had his heart wrenching in his chest...for a lot of different reasons. It would be ironic, he thought, if he finally found a way to connect with his son just as he lost the woman who'd made it possible for them to even talk with each other without arguing.

He couldn't let that happen.

As he strode toward the house, his pace was somewhere between determined and desperate. The front door was unlocked and he walked in without knocking, the way he had hundreds of times before. He didn't know the details of proper etiquette between feuding lovers and he didn't much care to learn. He needed to talk with Allie and he needed to talk with her now.

Her bedroom door was ajar. Burn drew a deep breath and without hesitating pushed it fully open, then was stopped in his tracks by what he saw.

Allie had changed a lot over the past weeks, but she hadn't become a different person. It just wasn't her style to waste time folding and hanging up clothes when she could be outside riding with him or working on her garden with Rory, and while she made an effort to keep the rest of the house neat, inevitably her room was a disaster area.

Not this morning. There wasn't a piece of clothing draped or tossed anywhere, not a single discarded magazine littering the floor, not so much as a hairbrush cluttering her dressing table. Apparently, while he had paced the night away, she'd cleaned. Whatever the explanation, the room was eerily, frighteningly tidy.

Panic clutching at him, Burn hurriedly pulled open a dresser drawer and the door of the closet. There were plenty of Allie's belongings in both places, and hope alone suggested that meant the worst had not occurred. Then, almost reluctantly, he lifted his gaze to the pegs above the bed, where she had enshrined her favorite piece of the antique lace she'd inherited from her beloved Aunt Verdy.

Sunlight dappled the wall, but the lace was gone, and Burn knew then that Allie was, too.

Evidently it had been more important to get away without seeing him than to take time to pack more than the bare essentials.

He bolted from the room, belatedly thinking to check for her pickup parked near his. It was no surprise to see it was gone as well. Burn's mind jumped from one possibility to another, none of them encouraging. She could have decided to drive all the way back to Boston, but it was more likely she would fly. That meant finding a flight out and buying a ticket, and that meant time. Time enough to stop her? Burn wasn't sure.

He knew she hadn't left during the night, because he would have heard her. That still left a window of several hours. He was trying to decide whether to phone the airlines individually or just drive straight to the airport and pray he could find her on his own when the sound of tires on the gravel outside drew his attention. He peered through the kitchen window, his heart nearly exploding with relief at the sight of Allie's pickup pulling to a halt.

He slammed open the back door, reaching the porch just as the driver's door swung open and Rhonda Sue climbed out.

"Rhonda," he said, his flat tone reflecting none of the disappointment, fear and frustration surging inside. "What are you doing here?"

"Driving back Allie's truck," Rhonda explained. "But then, I guess she didn't have a chance to tell you I'd be dropping it off after I took her to the airport."

Burn shook his head. "No. She didn't tell me anything."

"Oh." Rhonda shifted uneasily and nibbled the corner of her bottom lip. "Not even that she was leaving?"

"No...I mean, yeah, I guess she told me that much. Last night. I just didn't believe her or think it would happen so fast or something." He knew he sounded the way he felt—decimated.

"I take it you two had a fight."

Burn nodded.

"Burn, I sure hope it wasn't over Rory or the party or something I said or—"

"It wasn't," Burn broke in, shaking his head. "This had nothing to do with you or Rory or anyone else. Only me." He flashed a bitter grin. "What's new, right?"

"Hey, don't be so hard on yourself." She edged a bit closer to the bottom step. "You feel like talking?"

"Yeah. To Allie. Do you happen to know what time her flight is leaving?"

Rhonda nodded, her smile apologetic. "Eight-fifteen."

Burn glanced at his watch. Eight-fifteen on the dot. Then he looked up at the sky, which was clear, blue, endless.

"Figures," he muttered. Stuffing his hands in his pockets, he glanced at Rhonda. "Thanks for bringing back the truck. Come on, I'll give you a lift home."

"You don't have to. Keith will be along in a minute for me...unless you want me to hang around, lend a shoulder and all that?"

"No, thanks," he replied, shaking his head. "I think I'd rather be alone for a while."

"Sure. You know our number if you want company. Maybe I ought to take Rory for a few—"

He shook his head again, firmly. A sudden urge to hang on to whatever he had left assailed him. "Rory's fine right here."

"Yes," agreed Rhonda. "He is fine, really fine. Thanks to you...and to Allie, too. I already had so much to be thankful to the two of you for, and now, with the way she's insisted on helping out Keith and me—well, it's just too much to ever repay. Not that we won't repay her in full—in dollars, I mean—but the debt itself...well, it's just the kind of goodness that I only pray we can someday repay in kind."

Burn rubbed his jaw and squinted at her. "What are you talking about, Rhonda?"

"Oops. I guess you didn't know...about the loan?"

"What loan?"

"Oh, dear, maybe I shouldn't have said anything. Me and my big mouth. Keith is always telling me that one day it'll get me in trouble."

"No one's in trouble. Allie decides for herself how to spend her money. If she wants to lend some to you and Keith, that's her call to make."

"I'm glad to hear you say that. I'd hate myself if I went and stirred up more trouble for you both."

"You haven't."

"I'm just so thrilled and excited," she said, needlessly since both were evident in her broad smile. "I can't keep the news to myself. If not for Allie coming through with that loan, we'd have lost the ranch for sure. And soon. That would have just killed Keith."

"I'm happy for you, Rhonda, and for Keith. I know what that kind of losing feels like to a man."

"Yeah, well, at least you don't have those kind of problems, right?"

"No, I guess not," Burn agreed, thinking that, given a choice, he'd switch problems in a second. In fact, he'd swap the whole state of Texas to have Allie back. "How long have you and Allie been planning this loan?"

"That's just it," Rhonda replied, "we never planned it at all." Her eyes narrowed. "If you're thinking I asked her for money, you're wrong, Burn. I'd never impose that way, not after all she's done for Rory."

"I know you wouldn't, Rhonda. So it was all Allie's idea?"

"Every bit of it. She came over to the house bright and early this morning and said she'd been thinking for days about a way to help that wouldn't offend us. Can you imagine being offended by someone offering to save your home for you? Anyway, she'd been thinking and thinking and hadn't come up with anything, and so she came over and handed us the check outright on her way to the airport. Just like that. That's when I offered to drive her and drop the truck off afterward."

"I see," Burn said as Keith's truck appeared at the head of the drive. "I meant what I said before, Rhonda—I'm happy for you."

"Thanks," she said, waving to Keith. "I sure wish I could say the same for you. Do you know when Allie's coming back?"

"No," he replied, not even wanting to voice the thought that "if" might be more appropriate than "when." "I'll let you know when I hear from her."

"You do that. I'm going to have a big family dinner to say thank-you. In the meantime, if I can do anything...anything at all—"

"I'll call," Burn interjected, waving as she turned and climbed into the truck with Keith.

Burn already knew he wouldn't be making any calls. Not to Rhonda, because there was nothing she could do to help him...nothing at all.

And not to Allie, because he understood now that it wasn't simply a case of his finding the right combination of words to say to her. It was too late for words, too late to change what had happened, to go back and fix what had already been said and left unsaid.

Allie was finished. With the Circle Rose and with him. He didn't even need to look around inside to see if she'd left him a note to know how true that was. The spur-of-the-moment loan to Rhonda and Keith had been a gift to them and a message to him. He might not know Allie's financial standing down to the last penny, but from working on expenses and plans for the ranch with her, he knew that the money she'd lent them was the money set aside to make the upcoming balloon payment. Allie had meant it when she'd said she had no intention of making that payment, and using the money to save Keith and Rhonda's ranch had ensured that she wouldn't change her mind.

It was over, for them and for the Circle Rose.

There would be no solar pump in the spring, no grazing in the pastures along Pebble Creek, no generations of Traveler's offspring growing up alongside Rory and no more kids of his own. His and Allie's. He realized now that that too had been a part of the loosely framed plan he'd been carrying around in the back of his head for a while now. More pipe dream than plan, really, he supposed. Whatever it was, it had taken shape slowly and he'd been reluctant to examine it too closely for fear it would turn out to be pure fantasy.

It had started out with memories and his learning to come to terms with them. For a while it had seemed as if the ranch might be the solution for him and Rory, a way to bridge the future and the past. Only now, when it was too late for plans or dreams, was he able to step back and see it all as clearly as the cloudless sky overhead.

Allie had been at least partly right. Although he hadn't arrived at the Circle Rose that first day wanting the ranch back, he'd started wanting it soon afterward. Not in the way she thought, however; not as something she had and he didn't, something that could be manipulated or seduced from her. She was dead wrong about that. He didn't want the ranch from her any more than he wanted it for Rory. He wanted it *because* of them.

His feelings for this piece of land were all entwined with other feelings that he'd spent years running away from. And with his new feelings for his son and for the woman who was so much like the land itself—breathtakingly beautiful and just contrary enough to keep a man on his toes. He'd grown to love both Allie and the Circle Rose beyond reason. For him, it was an all-or-nothing proposition. He wanted Allie and he wanted her here. Without her, the rest meant nothing.

And suddenly, after half a lifetime of pain and resentment, Burn understood exactly how his father could have let it all slip through his fingers so easily.

It was a bitter lesson and one that didn't quit. It kept coming at him over the next few days, hitting harder and deeper all the time. For a while he managed to go through the motions of the daily routine he had once approached with such enthusiasm. But the work that had once been a reward in itself was now simply a way to anesthetize his pain.

Burn could think of a faster, less-strenuous method. Only his newfound sense of a father's responsibility kept him from spending the rest of his life in the nearest bar. He had to hold things together for Rory's sake, he told himself over and over, even as it got harder to drag himself out of bed in the morning and became sheer agony to think of facing another day without Allie in it.

Was this how his father had felt? he wondered over and over again. Was this how he had felt all those nights he had sat on the back porch alone, staring at the rose garden his wife had loved, watching it wither and die, one more piece of her gone?

Rory was keeping Allie's garden alive in anticipation of her return, and Burn was doing his best to sidestep his questions about exactly when she was coming back and why she didn't call to see how things were going without her. It wasn't done out of a sense of hope that she might just show up at the door and he'd never have to explain it all to Rory. He'd learned a long time ago not to hope for things that were gone for good.

If Allie loved him or missed him a fraction as much as he did her, she would have found a way to forgive him and start over. And if she were going to forgive him, she would have done so by now. He tried telling himself that this was all inevitable, the backhand of fate, and that it was probably for the best that it ended sooner rather than later, at least for Rory's sake. But that didn't make it hurt any less.

After a week had passed, Burn began knocking off work earlier and earlier in the afternoon and just sitting on the back porch until he heard the school bus. Keeping up the pretense that everything was normal while Rory was around was as much as he could manage. The growing neglect hadn't begun to show yet, but it soon would, and every day he told himself that tomorrow he would pull himself together for sure and get back to work. And every day he wondered if his father used to tell himself the same thing.

Allie had been gone for ten days when he didn't hear the bus and Rory took him by surprise as he rounded the corner of the house. Burn saw him stop short at the sight of his father sprawled in the old rocker in the middle of the day, and he didn't have to try very hard to imagine what was going through the kid's mind.

"She's not coming back, is she?" Rory said finally, dropping his backpack and climbing the steps to stand directly in front of Burn, making it impossible for him to sidestep the issue this time.

"I don't know," Burn told him.

"Did you guys have a fight or something?"

Burn nodded. "Something like that."

Rory inhaled deeply and stared at his sneakers. "Was it about me?"

"No," Burn said quickly, leaning forward in his chair. "It wasn't about you at all, Rory. Believe me."

"Then what was it about?" he demanded, his tone exasperated.

"It doesn't matter."

"It does to me. I—I miss Allie. It's just not the same around here without her."

Burn smiled faintly. "I know."

"Then do something."

"Got any suggestions?"

"I might if I knew what the fight was about."

"It wasn't a fight. It was just a misunderstanding."

"Then straighten it out."

"It's not that easy, Rory."

"Just because something is difficult doesn't mean you shouldn't attempt it. Unquote."

Burn had to smile at being lampooned with his own words. It made his face feel strange and he realized he hadn't smiled since Allie left. Progress, he thought, since he hadn't expected to smile ever again.

"You're right. The problem is I don't even know where to begin. I've thought about it and thought about it and I can't think of anything to say that I haven't already said to try and make her understand."

"Then keep thinking."

Rory turned and Burn thought he was walking away in disgust until he reached for his backpack, zipped it open and pulled out a royal blue ribbon.

"What's that?" Burn asked as Rory held it out to him.

"A blue ribbon," he said. "For the science fair. The pump won first prize."

Burn stood and whacked him on the back, then hugged him close, aware that he was grinning outright now. "Congratulations. I knew you could do it."

"Uh-uh," Rory countered, "we did it, and all because when you talked, I listened. Even when I didn't want to. And one of the things you said to me was pretty smart advice."

"What was that?" Burn asked, feeling like a fish being reeled in by a master and feeling damn proud of it.

"That when you have a problem to work out, you don't stop thinking until you come up with the solution. No matter how hard it is or how much you just want to quit and put on your headphones."

"I don't wear headphones."

"Don't make excuses."

Burn laughed as he recognized yet another quote from himself. Evidently Rory had been listening all along, just as Allie had said.

"I think I get the message. You're trying to tell me that where there's a will, there's a way?"

"No, I'm saying don't just sit there, think of something we can do to get her back...and keep thinking till you do."

"Well, I had thought maybe..."

He trailed off, turning the idea over in his mind. Actually, lately he'd been doing his best *not* to think about it, because it hurt too damn much. Now the seed of an idea that had been trying to break through erupted like a crocus in springtime. It wasn't exactly a battle plan, but it was a first step.

It had occurred to him that once the ranch was sold, Allie's tie with it would be broken forever. If he bought it, even with the intention of holding onto it for the two of them, it would just prove to her that owning the ranch had been his goal all along. If he let it be sold to someone else, what they had shared here and the plans and dreams they'd made would be gone for good.

The obvious solution was to not let it be sold, to make that balloon payment and keep the deed in her name as long as he possibly could. The problem was that the payment was more money than he had saved. Burn knew only one way to get his hands on as much money as he needed in the time he had to do it. It could prove to be an all-or-nothing risk in the truest sense of the word.

"Rory," he said, turning back. His son was watching him with such guileless expectation that he would somehow find a way to make everything all right that Burn knew, risky or not, his fate was sealed. "How would you like to see your old man ride in a rodeo? One of the biggest rodeos around, as a matter of fact?"

"I'd like it a lot," Rory said, not quite as enthusiastically as Burn had hoped. "But..."

"But what?"

"But Mom said only a foo—" He stopped abruptly.

Burn's eyes narrowed. "What did she say?"

"Nothing," Rory replied, his expression becoming blank. Evidently he figured that having his father at war with one of the women in his life was enough. "Nothing at all."

"Good. Then it's settled."

Chapter Fifteen

It always galled Allie to have to admit, even to herself, that her father was right. It was small consolation that this time he'd been only half-right.

He had predicted that using her inheritance from Verdy to buy a ranch would be a mistake and that one of these days her impulsiveness would land her in a situation she didn't know how to get out of.

At least he'd been wrong about the ranch.

Allie was more convinced of that than ever since she'd returned to Boston. She'd never been so homesick in her life as she was for the smell of fresh hay and the sight of a sunburnt horizon just outside her kitchen window. Not to mention the sight of the man she loved riding across that horizon at the end of the day. The heart had an agenda all its own, and no matter how hurt or deceived she felt by his duplicity, she still loved Burn as much as she had that night she first went with him to the bunkhouse.

Bunkhouse. She sighed as she gazed around at the jade and cream silks and brocades that adorned the sun room where she sat, doing what she did a lot of these days—nothing. There was certainly no bunkhouse here, and no need for her to cook dinner or mix wallpaper paste or pick up after herself. No need for her at all, really.

When she'd made the move to Bandera, she had given up her apartment in the city, which meant that moving back meant moving to her parents' brownstone on Beacon Hill. She wouldn't have thought it possible for a person to feel as cooped up in so many spacious rooms as she did there.

Her parents' hovering about protectively didn't help. They were clearly dying to know what had sent her home without warning and without either bag or baggage, but they were doing their best to remember that she was close to thirty, not twelve, and to refrain from prying. Allie was especially thankful they weren't pressing her with questions, since she didn't have much in the way of answers.

She knew only that the second part of her father's prediction, a variation on the same warning he'd been issuing her for years, had finally come true in a big way. Her impulsiveness in leaving the Circle Rose in such a hurry, with all her bridges in flames behind her, had left her in a mess she wasn't sure how to get out of. She'd been trying to figure it out ever since that moment during the flight home—somewhere over Chicago, as she recalled—when, like the mother in the movie "Home Alone," she had suddenly bolted upright in her seat and realized she had left behind one of the most important things in her life. At least she hadn't screamed out Burn's name—another small consolation. Maybe if she had, the flight crew would have realized she was crazy and turned the plane around.

Since returning to Boston, the only person with whom Allie had discussed even briefly the subject of Burn or her reasons for leaving Bandera in such a hurry was her sister, Lauren. Briefly, because Lauren's doctor's mind didn't tolerate lengthy discussions of romantic matters. Which, Allie decided later, was probably for the best, since her sister's no-nonsense advice had helped cut through to the heart of what she was feeling a lot more quickly and accurately than the sloppy, sisterly commiseration she had been sort of hoping for when she showed up on her doorstep toting a pizza. The woman should have been a surgeon instead of a pediatrician.

"Forget the hearts and flowers," she said to Allie over beer and pepperoni pizza in the stark black-and-white living room of her condo. "You bought a ranch, not a cowboy. If this guy isn't in the picture, can you still see yourself being happy there in five years? Ten?"

Allie had to think about it only for a moment before nodding. She'd found purpose and peace of mind in Bandera. Burn was a big part of that, but only part.

"Yes," she said. "What's more, Lauren, I can't see myself being happy in the same way back here, or anywhere else. There's something about the wide open spaces and having to depend on yourself because the closest neighbor isn't even within shouting distance that brings out a part of me I didn't know existed. A part of me I like and want to get to know a lot better. For the first time, I felt as if something I was doing really mattered." She shrugged. "That probably sounds weird to you."

"Not at all. I felt the same way the first time I walked into an examining room and faced a patient all on my own," Lauren told her, smiling at the memory. "I was scared as hell, of course, but I was finally doing what I wanted to do... what I'd dreamed of doing."

"Scared?" Allie echoed in surprise. "You?"

"Of course, me. Dreams are always scary when they're coming true, Allie. At least the important ones. You're always afraid you're going to mess up or crash before you pull it off. And they usually end up costing more than you ever expected in hard work and sweat—"

"I think I've got that part down pretty well," Allie joked, displaying her callused palms.

"—and swallowed pride," Lauren continued. "Believe me, I spent a lot of years swallowing mine as a med student before I got to walk into that examining room alone...and it was worth every gulp," she added, grinning.

"I think I'd rather swing a broom," Allie muttered, examining her calluses.

"Forget about what you'd rather do," Lauren countered. "You know what you *have* to do, don't you?"

"What?"

"You have to go back," she said firmly. "Maybe it will work out with Burn, maybe it won't. You're smart enough to figure out if he's worth the trouble. Maybe he's a con and maybe he's the real thing. But either way, that ranch is yours. Don't you dare quit. Fight for it, damn it."

Allie didn't want to quit. She wanted to do whatever it took to hang onto the Circle Rose. That wasn't going to be easy, especially not after she'd gone and lent the money for the upcoming balloon payment to Rhonda and Keith. They had been so overjoyed by her offer that she couldn't find it in her heart to regret having made it, even if it was going to mean a scramble to come up with the payment in time. That wasn't her most immediate problem right now.

She'd never been very good at saying she was wrong, but she was willing to give it a try...even if she had only been wrong in reaction to Burn's being wrong in the first place. As her father used to preach when they were kids, two wrongs don't make a right. In this case they didn't even make sense. Burn had explained that he'd put off telling her the truth because he was afraid she would jump to conclusions and overreact, and sure enough she had gone ahead and done exactly that.

Only afterward had she calmed down enough to give some thought to how very difficult it must have been for Burn to return to the Circle Rose. Belatedly she understood why he had so vehemently opposed any changes she proposed making in the house, the only real home he'd ever known, and why he had reacted so harshly the day he'd returned and found her resurrecting his mother's rose garden. She even had a better appreciation for his eagerness to escape his old bedroom in favor of the bunkhouse, which no doubt held fewer memories for him.

He'd told her that love could make a man do a lot of foolish things. So could pain, and returning to the ranch that represented so much heartache to Burn must have been very painful for him. It was easy for Allie to accept that he'd been telling the truth when he said he'd kept quiet about his ties to the Circle Rose because those old feeling were just too hard to talk about. Love alone made her willing to believe he'd been telling her the truth about the rest as well.

Pretending to be someone he wasn't had been a dumb mistake, and who knew more about making dumb mistakes than Allie? When you came right down to it, she realized, it wasn't who Burn had pretended to be that mattered most, but who he really was. During the weeks they had lived and worked together, she'd had plenty of opportunity to see for herself the kind of man he was.

Burn was the kind of man who delivered more than a day's work for a day's pay, who never looked for the easy way out and always did what he said he was going to do. He was the kind of man who could forgive Rhonda for keeping the truth about his son from him for so many years and wholeheartedly accept that son and all the aggravation and responsibility that came along with him. The kind of man who admitted he didn't know how to begin being a father and kept on trying anyway; the kind who would go out of his way to help a shoe store clerk he didn't even know. The kind of man she could love forever and keep discovering new things about him to love.

The same night she and Lauren talked, Allie decided that as soon as Burn called to say he was sorry, to ask for another chance or just to ask why the hell she'd left without a real goodbye, she would do as Lauren advised—swallow her pride and tell him she was coming home.

The problem was, he never called.

The days ticked past. At first Allie considered calling him, afraid he might not know how to get in touch with her. But common sense counseled that since she'd left her telephone book behind along with everything else, it wouldn't have taken much effort to find her if he wanted to.

Which opened up the possibility that he didn't want to, that perhaps her accusations had been right after all, and he was back in Bandera gloating over his victory. The very idea made Allie furious and more convinced than ever that the first step had to be his. It didn't quite stop her from racing for the telephone each time it rang, however. Even now the sound of it sent her careening from the sun room, shouting to Louisa that she would answer it. If it was Burn, it was perfect timing, with her father at work and her mother off shopping with friends. She had prayed for such blissful privacy.

She skidded to a halt by the phone in the den, took two deep breaths and counted to ten before lifting the receiver.

"Hello," she said, trying to sound both deliriously happy and slightly preoccupied, as if she'd been interrupted in the middle of something fascinating. She didn't mind meeting Burn halfway, but there was only so much pride she could swallow without choking.

"This is the long-distance operator. I have a collect call for Miss Allie Halston from Rory. Will you accept the charges?"

"Of course," Allie told her, not so much disappointed as surprised.

There was a crackling sound on the line and then the operator's voice said, "Go ahead, please."

"Hello, Rory?"

"Allie? You really are there. Wow, am I ever glad."

"I'm glad to hear from you. But how did you know to call me here?" she asked, resisting the urge to ask why he was calling instead of his father.

"I checked the phone in your bedroom and this was one of the numbers you had programmed for speed dial. You'd written Mom and Dad next to it, so I just figured I'd try you there first. I hope you don't mind...I mean, about me messing around in your room and calling collect and all.''

"Not at all. I'm thrilled that you went to all that trouble to talk to me.'' Which was more than some people seemed capable of doing, she thought bitterly. "I miss you, Rory. It's great to hear your voice.''

"Yeah, me, too. I mean, I miss you, too. And so does my dad. He misses you a whole lot, Allie. More than me, even.''

"Did he tell you that?'' she asked, winding the cord around her finger.

"He didn't tell me exactly, but I know it.''

"I see. So, tell me how everything's going on the ranch.''

"Good, I guess. I'm watering your roses every day.''

"Thanks. I knew I could count on you. How are those new calves?''

"Fine.''

"And how's old Traveler? Still struttin' his stuff?''

The sound of Rory's laugh brought back memories of the two of them sitting on the corral fence, munching apples and watching the bull who was so tough he was comical.

"Yeah, pretty much,'' the boy said.

Allie took a deep breath. "And your dad, is he fine, too?''

"I guess. Now, anyway.''

Allie heard the hesitancy in his voice and her heart twisted. "Rory, what do you mean, he's all right now, you guess? Has he been sick or something?''

"No, he hasn't been sick or anything,'' he replied quickly. "I guess I just meant he's okay for now. Allie, that's sort of why I called you, but if Dad finds out I told, he'll kill me.''

"Don't worry about that, Rory,'' she said, struggling to sound calm as her heart began to thud frantically in response to the edginess in the boy's voice. "Just tell me exactly why you called.''

"Okay, but I have to hurry 'cause I'm still at school and the last bell is gonna ring any second.''

"Fine, talk fast."

"It's about my dad trying to get enough money for some sort of big payment that's due."

"You mean for the ranch?"

"Right, for the ranch."

"So he is planning on buying the Circle Rose after all?" she asked, bitterness tainting the genuineness of her earlier concern.

"No, he says he's got to make the payment for you, in order to keep the ranch in your name or something until he can figure out a way to make you come back. And I really want you to come back, Allie, honest I do. But I'm worried about how he's going to try and get all that money in time."

"What do you mean, Rory? How is he planning to get it?" A confused jumble of possibilities, ranging from bank robbery to bullying it out of Rhonda and Keith, flickered through her mind. None of them sounded like Burn, however.

"He's going to compete again, Allie. In the rodeo, I mean. He's registered to ride in three events in the Reno Rodeo. I'm not saying he's too old or anything, but . . . Allie, I'm scared."

The Reno Rodeo? Burn, who'd been warned by a half-dozen doctors that another violent throw from a horse or a bull could shatter his back permanently, was planning to risk it in order to buy her a ranch she'd told him she no longer wanted? A ranch she'd been dumb enough to believe he wanted more than he wanted her? The man was crazy. Utterly, amazingly, wonderfully crazy.

"When, Rory?" she asked hurriedly as she heard the school bell ringing in the background. "When is he planning to ride in this rodeo?"

"It starts tomorrow," he replied. "In Reno. His first event starts at one. Bronco busting, I think."

Allie winced.

"I've got to go," he said. "If I get detention, I'll miss the bus, and Dad will want to know why."

"All right, Rory, but listen for just a second. Don't tell your father you called me and don't worry. I promise I'll be there in time."

Chapter Sixteen

Allie spent the next hour on the telephone with airlines and travel agents. She learned there was an intricate schedule of flights and split-second connections that just might get her to Reno by one o'clock tomorrow afternoon. However, she wasn't about to take a chance on breaking her promise to Rory and being stranded in Newark while Burn took the biggest risk of his life for her. There was only one person she knew who could arrange for her to definitely be on time, and if Burn was willing to put aside thoughts of his own safety and future, then she could certainly put aside her pride and ask for her father's help.

Richard Maxwell Halston III wasn't enthusiastic about the idea of chartering a private plane to fly his youngest daughter across the country so she could rescue some cowboy from himself, but he did it anyway.

"Allie," he called after her, as early the next morning she ran from the house to the taxi waiting outside to drive her to the airport. "Be careful."

"I will, Dad," she replied.

She could see in his eyes as he watched her go that he would have liked nothing better than to stop her from leaving, as he had in the past—stop her from becoming any more involved with a man he suspected had already hurt her badly. But he didn't try, and Allie knew that he understood, just as she did, that this time there would be no way even he could stop her. In the same heartbeat when Rory told her of Burn's crazy plan, she'd known that this was the real thing.

As she hurried out the front door and down the brick steps, she also knew in her heart that from now on she would only be returning here for visits. The Circle Rose was her home now. Far from being melancholy, she felt as if she'd finally reached an important milestone in her life, and with Burn waiting on the other side, she was eager to be on her way.

The private plane delivered her to Reno on schedule, but once she landed, she was on her own. With the airport and city crowded with visitors and participants in what was, according to the banners she saw everywhere, the wildest and richest rodeo in the West, just hailing a taxi was a major accomplishment. Allie was surprised to learn that, far from being a one-day or weekend event as she had assumed, the Carnival of the West, as it had been dubbed, was a full two weeks of "riding, roping, dancing and eating... and not necessarily in that order."

From the man at the hospitality booth at the airport she got directions to the fairgrounds and rodeo arena, and learned that the kick-off event Burn was scheduled to compete in promised to be one of the most well attended and dangerously exciting of the entire rodeo.

As her taxi inched along in line with what seemed to be every other car, truck and motorcycle west of the Mississippi, Allie found it easy to believe the "well attended" part of the man's prediction, and she did her best not to think too much about the other. Finally, after what seemed an endless ride, the admission gate came into view. She quickly paid the driver and climbed out, to hurry the rest of the way on foot.

The performance arena was surrounded by acres of carnival booths, food stands and small stages on which a variety of music, all country, was being played. Allie might have been moving through a vacuum-sealed tunnel, however, for all she heard, smelled or saw of the festivities around her. She received a map along with her ticket and made her way straight to the arena.

She faced her next hurdle when she tried to get past the gate marked Participants Only. She quickly discovered that cowboys aren't half as susceptible to strong, assertive women as most women she knew were to them. Backing off briefly, she freshened her lipstick, tossed her hair and unbuttoned the second button of the sapphire blue silk shirt she wore tucked into her favorite jeans.

This time she tried a different gate, and the big man standing guard smiled at her and responded to her request for just one little peek at the real, behind-the-scenes action with a wink and a real friendly "Right this way, little lady."

She might not know much about wild horses, Allie thought, but she was really getting the hang of this cowboy stuff.

Once inside, she stopped the first official-looking type she saw and asked if he could tell her where she could find Burn Monroe.

The man checked the clipboard he was holding and snapped, "Chute two," before hurrying on his way.

Allie went cold inside. Chute two. That must mean they were about to begin. Her fists clenched nervously as she looked around at the overhead signs identifying each numbered chute. She figured out where two should be and started running in that direction, weaving among men and horses, suddenly aware of the voice on the loudspeakers announcing the start of the event.

She saw Rory first, standing on the bottom rung of the gate in order to see over it. Burn sat on the top rail alongside the chute, his head turned away from her. As Allie drew closer, she became aware of the pinched, worried expression on Rory's young face, as well as the presence of three men holding ropes to restrain the horse Burn was to ride. Neither the men nor the horse looked particularly friendly.

All the way there she'd practiced what she would say—how she would firmly and sincerely appeal to Burn's common sense and his concern for his son, if not himself, and urge him not to do this. Now, startled by a sudden burst of noise as the horse and rider in chute one exploded into the center of the arena, and surrounded by an audience of men who fairly oozed testosterone, Allie froze, every pre-planned syllable she had walked in with suddenly turning to lead in the pit of her stomach.

"Allie," cried Rory as he glanced over his shoulder to scan the crowd and caught sight of her. He looked thrilled to see her, and more than a little relieved.

At the sound of her name, Burn turned instantly, and in the split second before the easy smile that she loved appeared on his face, Allie noted that he looked anything but easy and relaxed. Clearly he understood the magnitude of the risk he was about to take and was willing to take it anyway.

With a discreet squeeze of Rory's elbow, she climbed onto the gate beside him.

"Hey, Cowboy," she said to Burn. "Got a minute?"

"Just," he said. "What are you doing here, Allie? Boston not wild enough for you these days?"

"As a matter of fact, it's not," she replied, struggling to sound as casual as he did, wondering how he could manage it at a moment like this, with hundreds of pounds of straining, ill-willed horse about to be trapped between his legs. "I decided I do belong here in the West after all. So I thought I'd drop by to check out the action here, and maybe ask you a question."

"Yeah? What's that?" he asked, his gaze on her steady. Allie, however, couldn't take her own eyes off the man in the arena, who was hanging from his saddle as the horse dragged him in dusty circles.

As several men ran from the sidelines to assist him, she turned back to Burn, her throat thick with fear.

"Your question," he prompted.

"Have you entirely lost your mind?" Allie blurted, aware that the men holding the reins of Burn's horse had switched their attention from the action in the arena to the drama being played out right there in chute two.

Burn rubbed his jaw and adjusted his hat. "Probably."

"Don't bother to deny it," she went on, her prepared speech coming back to her in scattered bits and pieces. "No one in his right mind would do a thing like this on the chance, just a mere chance, mind you, of winning enough money to make some stupid payment on a ranch he once said he didn't even . . . " She stopped, frowning in bewilderment. "What did you say?"

"I said probably."

"You're up, Burn," said the burly man who stood at the opposite end of the chute, his hand poised on the latch.

"Give me a minute, will you, Ray?" Burn asked him. He turned back to Allie. "I said probably. But I was being modest. The answer to your question is yes, I've lost my mind. Over you. The chance I'm taking here today is the only chance I've got to get you back, Allie. There's nothing and no one else on this earth except you that could make me want to climb on the back of this animal," he said with a nod at the snorting, straining horse that seemed to sense the showdown was at hand and was jostling against the wooden chute.

"Then if you're doing it for me, don't do it!" she cried.

"I have to. I don't know any other way of saving the ranch for you, Allie . . . and saving the ranch is the only way I know to try and save us."

"Oh, please, Burn—"

"Let's go, Burn," the man at the gate said. "They've already announced you."

Burn stood and pulled on leather gloves that covered his wrists and the cuffs of an embroidered shirt Allie had never seen on him before.

"I don't care about the ranch," she told him, wishing she was close enough to reach him, to touch him. "Not as much as I care about us... about you."

"Same thing."

"No, it's not! The ranch has nothing to do with what happens to us."

"It has everything to do with us."

"Then we'll find another way to save it... or else we'll find a nice apartment or a houseboat. I don't care where we are as long as we're together," she said, the truth of that ripping through her like a shock wave. "All I care about is having you safe and healthy and alive. I love you, Burn Monroe." Her proclamation rang out in the suddenly silent backstage area. "And—and I'm begging you, please, please don't do this."

"Last call, Burn," the man said. "It's now or never."

Burn didn't even take his gaze off Allie long enough to glance at him as he said, "Never. Never again, Ray. Scratch me."

He pulled off his gloves and tossed them to a very happy-looking Rory as he carefully made his way along the chute toward Allie.

"Here," he said to Rory, "these might come in handy for you someday. I won't be needing them anymore."

"Does this mean you won't ride in the other two events you entered either?" Allie asked.

Burn's eyes narrowed quizzically. "How did you...?" He stopped and glanced from her to Rory and back. "Never mind. I think I'd rather not know all the details of how you came to be here. It's enough that you are."

He climbed over the gate, dropping to the ground outside and lifting her down beside him. Before Allie could say another word, he tipped back her head and kissed her long and hard enough to make her senses swim and draw the whistling attention of every cowboy on that side of the arena.

Allie felt his hands on her hips, pressing her closer, and she knew she should probably feel awkward or embarrassed, but all she felt was relieved ... and so much in love she didn't care if the whole world witnessed it.

"I love you," she told him again when he gave her a chance to speak. "I love you so much it hurts."

"I'm afraid that may just be my belt buckle sticking into you, sweetheart," Burn said, smiling wryly as he caressed her jawline with his thumbs. "You want me to back off a little?"

"Not a chance," Allie whispered and hugged him harder, this time lifting her mouth to meet his, losing herself in him all over again.

"That was quite a speech you made," he said when they both needed time to breathe. He was still holding onto her as if he might never let go.

"I meant every word."

"Except the part about the houseboat, I hope." He cradled her face in his hands and kissed her again, more gently. "Does this also mean you're willing to try learning to trust me again?"

"There's nothing to learn. I do trust you, Burn, with my heart, my soul—"

"The roof over your head," he interjected wryly.

"That, too, for as long as I still have one." She shot him a sheepish look. "I probably ought to tell you that I gave the money for that payment to Rhonda and Keith."

"I know. Rhonda told me," he explained. "Why do you think I decided I had to find a way to make the payment for you? I figured that as long as the ranch was still in your name, there was a chance you'd come back."

"There was never any chance of my not coming back," she said softly. "Rory's call just expedited things a bit."

"I've never been so happy with him for disobeying," he admitted, chuckling.

"I suppose I could always ask my father for the money," Allie suggested. "As soon as I pay him back for the plane he chartered to get me here on time, that is."

Burn shook his head, first in amazement and then, more firmly, in denial. "Absolutely not. I have a feeling I'm not going to be your folks' idea of a dream son-in-law to begin with. I'm sure not going to start off by borrowing money from your father."

"Son-in-law?" Allie repeated. "Is that by any chance your idea of a proposal?"

"Nope. That was a warning. The official proposal will come later," he told her, his smile seductive enough to make Allie shiver with anticipation.

"I see. Well, just for the record, the official answer will be yes."

Burn pulled her close and Allie melted against him blissfully, the familiar feel and scent of him dazzling her senses the same way they always did. Nothing had changed and yet everything had, she thought as her world tilted and condensed until it was completely filled with Burn and the sweetness of his mouth on hers.

Only the sound of Rory loudly clearing his throat injected a note of realism.

"You know, you guys," she heard him say, sounding embarrassed as only a fifteen-year-old can be, "there are more private places for this kind of stuff."

Now she did feel a bit awkward. Not Burn, however. He simply laughed and let her go long enough to throw his arm across her shoulders and anchor her close to his side.

"You're absolutely right," he told his son. "Do you think you can entertain yourself for a while?"

Rory tried to suppress a knowing grin. "Sure."

"Good. Allie and I have a lot to talk about."

"Sure," Rory said again, losing the battle with that grin.

Burn handed him some money. "If you need anything, find Frizzy. Otherwise I'll meet you at the entrance later, the same as we planned."

"Frizzy?" echoed Allie. "Isn't that the name of the guy who's supposed to be doing the cooking at the Circle Rose?"

"One and the same," Burn said, leading her toward the exit.

"Then maybe I ought to meet him and—"

"Later," Burn broke in. "You'll meet him soon enough anyway, since he replaces you as cook starting a week from Monday."

"Are you serious?"

"About your cooking? Always," he said, squeezing the back of her neck and sending tingles spiraling through her.

Allie jabbed him purely on principle.

"But how did you know we'd even need a cook come a week from Monday?" she asked. "I mean, if you didn't win the money and you couldn't make the payment and—"

"I hired him because I knew I'd win and I knew I'd make that payment and," he continued, stopping and touching her cheek as gently as if she were made of blown glass, his gaze intense and sober, "I knew that somehow I'd get you back again."

"How could you know all that?"

"Fate," he said simply, his warm lips brushing lightly, tantalizingly across hers. "We're meant to be together. I'm just damn glad I didn't have to get all bruised and sore proving it."

"Me, too," Allie said softly.

"Now, do you want to stand here talking about cooking or do you want to see the best little hotel room in Reno?"

Allie grinned.

The taxi ride from the fairgrounds to the motel seemed even longer to Allie than the ride there and soon turned into a steadily losing battle for them to make conversation and keep their hands off each other.

Constantly searching for new places to touch and caress out of sight of the driver, they spoke—when their lips weren't too busy to speak—of the long days apart and all the days that lay ahead for them.

"What do you think will happen when the bank finds out I don't have the money?" Allie asked as she sat with her legs across Burn's lap, his hand roving slowly and lazily and steadily higher on the inside of her thigh.

"Nothing as dramatic as foreclosure," he replied. "One thing I learned from my father is that losing a ranch is anything but a quick process. We'll put together some facts and figures and work it out. Together."

Together. Allie liked the sound of that nearly as much as she liked the sure, steady feeling of his hands moving over her, imparting fire even through the denim and silk that separated them.

They would work it out, together, and this time the Circle Rose would be not hers or his, but theirs. A few months ago she might have doubted they could pull it off, but she had learned since then that hard work and determination could perform miracles that mere money could not.

By the time they reached the Desert Motor Lodge, they were both aroused and impatient. The best little hotel room in Reno turned out to be little, indeed, as well as rather Spartan, but she had never been so thrilled to step inside any place in her life.

The instant Burn had shut and locked the door, he reached for her.

Allie went to him eagerly, barely aware of her surroundings. She was a different woman than the one who had pulled up stakes and headed West with no more than a sketchy dream and a legacy from another dreamer.

She smiled faintly as Burn's strong, sensitive hands coursed over her body, finding and caressing the curve of her hip. She thought how very much Verdy would no doubt approve of the new Allie and the magic her final gift had wrought.

Thanks to her aunt, Allie had come out here chasing an elusive girlhood fantasy and had found instead something real and rare and strong enough to last a lifetime.

With an urgency to match her own, Burn groaned softly and carried her to the bed. Excitement quickened her breath and made her senses hum.

He lowered her gently to the mattress, coming down beside her, his lips nuzzling her throat, his hands caressing her shoulders and breasts. Then he stopped and Allie looked up into the gleaming darkness of his eyes.

"There's just one thing I want to say before this goes any further," he told her.

For just a heartbeat, Allie's whole world went still.

Then, his rough tone endearingly tender, he said, "I love you, Boston. I'll love you forever."

And she was reaching for him with open arms, her heart racing with anticipation of the next hour and all the hours to come.

Passion marked the lines of his face in the shadows. She saw the longing in him and the love, and was reminded of one more change that he had caused in her. Now only one very special cowboy was her weakness . . . and her strength.

* * * * *

A Note from the Author

Alexandria Halston has received special treatment all her life. Beautiful, wealthy and spoiled, Allie is accustomed to having life roll out a red carpet before her and to having her path strewn with both lavish privileges and adoring men. In spite of all that, however, Allie doesn't feel particularly special. In fact, she feels like nothing more than a pretty face with an important family name attached, and suddenly it's not enough.

Allie longs to move mountains, to save lives, to do *anything* that ranks as exciting and important. She just hasn't a clue where to begin.

I think it's her spirit of honest ineptitude for anything the least bit practical that makes me root for Allie in a way I normally don't for drop-dead gorgeous women. Allie is creative and insightful and compassionate...she simply doesn't know it.

Luckily, a special aunt does recognize her potential and conjures to turn a painful loss into a dream come true for

Allie . . . even if it does seem more like a nightmare at first. She arrives at the Circle Rose ranch expecting to find adventure and romance. Instead she's greeted by sweltering heat and a man who appears to be totally immune to her charms.

For the first time in her life, the irresistible force of Allie's beauty and wealth encounters a truly immovable object . . . Burn Monroe. Initially, it's merely her penchant for having her own way that prompts her to stay and fight, but gradually something else takes over, something stronger and much more satisfying. Determination.

Allie learns the hard way that dreams—like life and love— require persistence, hard work and a little bit of patience. To her amazement, she discovers that given the right incentive, she's capable of all three. In giving to others, to Burn and Rory and Rhonda Sue, she receives the greatest gift in return . . . the gift of faith in herself. At last, Allie truly believes in herself, and she finds in Burn a man who loves her for the very special woman she is.

Silhouette

SPECIAL EDITION

COMING NEXT MONTH

#925 FOR THE BABY'S SAKE—Christine Rimmer
That Special Woman!
Andrea McCreary had decided to raise her unborn baby on her own.
Clay Barrett had generously offered a proposal of marriage, and soon
realized their arrangement would not be without passion....

#926 C IS FOR COWBOY—Lisa Jackson
Love Letters
Only the promise of a reward convinced Sloan Redhawk to rescue
headstrong, spoiled Casey McKee. He despised women like her—yet
once he rescued her, he was unable to let her go!

#927 ONE STEP AWAY—Sherryl Woods
Only one thing was missing from Ken Hutchinson's life: the woman of
his dreams. Now he'd found Beth Callahan, but convincing her to join
his ready-made family wouldn't be so easy....

#928 ONLY ST. NICK KNEW—Nikki Benjamin
Alison Kent was eager to escape the holiday hustle and bustle. Meeting
Frank Bradford—and his adorable twin sons—suddenly showed her this
could indeed be the most wonderful time of the year!

#929 JAKE RYKER'S BACK IN TOWN—Jennifer Mikels
Hellion Jake Ryker had stormed out of town, leaving behind a broken
heart. Stunned to discover he had returned, Leigh McCall struggled with
stormy memories—and with Jake's renewed passionate presence.

#930 ABIGAIL AND MISTLETOE—Karen Rose Smith
Abigail Fox's generous nature never allowed her to think of herself.
Her heart needed the kind of mending only Brady Crawford could
provide—and their kiss under the mistletoe was just the beginning....

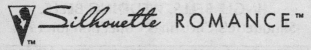
Silhouette ROMANCE™

'Tis the season for romantic bliss.
It all begins with just one kiss—

UNDER THE MISTLETOE

Celebrate the joy of the season and the thrill of romance with this special collection:

#1048 ANYTHING FOR DANNY by Carla Cassidy—Fabulous Fathers
#1049 TO WED AT CHRISTMAS by Helen R. Myers
#1050 MISS SCROOGE by Toni Collins
#1051 BELIEVING IN MIRACLES by Linda Varner—Mr. Right, Inc.
#1052 A COWBOY FOR CHRISTMAS by Stella Bagwell
#1053 SURPRISE PACKAGE by Lynn Bulock

Available in December, from Silhouette Romance.

SRXMAS

JINGLE BELLS, WEDDING BELLS:
Silhouette's Christmas Collection for 1994

Christmas Wish List

*To beat the crowds at the malls and get the perfect present for *everyone,* even that snoopy Mrs. Smith next door!

*To get through the holiday parties without running my panty hose.

*To bake cookies, decorate the house and serve the perfect Christmas dinner—just like the women in all those magazines.

*To sit down, curl up and read my Silhouette Christmas stories!

Join *New York Times* bestselling author Nora Roberts, along with popular writers Barbara Boswell, Myrna Temte and Elizabeth August, as we celebrate the joys of Christmas—and the magic of marriage—with

JINGLE BELLS, WEDDING BELLS

Silhouette's Christmas Collection for 1994.

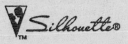

Jilted!

Left at the altar, but not for long.

Why are these six couples
who have sworn off love
suddenly hearing wedding bells?

Find out in these scintillating books
by your favorite authors,
coming this November!

#889   **THE ACCIDENTAL BRIDEGROOM**
by Ann Major
(Man of the Month)

#890   **TWO HEARTS, SLIGHTLY USED**
by Dixie Browning

#891   **THE BRIDE SAYS NO**
by Cait London

#892   **SORRY, THE BRIDE HAS ESCAPED**
by Raye Morgan

#893   **A GROOM FOR RED RIDING HOOD**
by Jennifer Greene

#894   **BRIDAL BLUES**
by Cathie Linz

Come join the festivities when six handsome
hunks finally walk down the aisle...

only from

SILHOUETTE®

Desire®

JILT

"HOORAY FOR HOLLYWOOD" SWEEPSTAKES

HERE'S HOW THE SWEEPSTAKES WORKS

OFFICIAL RULES — NO PURCHASE NECESSARY

To enter, complete an Official Entry Form or hand print on a 3" x 5" card the words "HOORAY FOR HOLLYWOOD", your name and address and mail your entry in the pre-addressed envelope (if provided) or to: "Hooray for Hollywood" Sweepstakes, P.O. Box 9076, Buffalo, NY 14269-9076 or "Hooray for Hollywood" Sweepstakes, P.O. Box 637, Fort Erie, Ontario L2A 5X3. Entries must be sent via First Class Mail and be received no later than 12/31/94. No liability is assumed for lost, late or misdirected mail.

Winners will be selected in random drawings to be conducted no later than January 31, 1995 from all eligible entries received.

Grand Prize: A 7-day/6-night trip for 2 to Los Angeles, CA including round trip air transportation from commercial airport nearest winner's residence, accommodations at the Regent Beverly Wilshire Hotel, free rental car, and $1,000 spending money. (Approximate prize value which will vary dependent upon winner's residence: $5,400.00 U.S.); 500 Second Prizes: A pair of "Hollywood Star" sunglasses (prize value: $9.95 U.S. each). Winner selection is under the supervision of D.L. Blair, Inc., an independent judging organization, whose decisions are final. Grand Prize travelers must sign and return a release of liability prior to traveling. Trip must be taken by 2/1/96 and is subject to airline schedules and accommodations availability.

Sweepstakes offer is open to residents of the U.S. (except Puerto Rico) and Canada who are 18 years of age or older, except employees and immediate family members of Harlequin Enterprises, Ltd., its affiliates, subsidiaries, and all agencies, entities or persons connected with the use, marketing or conduct of this sweepstakes. All federal, state, provincial, municipal and local laws apply. Offer void wherever prohibited by law. Taxes and/or duties are the sole responsibility of the winners. Any litigation within the province of Quebec respecting the conduct and awarding of prizes may be submitted to the Regie des loteries et courses du Quebec. All prizes will be awarded; winners will be notified by mail. No substitution of prizes are permitted. Odds of winning are dependent upon the number of eligible entries received.

Potential grand prize winner must sign and return an Affidavit of Eligibility within 30 days of notification. In the event of non-compliance within this time period, prize may be awarded to an alternate winner. Prize notification returned as undeliverable may result in the awarding of prize to an alternate winner. By acceptance of their prize, winners consent to use of their names, photographs, or likenesses for purpose of advertising, trade and promotion on behalf of Harlequin Enterprises, Ltd., without further compensation unless prohibited by law. A Canadian winner must correctly answer an arithmetical skill-testing question in order to be awarded the prize.

For a list of winners (available after 2/28/95), send a separate stamped, self-addressed envelope to: Hooray for Hollywood Sweepstakes 3252 Winners, P.O. Box 4200, Blair, NE 68009.

CBSRLS

OFFICIAL ENTRY COUPON

"Hooray for Hollywood"
SWEEPSTAKES!

Yes, I'd love to win the Grand Prize — a vacation in Hollywood —
or one of 500 pairs of "sunglasses of the stars"! Please enter me
in the sweepstakes!

> This entry must be received by December 31, 1994.
> Winners will be notified by January 31, 1995.

Name _____

Address _____ Apt. _____

City _____

State/Prov. _____ Zip/Postal Code _____

Daytime phone number _____
                              (area code)

Account # _____

Return entries with invoice in envelope provided. Each book
in this shipment has two entry coupons — and the more
coupons you enter, the better your chances of winning!

DIRCBS

OFFICIAL ENTRY COUPON

"Hooray for Hollywood"
SWEEPSTAKES!

Yes, I'd love to win the Grand Prize — a vacation in Hollywood —
or one of 500 pairs of "sunglasses of the stars"! Please enter me
in the sweepstakes!

> This entry must be received by December 31, 1994.
> Winners will be notified by January 31, 1995.

Name _____

Address _____ Apt. _____

City _____

State/Prov. _____ Zip/Postal Code _____

Daytime phone number _____
                              (area code)

Account # _____

Return entries with invoice in envelope provided. Each book
in this shipment has two entry coupons — and the more
coupons you enter, the better your chances of winning!

DIRCBS